THE WIDOW'S WEB

SUSAN MOORE

BLOODHOUND
— B O O K S —

To Lilu

PROLOGUE

The rise and fall of her chest slowed. Titus Creed watched her body soften into his LC4 Le Corbusier chaise longue. Of all the possessions he owned, this was his most treasured. He'd been searching a long while for an original one by Jeanneret and Perriand. Their pioneering designs had shaped the 20th century, and in his opinion, this recliner was their crowning achievement. It was a beauty, made in 1928, one of the first ever made, and it had cost him two hundred thousand dollars at auction.

Titus could have bought an expensive knock-off that would have looked pretty much the same and cost him only a few thousand dollars, but he liked the truest form of something, its original self. Fakery and copies were a dilution of creativity.

True to its nickname, the LC4 was a "relaxing machine," perfectly calibrated for hypnosis, with a design that mirrored the body's natural curves.

The wave of white leather now held Dr. Anna Jones, whose body was suspended, seemingly floating over the tubular steel cradle.

The breath work was done, and as he talked, using a slow,

melodic tone, he watched the muscles in her tense, rigid body relax.

It had been a tough few therapy sessions, even by his standards. One moment she was complicit, ready to open up, the next the steel trap door came down. And Dr. Jones was smart—therapy smart like him—and kept challenging the how and why of what he was doing.

Finally, she was beginning to let her guard down, allowing him to scratch at the surface of her deeply buried emotions.

He transitioned into the suggestion phase, stimulating her subconscious mind with questions he'd been meticulously formulating, crafting and noting since their first session. He was probing for the unconscious blocks that held trapped trauma at bay.

He was well-versed in her textbook reactions as he guided her through them—tears, choked words of sorrow, love, and regret.

Then he took her deeper. Her breathing slowed, growing more rhythmic and measured. He set aside his notes and leaned forward in his chair, his focus entirely on her. Her head began to move side to side, her eyes darting beneath closed lids. She was traveling down some long-buried neural pathway.

Suddenly her back arched against the curve of the recliner in such a sharp convulsion that he leapt up, ready to intervene. Her mouth opened, releasing a blood-curdling scream that had the receptionist and two of his practitioners rushing into his treatment room.

"Loni, stay here," he said, signaling the others to leave.

The poised, affluent figure in the photo that had made the front page of the *SF Chronicle* just weeks before, now lay awkwardly on the recliner, her body limp as a rag doll. He checked her vitals, keeping his voice a low, hypnotic hum. It was a tone carefully cultivated over years, a soothing balm that commanded a price as steep as its reputation.

He glanced over at where Loni was now sitting in a side chair, her face pale, hand shaking as she began writing her observation notes.

Dr. Jones' lips began to move, her words a slurred, disjointed whisper. He leaned in, his ear just inches from her mouth, straining to catch the fragments of her consciousness. "Sleep just a bit... Brad... So tired..." Then she was silent, her breaths becoming shallow and faint.

"Anna, where are you now?" he said.

The silence stretched out like a taut wire before she responded, her voice hoarse. "Dark. I can't see. Lifting. Someone's lifting me. Heavy."

She lay still again, her body seemingly lifeless. But he continued mining, navigating through the labyrinth of her mind. Suddenly, her fingers twitched, a spasm rippled through her entire body. She began to writhe on the recliner, her face a grotesque mask of pain.

"Get the hell away from me!" she screamed.

CHAPTER ONE

2019

Fog shrouded Stinson Beach. It was that time of year, June gloom, when the coast was cloaked in a moist marine layer, while only a few miles inland the earth baked under a cloudless sky. Inside the glass and steel modernist abode of the Jones' household, Anna began her morning coffee ritual.

Brad had already warmed the machine, making his custom espresso before heading out to run and surf.

As the milk frothed Anna checked her email, scrolling quickly through the endless stream of flotsam and jetsam from the digital world. New threads, old threads all spooling through.

She fought the urge to open one or two of them and dive in —knocking the balls back into someone's court. Wait until later, after school drop-off.

Cup in hand she padded across the limed oak floor and out onto the cool ash decking. It was still early, her favorite time of day, when spaciousness and stillness lent promise to the day ahead. She took a sip of cappuccino. The first taste was always the best—a bittersweet jolt to a sleep-laden palate.

An ocean breeze whispered through the newly installed wild grass border that their landscape designer had recommended to soften the house's brutalist lines. She pulled the collar up on her cashmere robe, and looked out to where the rhythmic rumble of Pacific waves pushed and pulled the golden grains of Californian sand. Today already had a good vibe to it.

She ran through her schedule, pausing on the noon exec team Zoom with Xomftov, a tech start-up. She still wasn't certain how to pronounce their name. It was another fangled word, on which they'd no doubt spent a fortune creating with a big-name brand agency.

The CEO was in his early twenties, textbook cockiness from someone that age with a revolutionary idea (weren't they all?) that had the promise of being a game changer in the financial markets. Venture capitalists had rushed in like bees to a honeypot, funding him and his arrogance to a tune of forty million dollars, before he'd even shown a dime of revenue.

Everything had been going swimmingly until he'd unleashed his repressed emotions, in a hot and heavy exchange with an online sex worker, late at night at his desk, making the rookie error of not bothering to check if anyone else was burning the midnight oil.

The project manager had walked in to share her updated Gantt chart. The fallout had legal and human resources scrambling. Hence the call to herself, cyberpsych troubleshooter Dr. Anna Jones.

She sipped her coffee, relieved she was the old guard, the ones who no longer had to deal with all the drama that went down with pioneering the digital storm that now governed the new age AI.

Way off in the distance she became aware of a dog barking, its tone insistent.

She headed up the centerpiece of their home, a spiral staircase made of bladder-molded glass and carbon fiber. Brad had become obsessed with its design, driving their architect to the point of madness, creating draft after draft of detailed drawings, until he was satisfied that the result was an exquisite, optical illusion of a double helix. She'd have called it done with one.

The door to Jack's bedroom stood ajar. She pushed it fully open. Testament to teenage hormones and growth spurts, he was dead asleep under the duvet.

"Morning. Breakfast in ten," she said.

"Gui, come on."

She waited for the usual ripple of activity from their long-legged fox red Labrador squirreling out of her sleeping spot at the bottom of the bed. Nothing.

"Hey, Gui." She lifted the edge of the duvet.

No dog. Must have decided to buck the trend of lying in, which she'd adopted as part of her being over a decade old. Probably had gone out with Brad, like the old days. Not the best idea since she had bad hips.

Anna headed back down the stairs into the kitchen, took a jar of granola off the shelf. She opened the fridge to retrieve a bottle of organic milk. The noise of the dog barking came through the open door to the deck. No doubt someone had lost it on the beach...

Brad. She'd bet anything he'd put on his AirPods and forgotten Gui was with him. Head in the clouds. Hell. She marched onto the deck and unleashed her hi-lo whistle. The barking ceased.

She whistled again and stood, waiting for the familiar sight of a loping lab appearing out of the mist. Brad had to be more careful.

The barking started up again, accompanied this time by insistent whining. An image of Gui trapped, most likely in someone's yard that she'd managed to access but not exit, flashed through Anna's mind's eye.

Shit. She pulled on her trainers and broke into a swift jog across the sand, towards the source. She'd bet anything Gui was in the Weizmann compound. They had a side gate that the gardener sometimes used, the only access point in a beachfront steel and glass-plated fortress. That'd be a long conversation with Leila Weizmann about leash laws and badly behaved, wandering canines. If she was lucky, the Weizmanns would be at their place on Nob Hill, and she could deal with their housekeeper.

As she closed in on her target, she realized the barking wasn't coming from up on shore. It was down, somewhere in the thick band of fog at the water's edge.

The caffeine jolt kicked in. Anna quickened her stride, a gnawing angst working in the pit of her stomach.

Up ahead, through the gloom, she could make out the specter of her dog, glistening with water.

"Gui, hey!"

The dog didn't move. Instead she whined, shifting from paw to paw, as the waves came rolling in, leaving a frogspawn froth in their wake.

Anna raced to her side. She reached out to stroke her head, but Gui shook it off. Maybe this was senility hitting its first home run. They'd have to properly fence the garden in to stop it happening again.

Gui barked up at her and then looked out to sea.

"What?" Anna said, following the Labrador's gaze out to the heaving indigo swell. "What is it?"

A wave crested and crashed. She blinked, clearing her line of sight. The dip exposed a dark object bobbing out in the water. The shape looked to be half-submerged, like a fallen log. She squinted, trying to make out the shape. A glimpse of dark wet hair.

"Fuck." She kicked off her trainers, tore off the robe, and ran

8

into the water. The cold took her breath away; the thin silk slip providing poor protection against its icy grip.

She dove under an oncoming wave, coming up the other side, adrenaline kicking in as she broke into a freestyle crawl. With every shoulder rotation and arm stroke, her paddling palms pulsed and pushed through the dark water.

She paused to look up, to where the shape lay bobbing only meters away. The floodgates opened. An icy dread came coursing through her veins.

With a Herculean spurt she reached it, flipped the wet-suited form, bringing Brad's face to meet her own. His eyes were closed, his skin pale, almost blue.

"Brad! Brad!"

Nothing. Unconscious.

She had to get him to shore quick. It'd been years since she'd got her life saving certificate, but somehow she remembered the drill, hooking her arm over, across his shoulders, tucking her hand, pushing her frigid fingers under his armpit to grip onto the wetsuit.

"I've got you," she said.

His leonine head lay heavy on her chest. She could feel the fanning of his dark hair against her skin.

A wave pulsed them towards shore, before a sharp undertow cut in, pulling them back out.

"Come on," she said, fighting to keep afloat.

Way out their depth, both of them. The fog was thickening, blurring the lines of sea and sky.

Don't panic.

Swim.

Kick.

Breathe.

Another wave came pulsing towards them, fueled with raw ocean power. Surf lessons. She'd only had a few. Her talent lay in other things was how she'd framed her inability to stand up. What did that instructor say? *Ride the wave, you gotta ride the wave, Anna.*

She arched her back, pushing Brad and herself up to the surface, her arm cutting through the numbing water.

A sweeping surge lifted them.

Stay in the frame of the wave. Keep kicking.

The freight train rolled towards the shore. Above the thunderous roar she could hear shouting. Brad's head bumped her under the chin as they reached the crest, sending them into freefall. A still life snapshot.

CHAPTER TWO

Kobe was in "the dugout" as he liked to call his table under the stairs. It was the one everyone else avoided since it sat only one, on a hard stool, with a partial view of the counter. He favored the covertness of its location. It was a place of solace, yet in the beating heart of Silicon Valley.

From where he sat, he could watch and eavesdrop on the tech glitterati as they ordered their organic, oxygenated, Quorum food and drinks that were formed specifically to each person's gut health. Quorum's app-based nutrition had taken the tech world by storm. *Go with your gut, choose Quorum*—that was the strapline that had them lining up in droves. And here he sat, picking and sifting through their counter and table chit-chat to find eight bits of succulent news for his daily ByteBeat column.

Journalism wasn't what it used to be. Gone was the authorial tone that ignited heated discussion in the Otieno household. The paper portal to the world's events had been read by his parents over breakfast, and later dissected over dinner. When he and his brothers had been old enough, they'd joined in the ritual; volleying political, domestic, and economic viewpoints with a fervor that unnerved any invited guests.

It had fueled him to get a US scholarship to study journalism at UC Berkeley. And in that move he'd mapped himself a career path to investigative journalist for the *Washington Post*.

After a short spell at the *SF Chronicle* (they'd made him redundant six months in), he'd hopped on the tech track, interviewing and writing pieces for *Code Life* magazine. This hadn't been driven by any burning desire to report on the tech field, rather it was the only way he could pay his rent and food bills. With his talent for bringing humor into what was often dry as dust material, he'd been given his own column.

It didn't make him enough money to buy his own home, he doubted it ever would, based on the rocket-like trajectory of local property prices, but it gave him freedom to roam and write wherever he chose as long as he delivered eight juicy bits of news a day into subscribers' inboxes.

It sounded like low hanging fruit, except for the last few months, where regulation, layoffs, and market corrections had stemmed the flow of salient news.

If he was honest, he'd got into the habit of hacking together different news pieces and viewpoints to reach his eight a day. Worse still, today he was hacking around with six different sources already written on the Japanese art of acceptance in difficult times, to make his own. Plagiarism in action. Something he'd vowed he'd never do. But the competition to break a story before anyone else was crushing these days. Every person armed with a smart phone could publish at anytime from anywhere.

There was no time anymore for digging in, under the bones, to get to the marrow, to add slant and style to a piece. He worried he was fast becoming as irrelevant as a soundbite himself.

What he needed was a miracle, an untapped source with a story that would light the world on fire...

"Hey, Kobe, can I get you another one?"

He looked up to find Nora standing with her iPad at the ready.

"Nah. Gotta get going. You got anything for me?"

She leaned in, close to his ear. "Table four are from PalmaTouch. Their beta testing's for shit. App's crashing. They need more investment or they're done for."

His mind raced down the mental list of hot start-ups. He pulled a crisp twenty dollar note from his pocket and passed it to her. This was his daily grind—a cash spot fee for his network of hospitality staff who fed him fresh material. Fifty-six bullet points a week to fill his column was a lot of news to find.

He packed his laptop into the rustic faux leather messenger bag he'd recently acquired. He'd have liked it in real leather, but that would have added another zero to the transaction. Things were pretty tight right now with the cost of living spiraling upwards.

He pulled his cap on low and navigated through the heaving tables to the door. The cap position was for anonymity. He'd reasoned with himself many times how stupid he was to think he even needed to do that because no one knew him anyway, but some stubborn pride of wanting to be "someone" always won over.

He slowed his stride past table four. A woman dressed head to toe in khaki, like she was a part of a desert militia, was sitting opposite a young, skinny guy. He still carried the angst-ridden marks of acne, which blazed in a livid carpet up his neck and cheeks, no doubt inflamed under the stress of data testing.

"We're fucking screwed unless LVP bail us out, and that's a long shot," she said.

"Give me another couple of days."

She leaned in, grasping the teaspoon in her fist like some weapon with which she would unleash hell upon the victim in her sights. "We don't have any more time," she hissed.

Lyle Venture Partners. Hell would freeze over before LVP would bail out someone with an amateur code base. Kobe thought for a split second about telling this pair that, but then he wouldn't be impartial, he'd be affecting an unfolding story.

He increased his pace, heading out past the vertically farmed wheatgrass wall, into the heat of another bright shiny day in the tech capital of the world.

It wasn't hard to spot his car amongst the Tesla-saturated lineup outside. His white 2010 Toyota Corolla with a dented wing had the air of a fallen angel.

He unlocked the door and was greeted by a furnace blast of trapped air. Maybe the car could do with a dose of Quorum probiotics like him.

He fired up the engine, set the air con to max and pulled out into the stream of traffic. Two years. He still had two years of car payments on this machine before it could wholly belong to him. The interest rate alone was a killer, but he'd had a couple of credit rating dips that had dictated his subpar loanability metrics.

He pulled up at a stop light alongside a convertible Aston Martin, top down, a guy at the helm in a tailored sports jacket and open-necked blue shirt. A venture capitalist, had to be by the caliber and polish of the driver and wheels. The guy looked young, mid-twenties. Another spear to the heart of the hacking journo pushing thirty-plus in the slow lane.

To combat his plummeting mood, Kobe hit play on the Corolla's stereo. The loose, nonchalant fluidity of Miles Davis' "Venus De Milo" flowed in through the speakers. He tapped his fingers on the steering wheel. Fuck eight bits of bite-sized tech fodder a day! He was a writer, a true artist. He would be a somebody, cap pulled down, but head held high.

A car horn blasted through his internal fervor. Hell, he'd gotten himself so distracted he was headed onto the freeway at thirty-five miles an hour. With his foot on the gas he moved into the fast lane. His cell pinged, the custom drum roll signaling an incoming tide from his boss. He glanced at the dashboard clock, column was twenty minutes late, and still missing its eighth bit. He still had another fifteen minutes to reach his studio apartment in East Palo Alto. He was screwed.

Only thing for it was to take the next off-ramp and pull in at the Wendy's parking lot.

There wasn't a tree in sight to shelter under so he pulled up close to a towering dumpster to give him a fraction of shade.

He switched off the engine, pushed back his seat as far as it would go and flipped open his laptop. Ukeireru versus PalmaTouch —one was already done to death online, the other was a wisp of story with zero investigative underpinning. His boss had already given him a warning on the diminished quality of the column. A bead of sweat broke out on Kobe's forehead. He closed his eyes. Ukeireru versus PalmaTouch. Shit versus shit. Five minutes was all he had.

And when the pressure's on... a memory swept in. A canoe trip years before. His mom had arranged it for her and her three boys in an effort to boost their knowledge of the natural world. He'd been seven at the time, his brothers older.

The guide had strapped them all into bright orange life jackets and paddled them out to where a flock of flamingos stood peacefully balancing on spindly legs, beaks dipping in and out of the water as they filter fed for shrimp and insects.

His mom and the guide were in raptures. The guide called for silence, putting them into some sort of stealth mode so they could get close in. Personally he wanted to stay well back since the flamboyance was growing pinker, more menacing by each stroke of the paddle. He'd shrunk down low in the boat, keeping his hands well away from the sides, while his oldest brother kept trailing his fingers in the water.

Out of the corner of his eye he glimpsed a faint ripple coursing through the water just to the left of the canoe. Seconds later a telltale reptilian outline surfaced.

He opened his mouth to warn the flamingos, but it was just at the moment when the creature leapt above the surface, jaws wide, clamping down on pink feathers with a crunch. This visceral act unleashed mayhem, as the flamboyance took off, painting the sky a lurid pink.

His cell pinged, pulling him out of his reverie. A text from Sam, a waitress he'd had in his inner circle for a long while, but who'd defected the valley in favor of beach life up in Marin.

> Hey Kobe, tip for you, you can pay me when you get here $$$.

She'd attached a photo. He clicked on it. The curl of a cresting ocean wave. He zoomed in to where a woman in a ghost-white slip was clutching a guy in a wetsuit. They were mid-air, freefalling towards the turbulent, churning water below.

CHAPTER THREE

Brad's face had a waxy sheen to it, making his pale skin almost translucent. His dark hair was still damp. The frown line that had formed a deep furrow across his brow years before, when TopMatch was screwed on funding, had vanished. It struck Anna that this was the first time she'd seen him relaxed for a long time.

The roar of the wave lingered in her head. The drop off its crest had sent them plummeting into a turbulent froth. She'd lost her grip on Brad, and with it the air in her lungs. She'd been certain they were going to drown.

She reached out, hand trembling, to adjust the collar of his wetsuit. Her knuckles grazed the cold skin of his cheek. The Isurus' hi-tech fabric, with its thermal layer lock, hadn't kept its promise. He was stone cold.

"Ma'am."

She looked up. A Marin County cop was standing next to her.

How do you tell a child he's lost his father? A wave of coffee-tinged nausea came sweeping up. She leaned over, vomiting onto the sand, cold and compressed from where the Pacific was beating its retreat.

The cop crouched down, put a comforting hand on her shoulder. The touch tapped a well of tears. Her eyes misted over. The world about her began to spin.

Certain she was going to vomit again, she pitched forward, feeling herself falling into a spiraling black hole. Brad's waxen face flashed through her mind's eye, then another, a shadow face, whose appearance brought with it more dread than death itself.

Jack lay in bed waiting for his mom or dad to get to the front door and stop whoever it was from banging so loudly on it. One of them had to have opened the main gate for the person to get this far, so why in hell hadn't they let them in?

He pulled the pillow over his head, but it did little to dull the sound. There was only one solution. He rolled out of bed and made his way sleepily across the room, to where he'd left his noise-canceling headphones.

"Jack!"

A stranger's voice was calling his name from outside. He looked back at his bed. Gui. He bet the dog had escaped again.

Yawning, he threw on his sweats and headed down the stairs, expecting to find a neighbor with his dog in hand. Instead, he was surprised to find two cops on the doorstep.

"Jack Jones?"

"Yes."

"There's been an accident. Your mom asked that we come and get you."

The taller one went on to explain it had happened on the

beach, that he was needed there right now. Despite their calm demeanor, unease washed over him.

They escorted him out, down the beach, speaking in hushed tones. Up ahead he could see the flashing lights of an ambulance at the water's edge. Dread formed in the pit of his stomach.

"One moment, son."

A paramedic appeared. "Your mom's not feeling so good. She's resting," he said, steering Jack by the arm around to the open back door of the ambulance, to where his mom was lying on a stretcher, wrapped in blankets, her eyes closed.

"Mom?"

"She's in shock. We gave her a sedative. She's okay," said the paramedic.

Dad. Mom was in the ambulance. Where was Dad? He turned, looking out towards the roar of the ocean, to where a group of people were gathered in the swirling mist.

Before the cop could stop him, he jumped out of the ambulance and ran over, just as his dad was lifted into a black body bag.

CHAPTER FOUR

Kobe pulled the Corolla into the parking lot of the Ranch Cafe just as an ambulance sped past, lights flashing. He turned down the air con—wasn't needed in a place like this—and listened to the last few bars of "So What".

Once the last note was played, he picked up his bag and climbed out into the cold, damp morning air. Why the hell Sam had wanted to move out of the sunshine belt to this mist-shrouded enclave of old money, and New Age idealists, he'd no idea.

"Hey, Kobe." Sam was waving at him from an outdoor terrace lined with driftwood tables. A rustic sign, "Ranch", was swinging in the ocean breeze on an iron chain above her head.

He pulled the collar up on the navy jacket kept in his car for meetings, and headed up the steps. Definitely overdressed in a sea of hoodies and plaid shirts, but he'd freeze to death otherwise.

Sam led him to a table at the far side, away from the other diners. He took a seat with a view out over the beach. Not that you could see anything, but he could hear the distant roar of the ocean.

"What have you got for me?" he asked, after a couple of pleasantries on her new life.

"You'll be stoked you came up," she said. "I'll get you a coffee."

Before he could reply she disappeared back inside, the screen door banging in her wake. He wondered why the bother —no self-respecting airborne insect would inhabit or be passing by; they'd be over the hills basking in the inland sunshine. Had to be because of the ranch vibe; a screen door to add authenticity to the dining environment.

He'd been preoccupied when he'd arrived, but now with a few minutes to spare, he took in his surroundings. What at first glance looked ramshackle was in fact carefully curated. The driftwood tables were polished, held together with brass nails and wooden pegs. The cane chairs were lined with linen cushions. Optional tweed throws were stacked in a neat pile next to the entrance.

Now he was looking with a more investigative eye, he saw that the crowd was equally polished. The guy closest to him was wearing a Loro Piana hoodie, three thousand bucks on that price tag.

Beyond them sat an older guy, who symbolized the wealth and status of the area. Looked kind of familiar.

"Americano, one sugar," said Sam, landing a hand-thrown ceramic cup in front of him, the word "Ranch" stamped into its side.

"Thanks. I recognize that guy over there," he said, with a nod of his head in his direction.

"Joel Weizmann."

"Thought he lived in the city."

"Yeah, but also has a place on the beach here. His wife's a bitch, but he's okay."

Naive of him to assume Weizmann had only one abode.

The guy ran one of the biggest corporate law outfits in the Bay Area.

"I didn't take the photo, but I know who did, and he'll give you an exclusive."

"What's the story?" he said, taking a sip from his cup. Damn fine brew. He'd be hard put to find anything equal to that outside of his own kitchen.

"The woman was out there rescuing the guy."

"So?"

"It's Brad and Anna Jones."

"Poster kids of the dot.com boom?"

"Yeah. They live up the beach. My roommates pulled them out of the water. He had already drowned."

Kobe shuddered. "Your friends?"

"JT and Coop have just finished up with the cops. They're back at the apartment, pretty shook up, but ready to talk."

"How much?"

"Seven fifty. Photo exclusive to you."

He whistled air out between his teeth. "Jeez. I'm a columnist..."

She smiled. "Yeah, but I know you need a break, just like we all do. You get this, you'll get those eyeballs you're always talking about."

Kobe did the mental math, his financial landscape flashing before him—his journalist's drip-fed bank account, three credit cards, two maxed, his rent, the car, health insurance...

"Come on, Kobe, your boss'll pay you back."

"Boss is a tight ass. Says it goes against principle to pay for a story." In saying this he already knew the answer. "Where's the nearest ATM?"

"Fifth and Lincoln. It's on your way."

He reached for his phone.

"Coffee's on me. I'll text you the address."

He pulled up outside a low-rise, low-rent apartment block that looked like some sagging fifties motel. The cars here made his look like a luxury ride.

Following Sam's directions he made his way up the open stairwell to the second floor. Number nine had a long line of surfboards stacked outside the door. A couple of them had wet sand clinging to the wax. Nineties music floated out on a cloud of weed smoke through the open window.

He knocked.

A young guy in a T-shirt and board shorts opened the door. "Hey, man, you Kobe?"

"Yeah."

JT high-fived him, led him into a sitting room with two worn couches that matched the mood of the building. Another guy lay across one of them, drawing heavily from a bong.

"This is Coop."

Kobe nodded over at him.

JT flopped down on the coconut mat rug next to a brown, cracked tile coffee table. "You got the cash?"

Kobe patted his jacket pocket.

"Show me what you got."

"It was bad, man," muttered Coop, eyes partially closed, headed into a mind-muffling stupor.

"Coop got it the worst. He worked on the dude. Didn't know he was already dead."

Coop let out a guttural moan before sucking back on the bong.

JT passed Kobe his phone. His hand was shaking. It was open on the photo reel. The last four were successive shots of the photo Sam'd sent him earlier. Brad and Anna Jones, falling through the space between the wave's crest and the turbulent waters beneath.

"Okay if I record this?"

JT nodded.

Kobe gave the surfer back his phone, retrieved his own from a pocket, opened a new audio file, along with his notebook, and set to work, asking the leading questions.

The gist he got—they'd been about to head in to catch their first wave of the day when they'd spotted the Joneses, caught in the thick of the surf.

JT and Coop ran in, dragged them out.

Interview over, photos and copyright transferred, originals deleted from JT's phone, Kobe climbed back in his car, $750 lighter, armed with the story that could change everything.

CHAPTER FIVE

Jack sat on the top step of the glass staircase. He had no idea what time it was, or how long he'd been sitting there. Gui lay at his side, her head resting in his lap. He ran his fingers through her warm fur. His dad was dead.

The door to his mom's room was open. He could hear her low inhale and exhale. He closed his eyes, willing her to wake up, to tell him that this was just a nightmare. He'd find himself back in his bed, waking up to a normal morning.

The dull buzz of his phone vibrating again on the desk in his room. Ever since the beach he'd ditched the deluge of incoming messages. News traveled fast, and he was just learning that real disasters spread like wildfire. He guessed Alicia would have heard by now, over the bridge in the city. He bet her whole school knew what had gone down. But he was so strung out, numb, that right now the only person he wanted to talk to was his mom.

Downstairs, in the kitchen, he could hear Caitlin, his mom's best friend, speaking with a cop. Finally he'd get to know what had really happened out there. No one would tell him anything until an adult family member was present—a conscious one—and Caitlin was the closest person they had to family.

"They think the swell brought a rogue wave with it. He fell, and the board knocked him unconscious," the cop said. "The dog alerted Mrs. Jones, but by the time she reached him it was too late."

"Oh my God."

No shit. He looked down at Gui. A lump lodged itself in his throat, blocking a sudden overwhelming feeling in his chest, as if his heart was about to explode. Gui nosed his hand.

The front door banged shut.

"Hey, Jack, can I get you something to eat?" Caitlin was standing at the bottom of the stairs, wearing her work suit.

"I'm fine," he said, getting up to retreat to his room.

The last thing he needed was sympathy.

Anna stirred. Her head felt as if it'd been stuffed full of cotton wool. Her eyelids were leaden, glued with the slick of sleep that had hardened after long hours of sedation. The room was dark. Had to be the middle of the night. Rolling over, she reached out to the other side of the bed, searching for Brad.

Smooth, cold sheet.

The blunt force of reality knocked her out of slumber. In its wake came the flood of sharp, brutal memory. Adrenaline kicked in, replaying her time in the swell, trying to rescue him. But he was gone. He'd been gone before they'd reached him. The Pacific had made her a widow.

Heart thumping, she fumbled along the edge of her nightstand, her fingers grazing the control panel. The thick blinds slid upwards. The water reflection of moonlight filtered into the room. How the hell had she got here?

She slid out of bed and made her way slowly to the bathroom. The mirror never lied, not this one, where a daylight filter showed up every pore, line and blemish. Brad had always joked that he'd have it removed one day when they were finally too old to care.

She'd aged ten years in less than a day. Her skin was blotchy and swollen, her eyes bloodshot. She ran her hands through her hair, feeling gritty grains of sand loosen and fall to the limestone floor.

She turned on the shower and stepped under the stream of warm water. A wave of dizziness washed over her. She sat down, letting the water soak in through the toweling robe someone had put on her earlier. The rainfall, tapping on her skull, blunted the ricocheting thoughts trammeling her mind.

A figure appeared behind the wall of glass, now beaded with water.

"Cait?" she said, not sure if she was hallucinating.

The water shut off.

"Oh God, Anna. I'm so sorry." Caitlin grabbed a large bath sheet in one hand, and reached down with the other, helping her up. She removed the sodden bathrobe and wrapped her in the towel.

"I came as soon as I got the call. I'm so sorry about Brad. It's utterly tragic."

Anna reached for a hand towel. The scent of Brad's oud and cedar scent accompanied it. She buried her face in its folds, willing him to walk in and tell her that this was all a nightmare.

"Jack?"

"I checked on him a few minutes ago. He's asleep for now. Come on, you're shivering. Let's go down and have a cup of tea."

Anna looked in on Jack as they passed his room. Gui's head was resting on the pillow next to him. Neither of them stirred.

At the bottom of the stairs Caitlin headed to the kitchen. Anna slowed, pausing outside Brad's study. The door was closed like it often was at night, when he was burning the midnight oil.

She couldn't bring herself to go in there now. Later.

Along with the tea, Caitlin passed her a blueberry scone. Anna pushed it to one side.

Caitlin moved it back. "You've got to eat; you're going to need your strength."

Anna took a bite, grimacing at the act of normalcy, when her life was so far from it. The kitchen clock was moving its hands glacially—10:15pm. She'd got a whole life to carry on living after this, and if time moved this slowly from now on, it was going to be torture.

"I spoke to the police officer who brought you back here with the paramedics. She said she'd be in contact again when the inquest was done."

"Inquest?" Her pulse raced.

Caitlin squeezed her hand. "A formality, the officer said. Oh God, sorry, Anna, I just wanted to tell you what's been happening."

Anna took a deep breath. "Jack? He knows?"

"He was at the beach. He knows. Didn't want to talk with me about it. He'd been waiting for you to wake up."

Tears pricked her eyes. "I can't believe Brad's gone, Cait. He called up the stairs this morning before he went out, asking if I wanted a coffee while he was making his. I said no, I'd get it later. I should have said yes. If I'd said yes, this wouldn't have happened."

"No guilt. No thoughts of what if." Caitlin squeezed her hand, continuing with her update... the beach, the police report.

It was after eleven when Anna crawled back between the sheets. She lay there in the silence, waiting for sleep to shut down the horror of the day that was on constant replay in her head.

Twenty minutes later she gave in, reached for the newly prescribed pills at her bedside and popped two out of their blister packaging.

ByteBeat Exclusive by Kobe Otieno

"Hanging Ten—TopMatch Founder's Final Ride"

(PHOTO—copyright ByteBeat)

Brad and Anna Jones, poster kids of the dot.com boom, found themselves in turbulent waters out at Stinson Beach earlier today.

A suspected rogue wave toppled tech giant from his daily ride on his $75k Satoshi longboard.

Celebrated dot.commer and cyberpsychologist wife, Dr. Anna Jones, battled treacherous conditions in her $1k silk La Perla slip to rescue her husband of sixteen years.

Stinson surfers, Coop and JT, pulled them from the ocean.

Trauma doubled down after resuscitation attempts on Brad Jones were futile.

"Coop got it the worst. He worked on the dude. Didn't know he was already dead," said JT, during an interview at their retro rental apartment.

The accident occurred down the beach from the couple's $45m home.

The couple scooped a $250m payday in 2001 with the IPO of dating juggernaut TopMatch.

CHAPTER SIX

SIX MONTHS BEFORE BRAD'S DEATH

The furnace of the desert and fire inside him was so perfect that Brad couldn't think of a time when he was more at peace. Crystal meth ignition of his brain, and the dopamine was hitting its high notes, generating a high that knew no bounds.

The weight of his existence had sloughed off about an hour ago when he'd taken his first hit. His annual trip out of himself was underway.

Sometimes he contemplated going down the rabbit hole forever. He'd got the time, and God knew he had the money. He could even, if he put his mind to it, load up his 3D printer with a cocktail of raw materials and print out his own drugs. Custom created and designed. He could go *Breaking Bad*—but with deeper pockets, style, etc. and take over the West Coast supply chain.

"Hey, you up for a ride?"

He looked up from where he was sitting in cross-legged contemplation, out on the wooden deck with a view across the searing heat of The Playa. He liked this perch. Removed, yet in the thick of it. Dwight was standing, dressed in a pair of camo shorts and his signature leather waistcoat that he'd worn to the last sixteen years of Burning Man.

It suddenly hit Brad that they were veterans now, the old guard who rocked up year on year to play fast and loose, giving over to hedonism.

His phone pinged with the custom ringtone that meant only one caller. "Hey, A," he said, picking up.

"I'm in the car with Jack."

"And..."

"We did it, Dad!"

"Nice one, Jack. Score?"

"Five-one. I scored the final goal."

"Awesome. You on your way home?"

"We're going to Ranch for dinner," said Anna.

"When are you coming home, Dad?"

"A few more days." A pang of guilt cut his buzz. "Tell you what, we'll take the bikes up Mount Tam, do a freefall ride."

"Cool!"

Guilt erased.

"You take care up there."

She had a way of letting him know that as much as it was way out of her comfort zone, she knew the terrain. He did a quick mental recap of her study projects over the years to check if Burning Man had ever fallen under her cyberpsych microscope, but he was pretty sure it hadn't... yet.

"Will do."

They hung up.

He took another shot of tequila and zeroed in on the stars of Orion's Belt, fanned across the desert night sky. Up there so tiny, but in reality each one several times more massive than the sun.

And then he was young again, seventeen years younger. Raw, unchecked energy was flowing through his body. He was sitting at his desk in the TopMatch headquarters, with the sun setting on another day in South Park, San Francisco's tech sweet spot, which in many ways was more home to him than his small, sparsely furnished rental across the city.

He was wrestling with an unstable codebase. The progress was slow. His engineering team had failed to help him find the root cause, and had, one by one, peeled away and gone home. But he, code master supremo, was unyielding, knowing that somehow he'd find that bastard line of code, and slay it with his keyboard.

"Hey, man, we've gotta get going."

He glanced up to find his operations manager, Josef, standing by the wall switch, ready to flick off the main lights.

"Huh?"

"Nathan's party."

"I'll catch you there later."

Josef turned off the lights, plummeting the office into gloom and shadow. Only the ghostly glow of the desktop screen gave any illumination of the toil still underway. But he didn't leave. "Not this time, Brad. You owe me for the last two 'I'll catch you later'. The no-show ones. Remember?"

Brad shifted in his chair, cramped from being sat in it for hours. He reached for his coffee cup, but the contents were stone cold. Time had warped on him again. "I promise I'll make it."

Josef walked over, pulling on his leather jacket. "Leave it. Vlad's back in tomorrow. He can pick it up."

"I'm close. I can push it over the line."

"Listen, you hired me to operate this place. You're a part of that remit. You have gotta get a work-life balance going, otherwise you'll burn out. And if you burn out then we all go with you."

The cab dropped them outside Nathan's building in the

heart of The Marina. Fog had sucked in from the Pacific and was obscuring the old Victorian building.

Still aggravated by the code issue, Brad poured himself a double vodka on the rocks and headed straight through the crowd and out onto the balcony. A few engineers from Nathan's company were huddled at one end. He let the iced spirit wash over his tongue, and tuned into their tech talk.

"Want a toke?" said Josef, passing him a joint.

"No thanks. Keeping sharp."

As the vodka stemmed the tide of work in his brain, he turned his attention to the crowd through the window. A few of them were now dancing on the stained woodblock floor to Nirvana. The old, beat up La-Z-Boy couches that he and Nathan had sat in a couple of years back, for days on end discussing business ideas, had been pushed up against the walls. The 70s dining table had been repurposed into a bar, loaded with a couple of kegs, flagons of vodka, and a pitcher of ice.

Through in the tile kitchen he could see Nathan. Hard to miss him in his blue blazer and chinos amongst a writhing mass of jeans, T-shirts and sneakers.

Caitlin was with him, looking equally out of place in five-inch heels and short black dress. She wouldn't be there long. He gave her another five minutes before she headed off to some fancy restaurant. As if on cue, she stepped out into the main living room, but instead of heading for the door she crossed the room to speak with one of their database engineers.

Back in the kitchen he watched Nathan step to one side, and in that movement he undid everything that Brad had resolved to leave until later in life, for when he had time and money.

A tall, blonde woman with Nordic features was being talked at by Nathan. The way she was listening, nursing a plastic cup, unblinking look, mirrored how he often felt when Nathan got underway with his spiel of world-conquering ideals.

Brad knew only one thing. He had to rescue this woman. "Nathan, you're killing her," he said, walking into the kitchen.

Nathan turned and laughed. "Hey, man, good to see you."

They clapped each other on the back.

"Secure your next round?" said Nathan.

"Getting there. Couple of VCs sniffing around." He turned to the woman. "Has he told you how he's going to revolutionize the way that banks communicate with their customers in a synergistic play?"

She smiled.

"Exactly."

"Brad Jones," he said, shaking her hand. She had a firm grip, looked him in the eye. Blue eyes. Piercing, glacier blue. Damn.

"Anna Hartley."

A girl appeared at Nathan's side. She hooked her hand around his upper arm and levered him out of the conversation in one swift move, ignoring Brad and Anna.

"Wow, was it something we said?" said Anna.

He looked at her, unfazed. "Welcome to California. English or Australian?"

She stifled a yawn. "Sorry, it's not you, I only came in from Sydney a couple of nights ago. But originally from London."

"Friend of Caitlin's?"

"Friend of a friend. Kelly and I were working together at the same marketing company in Sydney. She was at uni with Cait, and put me in touch. I'm guessing you work with Nathan the way you know his business?"

"We did a start-up together a couple of years back, but it never got off the ground. We went our own ways. I founded TopMatch." He paused, expecting a sign of recognition, but her face was a blank. "We're taking matchmaking and dating online."

She looked so horrified he wondered if she mistakenly thought he was making a pass at her. "We carefully vet the users..."

"Online? How could you begin to match people through technology? We're human beings."

"Who sometimes need help. We're developing algorithms that have had success in—"

"Where's the romance in that?"

Brad ran his hand through his hair. He was used to a receptive audience, curious to know where the magic happened in the code. "We've had our first marriage." He knew he was sounding defensive, but she was unnerving him.

"A marriage? Is that how you measure your success?"

"I see you two have met," said Caitlin, appearing at Anna's side.

Anna looked at her. "Would you go online to find love?"

Caitlin shrugged. "Since I've got Mark, no. But if something happened, maybe I would. How's your stable of hot guys on TopMatch?"

"Once we've broadened our content offering I'll let you know." Brad looked back at Anna. It wasn't often anyone challenged him like this. "Can I ask a favor?"

She took a step back, hand up. "No way am I signing up."

He shook his head. "I would never ask that. It's our content. I mean, not the clients, it's the content, the stories. We're struggling to keep it fresh. I need an honest, brutally honest opinion, on what we've got, and you seem like the ideal person to give that."

She was frowning.

"Of course, we will pay a consulting fee," he added.

Caitlin raised her cup. "Cheers to that. You needed a new gig, Anna."

Two days later Anna walked into their South of Market warehouse office. He didn't often think of how an outsider viewed their setup, but as she came in through the door in stilettos and a gray tailored business suit that clung to every curve on her body, he noticed how she glanced at the raw concrete walls, the fifty jeans wearing, sneaker only, T-shirted people hunched over computers perched on folding tables, how she stepped across rivers of electric cables.

"I should have tamped down on the office wear," she said.

He smiled. "They'll think you're a VC and take everything you say very seriously. Coffee?"

She nodded. He led her across to the makeshift kitchen screened off by a few sheets of ply that Josef had bought. He grabbed the filter jug off the warming plate and poured her a steaming cup of thick, black coffee.

"Help yourself to anything. We keep everyone here fed and watered at all times of day and night."

"You're a twenty-four-seven operation?"

"Depends. We're putting out a new release later today. Problems on the testing, though, so a few of us pulled an all-nighter." He yawned. "I'll catch up on sleep tonight. Community are looking forward to meeting you. Follow me."

He led her to the back bank of desks. "This is Rain, our community manager. She's going to show you what we've got and how we do it."

And that was it. Instant work-life calibration. Anna Hartley moved into the company, his apartment and his life.

CHAPTER SEVEN

2019

"Mom, hey, Mom, you gotta wake up! Cops are at the door."

Anna dragged her head up off the pillow. She'd been up pacing, unable to sleep half the night, having read that reporter's latest ByteBeat. He seemed to have lit a fire underneath the story of the Joneses, and was trending in major news feeds. Why the hell did he want to invade their lives?

"Mom!"

She swung her legs out of bed. Glancing at the mirror, she saw a grief-stricken woman staring back at her, eyes hollow and cheeks pale. She threw on Brad's old toweling robe over her PJs, the familiar scent of him enveloping her like a ghostly embrace.

Following Jack down the glass steps, she approached the double-height oak door that stood between them and the world outside. She paused at the security screen. Three cops stood on the other side, their expressions stern and unreadable. None of them were familiar. Two were in uniform, their badges glinting in the morning light, and one wore a black jacket, his hands tucked casually into his pockets.

Anna took a deep breath, steeling herself for whatever news they brought. "Hey, Gui, it's okay," she said, stroking the dog's head to calm the barking. "Why don't you take her upstairs with you. I'll handle this."

"You sure?" said Jack, putting his hand on her shoulder.

She opened the door. A cool breath of ocean fog came rushing in, breaking through the warm barrier of climate-controlled air.

"Mrs. Jones?" The cop in the black jacket held up a silver badge.

"This is she." Sounded formal, but right.

"Detective Ron Jaramillo. Can we come inside?"

"Is it urgent?"

"Important. We have the medical examiner's report on your husband."

She frowned. "He drowned."

"I'm afraid there's more to it."

That fleeting dark shadow she kept glimpsing in her mind's eye, flashed across her vision. A shudder ran through her. She led them into the kitchen. "Can I get you coffee?" she said, on autopilot.

At least if they accepted it'd give her time to recalibrate her fast scrambling mindset.

"Sure, thank you, ma'am," said Ron, answering for them all. He was evidently in charge. As she operated the coffee machine she wondered what "more to it" meant. There hadn't been any signs of shark attack; Brad was fit, athlete fit.

She passed out the cups, along with the milk jug and cane sugar jar, before making one for herself.

They sat at the driftwood kitchen table, that she'd bought from a surf guy who made them up in Bodega Bay.

One of the cops handed Ron a file. He pulled out a sheet of paper. "Office of the Medical Examiner: AUTOPSY REPORT" was spelled out in strong black type across the top.

He laid it flat on the table, smoothing it out, although there wasn't a crease in it.

She took a sip of coffee to calm her nerves.

"The report states they found high levels of ketamine in his blood."

Her brow knitted. "Ketamine?"

"Anesthetic, ma'am. We've checked his medical records and none has ever been prescribed."

"That's impossible." The palms of her hands burned as she tightened her grip around the steaming cup. Ron was now looking at her intently. She knew the read, he was looking for tells in her body language.

"Did your husband take drugs recreationally?"

"No. Maybe when he went to Burning Man, but that was only once a year. Rest of the time nothing but the odd drink."

"Did he suffer from depression?"

"No."

"The ketamine went in by intramuscular injection into his thigh. The levels were too high in the bloodstream for the body to safely break down the toxins. About seven minutes in from taking it, long enough to paddle out, he lost consciousness, and with that fell off his board, and drowned."

Her head was spinning. "My husband was NOT depressed. He would never leave us!" She knew her voice was rising, but she couldn't stop it. One of the cops put a hand on her shoulder. God, she was fed up with people trying to console her. She shrugged it off.

"Ma'am, I understand your confusion, but the facts are stated here." He pushed across the report, directing her gaze with his finger:

From the anatomic findings and pertinent history I ascribe the death to: DROWNING

Due to or as a consequence of: EFFECTS OF KETAMINE

Manner of death: SUICIDE

How injury occurred: Submerged in water after lethal injection of Ketamine.

Anger came bubbling up. Anna slammed her cup onto the table, coffee spilling to form a dark pool on the wood. "No way. He would never have done that in a million years. Drugs? Taking his life? You've got the wrong man." She was shaking now. Grief rising.

This time the cop took her by the arm, guiding her to sit back down. "Ma'am, I understand this is a big shock for you, but this is certified by the medical examiner." He reached into the folder, extracted another piece of paper and placed it next to the autopsy report.

"This is a search warrant issued by a Marin County judge earlier today. We need to search the property for evidence of illegal drug abuse."

———

The fog had now thickened, enveloping the glass house. In any other situation Anna would have enjoyed the eerie white light coming in through her and Brad's bedroom window. Shades of white on white, giving the room a cloud-like quality. Instead she felt like she was in a padded cell.

Since the cops had left, she'd scrubbed herself head to toe in a scalding hot shower, trying to wash away the grief and anger.

She pulled on a pair of jeans, marl gray T-shirt, and thick knit cashmere sweater, trying to hold back the meltdown that had been brewing since the cops had discovered two large vials of liquid ketamine, stashed at the back of Brad's desk drawer.

Jack didn't know yet. He'd been hooked into a game with his friends. She wasn't sure how to tell him, let alone how she was going to deal with it herself. Suicide? Brad would never do that.

She needed to speak to Caitlin. Grabbing her phone off the dressing table she headed onto the landing. Gui's tail thumped on the oak flooring. The Labrador got to her feet and went to greet Anna, who reached down, running her hand through the thick fur. Thank God for the dog.

Jack emerged from his bedroom door, his hair still damp from the shower. "Alicia's at the gate."

"What? How?"

He was already halfway down the stairs. "She got a ride over."

Christ, that was all she needed right now. Jack's girlfriend, or almost girlfriend.

"It's okay, right, Mom?" He paused at the bottom of the stairs, looking up at her.

"Yes, yes, of course. Just for a while. Not too late though."

He went to the door and opened it. Outside she could hear car doors opening and closing. Footsteps.

"Jack, I'm sorry!" Alicia, all long dark hair, still wearing her St. Mary's uniform, came running inside, straight into his arms.

A second later a tall, well-dressed man with the looks and casual elegance of a Ralph Lauren ad appeared in the doorway.

Hell no.

"Jack, we're so very sorry for your loss," he said, waiting for the young couple to part long enough for him to shake Jack's hand.

"Thank you, Mr. Lyle," he said. "My mom's..." Jack looked up to where she was standing on the top step. Scott Lyle followed his gaze.

There was nowhere to hide. She had to suck it up and go down.

Alicia gave her a hug, saying once again how sorry she was. In the next second she and Jack disappeared into the snug off the main sitting room.

"I'm sorry, Anna," said Scott Lyle. "I cannot imagine what you must be going through."

"Thank you."

"What time suits to pick up Alicia?"

"Um, a couple of hours. No later please. It's been a long day."

"Understood. I'll send my driver." He headed outside. She closed the door and took a deep breath. She wouldn't be able to hold back the tide of the outside world for long. Private grief was going to give way to public intrigue. How long could she keep a lid on Brad's suicide?

CHAPTER EIGHT

Kobe sat back in his chair. He was still in his sweats at 11am. First time in a long while that he didn't have to be perched at his listening post in the cafe, trying to gather pieces of gossip and intrigue to fuel his ByteBeat column.

Now the news was coming to him. Ever since the scoop on the Stinson Photo, as it was now known. He was at the epicenter of a whirlpool. Fragments and memories came flooding in through all his comms channels, shining a light on the old days of the tech boom when Brad and Anna Jones had hit the big time.

His ByteBeat column had gone viral, hitting national and international news channels. His boss had paid him back for the photo, licensed it out, providing a big payout for *Code Life*. And just now he'd got the pay raise he'd been campaigning for the last eighteen months—instantly, just like that, when his subscriber base had gone north of 250K followers.

He stood up and walked to his fridge, opening the door on what was a post-apocalyptic variety of old takeouts, bottles of ancient sauces, and tubs of random spreads that'd caught his eye on his rare outings to a supermarket. Grabbing a garbage bag, he reached in and systematically cleared each shelf and rack, until it was empty. Clean slate.

He'd used the Quorum app to sign himself up for their "Daily Quorum" to be delivered to his doorstep each day, with the first dose coming any minute. Not a cheap subscription but hey, he deserved it.

Another swath of messages came spooling in. More material that hadn't cost him a dime. He flicked down the list, stopping at one from "Lana Fernandez". Name looked familiar. Lana... he put down his phone and went to the window.

The only reason he'd signed up for this apartment—apart from the low deposit—was that he could see a sliver of the Dumbarton Bridge between the two apartment blocks opposite. Those concrete struts rising over the Bay were a reminder that one day he'd be living somewhere with a panoramic view of the Golden Gate Bridge. Small beginnings but major goal setting.

As he watched how the sun painted it in light and shade he pondered on the name Lana Fernandez. Hadn't been in the column, definitely hadn't dated her, *Code Life*... early days... Bingo!

Lana Fernandez, the designer who had brought the editor a graphic that had so impressed him he'd used it on the front cover. But it turned out it wasn't hers. Someone else had spent months creating it, and she'd passed it off as her own. The editor fired Lana and the incident cost the magazine a slice of reputation, and compensatory dollars.

Interest piqued, Kobe went back to his phone to see what she had to say. A smile formed on his lips and he hit her number. "Hey, Lana, Kobe. Long time no speak."

"You got my message then?"

"Yeah. Interesting stuff. I'll confess I'm gun-shy on using you as a source after what you did at the magazine."

She had the balls to laugh. "Past history. I don't do that kind of shit any more. I'm as true as they come."

"You got backup on this?"

"Kept printouts of a few email threads, got a few photos from back in the day. Got them in the basement."

"Okay."

"A thousand and they're yours with an interview."

"No. You know *Code Life* doesn't do payouts for information. Goes against the grain."

"Well as I see it, this is juicy stuff you're getting, and it's about time I got a payout from you guys since you never settled on my final paycheck."

His door buzzer went. He crossed the room and opened the door. The Quorum delivery driver handed him his first daily dose. He ripped the top off and downed half of it. Why did the universe bring people like this back into your life a second time?

"And, to sweeten the deal, I'll tell you about me seeing Brad Jones up at Burning Man only a few months back."

"Text me your address and I'll come by." He hung up.

ByteBeat by Kobe Otieno
Featuring exclusive interview with ex-TopMatch Creative Director,
Lana Fernandez
"Man of The Playa"
*(PHOTO—Living the high life at Burning Man. Brad Jones on his
$10K T-Bike, copyright Lana Fernandez)*

TopMatch founder had a penchant for letting loose during his annual hiatus to Burning Man. "He was out of his mind when I met him," said Fernandez.

Jones and TopMatch investor Dwight Laroy founded

Burning Man's ADTIBE camp during TopMatch's race to IPO. Home for the nine days of burn up in Nevada's Black Desert is a custom-built UFO complete with bar and sound stage.

ADTIBE's bar is one of the premium stocked places for the post-economic tech crowd to gather and shoot ideas. "I know they budget over $500K: the bartender told me while he mixed me a Martini," said Fernandez.

And now we hop in the time machine again to those heady days around the millennium, to South Park, where dating giants of the day, TopMatch and LoveLink, went head to head in their domination of the online dating space. (You gotta remember here, readers, that this was pre-swipe when your best chance of finding love was in the bar next door.)

Their rivalry reached an all-time head when LoveLink CEO, the late Vikrant Chomodsky, moved his entire team into the floor below TopMatch's HQ, piggy-backing onto a state of the art new internet pipe that Jones had just installed in the building, using his latest funding round dollars.

This move triggered an all-out battle, resulting in a fight between the two CEOs in the back stairwell.

"It was one hell of a fight," remembered Fernandez. "Anna finally broke them up by setting off the fire alarm. Trouble was, a rogue sprinkler went off up in the TopMatch server room. Damage was intense but they couldn't get an insurance payout so Brad had to sell his BMW to cover it."

TopMatch was known for its free-flowing Friday nights where it was an open invite to local dot.coms to drink and dance in the open space warehouse top floor.

"It was a shit show," Fernandez recalled. "Brad went wild, went down to LoveLink's offices and had it out with Vikrant, who of course denied it all. No surprise that his company suddenly rolled out a whole load of new features that pushed LoveLink to number one in the dating sphere."

CHAPTER NINE

Despite the neurological consequences, Anna couldn't help herself. She was lying in bed doomscrolling through the comments people had posted on the ByteBeat column. The trolls were out in force.

Vikrant and Brad's rivalry she knew about, but Burning Man, she'd always gone along with a "don't ask, don't tell" approach to Brad's few annual days of hedonism. Now Lana had ripped the Band-Aid off, she was learning at the same time as the rest of the world about what really went on up at the festival in the desert. It was the *out of his mind* quote that had punched her hard in the gut. She'd been brushing her teeth, trying to scour away grief and anger when her phone had pinged with the fresh column. Caitlin had told her not to subscribe, that she'd filter the outside world for her, but Anna had signed up anyway because whatever was being said she wanted to hear it uncensored.

Those four words. Was that how he had ended it?

She scrolled back up to the column itself and ran her finger across the photo. It was a side of him she didn't recognize. Their family vacations were spent skiing, hiking, with the occasional tropical beach getaway to some five-star retreat. The man in the photo was not that husband or father. Fresh tears came, blurring the image.

The day had stretched out like a bleak, endless road. She'd broken the news to Jack that morning, the word *suicide* detonating an emotional bomb. Raw and uncontrolled grief echoing through their home, and then the questions had come— the whys, hows, what-ifs.

They'd pulled Brad's office apart, scrambling through files and books, trawling through his laptop, hunting for clues, reasons, anything that could explain the inexplicable. But they'd found nothing. Just the remnants of a life cut short.

That was when Jack had lost it and turned on her. "It's all your fault!" he'd screamed, his voice hoarse from crying.

She'd stood there, taking the brunt of her son's accusations. She could have fought back, but Jack's eyes mirrored her own pain.

When he'd finally run out of steam, he'd turned and run up the stairs, slamming his bedroom door shut. It'd taken everything in her not to rush after him.

Now here she was overloading her brain with the trolls' vile comments. She stuffed her phone into the bedside table drawer, out of sight. ByteBeat was poison.

10pm. The echoes of the argument with Jack still hung in the air, raw and unresolved.

She got up from the bed and walked out onto the landing. The silence of the house had a tomb-like quality to it. She took a seat on the top step of the staircase outside Jack's bedroom door.

"Jack," she called out. "We have to talk."

She heard Gui's paws land on the wood floor and patter across. There was a groan, followed by Jack's footsteps.

The door opened, revealing his silhouette against the dim light of his room. He stepped out, his eyes red but dry, his expression guarded. He was a mirror of Brad in that moment, the same defiant stance. "What's there to talk about?" he said. "Dad's gone. You can't change that."

She stood up. "No, I can't. But we can't tear each other apart, Jack. It won't bring him back."

He looked away, his hands clenching into fists. "I don't understand. Why he did it. Why he left us."

She took a step towards him. "Neither do I. But blaming me won't give us answers."

His eyes were full with pain and anger.

"Your dad loved you. More than anything. And he loved me. We have to keep living, Jack. Even when it hurts."

Jack's facade crumbled. "I'm sorry, Mom. I'm really sorry."

She pulled him in tight, and in that moment she made a silent vow. She'd dig in deep and get to the truth because the hell that was illustrated in that article was not her husband.

CHAPTER TEN

FOUR MONTHS BEFORE BRAD'S DEATH

A warm evening breeze blew across the raised stone terrace of Roaring Bear winery where a crowd of women in their twenties and thirties were enjoying a tasting. The winery's owners were personally pouring, helping the amateur palettes navigate the notes and tones of their finest vintages. Anna watched how Caitlin and Mark held their audience captive as they shared their passion for each bottle's contents.

"Think that's our next move? Quit the coast and set up a winery up here?" said Brad, his hand on the small of Anna's back.

They were standing to one side, taking a moment out of the evening's proceedings.

She laughed. "Think we leave that to the professionals. Speaking of which, who's doing the speech before the awards? You or me?"

He leaned in close to her ear. "I'll leave that to Dr. Jones."

"Okay, then you're on the hook for the aftermath."

They clinked glasses and drank the RB Mk II Cabernet that Mark insisted was their go-to for the night.

It wasn't the first time that Anna wondered how a man who

had been top of Silicon Valley's sales team league for a decade, could move so effortlessly to become a man of the soil and vine. He'd cashed out his stock, ditching everything that didn't connect him to the natural world, except Caitlin.

They'd moved to Napa when she and Brad had opted for Stinson. Instead of sales forecasts Mark had moved into biodynamic farming. The results were a vineyard that produced award-winning wines.

"Why doesn't Cait stick to this full time? She'd look a hell of a lot less stressed," said Brad.

"You know Cait, can't quit the sales game. She likes the stress, says it keeps her edge, otherwise she'd get bored to shit up here."

They looked out past the tasting to the rows of neatly pruned vines, rolling out as far as the eye could see.

"It's so tidy. Like some perfect green wave."

"Yeah, but give me the ocean any day."

"That's because you surf."

He turned towards her, blocking the view. "Shine worn off our beach?"

She shrugged. "No, but is that it? Do you think we'll be on the beach for the rest of our lives?"

"You having some existential crisis about our future?" he said.

"No, just wondering if it's as good as it gets."

He frowned. "We built the forever house, remember?"

"You built the forever house. Remember how you obsessed over it? The staircase."

He jolted, wine sloshed up and out, hitting his white shirt. "Fuck!" he said, loudly.

A few of the women nearest turned around.

Anna reached out to blot the spreading red stain with her cocktail napkin, but he brushed her away.

52

"It's fine, I've got it," he said, and walked off into the building.

———

Dinner was served. The meal was a triumph, Mark could tell by the sated expressions on the diners' faces. All except Brad, which was unusual since the guy was obsessed by fine wines and food.

"Hey, buddy, Merlot didn't work with the mille-feuille?"

Brad looked across at him, instantly replacing the frozen mask with a smile. "Worked great. You guys knocked it out the ballpark. Thanks again for hosting this."

"No problem. You know Cait and I like to help out where we can."

Their conversation was interrupted by someone tapping a spoon against a wine glass. Caitlin stepped up onto the wood podium they'd hired. Mark smiled. Man, she looked hot in that dress. If he played his cards right, maybe he'd get lucky tonight.

"I'd like to say how wonderful it is to have you all here tonight at Roaring Bear. Brad and I are delighted to share this special place with you all on such a special occasion..."

It was great seeing his wife in action, holding the audience in rapt attention. If she was selling something to them now, hands down, they'd buy it. That was why she couldn't let the job go that had her up at 5am to catch a flight. She was addicted to the close.

Next up came Dr. Jones of the Jones Foundation. He had to admit he was surprised when it was Brad, not Anna, who had set up the foundation to champion the cause of helping women achieve their potential in science and technology. He'd done it shortly after TopMatch's IPO when Anna had been heavily pregnant. He'd always thought Brad was more of a moonshot kind of guy who would've gone full philanthropic on something like finding life on Mars.

He enjoyed the Merlot and listened to Anna's deep-dive speech into what the Jones Foundation awards were about, and how important it was that mental clarity and health were maintained in the ever shifting sands of tech. AI was the next frontier and there had never been a more important time than now for the female gaze to imprint on the industry. The resounding cheer from the audience was testament to an ability, just like Caitlin's, to captivate and corral.

As she spoke he could see Brad out of the corner of his eye, watching her up there on stage. He might as well have been watching the news, the way he was sitting, glazed over. First off, Anna was stunning. Always had been in some kind of Viking way. She wasn't his type, not like Caitlin, but he knew the effect she had on other men. Back in the day when the four of them had been out on the town, guys had pulled him to one side asking what the secret was to get girls like theirs on their arms. He'd always joked it took a big lasso.

Hell, marriage was a long game. He knew that. But having a firecracker wife made it a thrilling ride.

It struck him now, in this very moment, that although he'd known Brad over twenty years, he didn't really *know* him. They got along because of Caitlin and Anna, and of course the kids, but beyond that, they didn't hang out even though they were both keen mountain bikers.

CHAPTER ELEVEN

2019

Caitlin stepped out of the car, not pausing to take in the view over the chaparral-covered hillside, the roof tops of Stinson Beach, and beyond, to the pale gray churn of the Pacific. The traffic on the 101 had been stop and go, leaving her with only minutes to check on the flowers before everyone arrived.

She entered the whitewashed chapel, her stilettos clicking on the flagstone aisle up to the altar. The moment she'd found this place, built by the original settlers, she'd known this was it.

"Suits Brad's pioneering instincts," Mark had said, when she'd shown him the photos.

She knew Brad hadn't been religious. He'd been raised in a commune somewhere in Oregon. She remembered the heated debate between him and Anna when choosing the location for their marriage. His atheist leanings had led to a compromise of them exchanging their vows in a local redwood forest.

But since Caitlin had taken the funeral into her own hands, to help out Anna, who was reeling from Brad's newly ascribed cause of death, she felt a place like this gave a feeling of salvation and peace.

As she checked on the lily and white rose arrangements that

she'd engaged the floral designer to create with an eye on the theme of "an unexpected ending", her mind drifted once again to the fact that Brad had taken his own life. God, it was ghastly. Unthinkable that he'd left Anna and Jack. No note, no closure, just a great big mess left in his wake. And Jack had been so silent. She was worried about him. Thank God for the dog. It deserved a service medal.

It was her mission now to pick up the pieces, and put Anna back together again. Or at least to try, because in reality she herself was frightened her friend might never recover.

But fear was not an option. Not now. Not when Anna and Jack needed her the most. She took a deep breath, steeling herself for the task ahead. She would be the rock, the steady hand, the unyielding support. She would navigate this treacherous landscape of loss and longing with them one step at a time.

The chapel filled, the air thick with the hushed whispers of mourners exchanging condolences. Caitlin took her seat beside Anna, clasping her hand, her gaze sweeping over the gathering crowd. She knew that among the sea of faces, only a handful knew the truth—herself, Anna, Jack, Dwight, and Mark.

The weight of it was a heavy shroud. To the world, Brad had been claimed by the sea, swallowed by the relentless tide. A tragic accident, a life cut short by the capricious whims of nature. Mark had helped create the narrative, a lie that was easier to swallow than the bitter truth. Anything to get them through this.

Caitlin's eyes met Dwight's across the aisle, a silent understanding passing between them. Anna had asked the police to hold the truth "in process" for as long as possible, to keep the lid on the ugly reality. But how long they could maintain this facade, she didn't dare guess.

Dwight stepped up to the pulpit. He looked out, his eyes lingering briefly on Anna and Jack. Caitlin tensed.

"Brad was a man of extraordinary talents," he began, his voice echoing through the chapel. "He built an internet phenomenon from the ground up, his brilliant mind and big heart driving him to create something that would touch the lives of millions. He was a man who loved deeply, who lived passionately, who inspired those around him to reach for the stars. He also founded and spearheaded the Jones Foundation, championing the cause of helping women achieve their potential in science and technology."

His voice was steady, his words measured, as he painted a picture of a man who had been a visionary, a pioneer, a friend. But Caitlin knew it was a story with gaping holes.

He left out any mention of the annual Burning Man pilgrimage. He left out the truth, the harsh, unfiltered reality of Brad's final moments.

Finally, he stepped down from the pulpit. The chapel filled with an orchestral arrangement of The Doors' "Riders On The Storm" played by a few members of the SF symphony, who Caitlin had engaged for the service. Anna had chosen the song, it'd been one of Brad's favorites.

Caitlin dared herself to finally look at Anna. The tears were streaming down her cheeks, silent sobs racking her body. Reaching into her pocket, she passed her a tissue, vowing to herself that they would keep the lid on the truth for as long as they could. Because that's what friends did. They stood by each other, through joy and sorrow, life and death.

CHAPTER TWELVE

The Pelican Inn loomed out of the fog like a spectral apparition as the limo crunched to a halt on the gravel. Anna stared out of the window, her eyes glazed. The world looked blurred and indistinct.

She stepped out of the car, the chill air wrapping itself around her in a cold embrace. The scent of woodsmoke came drifting in, and she could hear the murmur of voices, clink of glasses, and forced joviality of a gathering determined to celebrate Brad's life.

The question still plagued her. Why? Why had Brad done this? Why had he chosen to leave her, Jack, and this world in such a brutal way? And with that question came wave after wave of anger. But beneath the anger, there was something else. A nagging doubt. What if he hadn't done it?

She walked into the pub, and headed straight to where Mark and Dwight were standing at the bar, their heads bent together in hushed conversation.

"Anna," said Dwight, putting his hand on her shoulder. "How are you holding up?"

She shrugged. How was she holding up? She was drowning,

that's how she was holding up. "I need to know. I need to know if there's a chance, any chance at all, that Brad didn't... that he couldn't..." She couldn't bring herself to say the words.

Dwight glanced at Mark. "Anna," he said. "We've been over this. We never touched ketamine, not at Burning Man, not anywhere. Brad never showed any interest in that stuff. He was always so careful, controlled, just a hit of weed every so often..."

His voice trailed off. She turned away, her gaze sweeping over the crowded room, the faces of friends and family, gossiping in small cliques. One of them caught her eye, waving her over.

How many hands she shook, hugs she was given, she'd no idea. The faces blurred into an indistinguishable mass, the words of condolence merging into a monotonous drone. "So sorry for your loss." "He was a great man." "If there's anything you need..." She accepted them all with a grace born out of numbness.

She caught sight of Jack across the room, his friends huddled around him like a protective shield. Alicia was there, her arm linked through his, her head leaning against his shoulder. They were a tight-knit group. She watched as they retreated into the library room at the back to watch a movie.

She wished she could do the same, curl up in a corner, pull a blanket over her head, and block out the endless tide of sympathy.

"Anna, how are you?"

She turned from where she was standing at the window, holding a cup of tea that Caitlin had given her when she arrived.

Scott was standing there in a dark suit, hair wet from the rain outside. Weird she hadn't noticed him earlier.

"Sorry to miss the funeral. Something unavoidable came up so I sent Alicia on ahead with my driver."

He leaned in and kissed her cheek. For a second she was

paralyzed. It was the same cologne blend that Brad had worn—$500 a bottle of Tom Ford's Oud Wood.

"Alicia told us what had really happened. You must be all the more devastated."

That jolted her back into the present. She'd sworn Jack to secrecy. "Jack's not meant to have told anyone. Yet."

Scott held up a hand. "Of course. But when Alicia came back very upset the other day, she shared it with Kristy and me. It'll go no further than us. I promise."

Anna exhaled so heavily, the china cup rattled on its saucer.

He reached out, taking it from her hands. "Tea's stone cold. Sit down," he said, guiding her to the sofa. He signaled a waiter, and in the blink of an eye a glass balloon of brandy arrived on a silver tray.

The power of the Lyle family had everyone jumping to attention. He passed it to her. "Drink."

It wasn't a question, it was an order and if she'd been her normal self, she'd have challenged him. But right now she didn't have the strength so she put the glass to her lips. The brandy lit a warm trail right down her throat into a stomach that hadn't seen food for twenty-four hours. The effect was immediate.

"Thank God," she said, taking another sip.

He gave a thin smile.

"Dad. You ready?"

They looked up to find Alicia walking in. She commanded the same sort of attention that her father did. If ever Anna thought she and Brad were wealthy, and that Jack was over-privileged, then they were eclipsed by the Lyles. Alicia was a chip off her mother's block—a society doyenne in the making.

Scott Lyle stood up. "If there's anything you need, just ask," he said, heading out.

Later, when they'd got back to the house and changed into sweats, Caitlin handed Anna a business card. "Okay, it's time. I've made you an appointment for tomorrow."

"For what?" Anna glanced down to read *Titus Creed, Grief Counselor and Clinical Hypnotherapist.* "No way. I want to process this on my own, thanks." She dropped the card on the coffee table like it was red hot. "I do not need anyone else going inside my head."

Caitlin refilled her wine glass. "Drink some more and let's at least talk about it."

"There's nothing to say, Cait. I'm not up to it."

"You're not up for it, but you know you need it."

Anna knew that tone. She'd heard it a million times over the years. It was Caitlin's tic, the one which silently broadcasted, *I'm not leaving until you say you'll do it.* She picked up the glass and took a sip of the chilled white wine. Now she could finally relax, lift the public mask of "Brad tragically drowned".

"He'll not find much in there but misery, anger and bewilderment. I mean, how the hell did my husband stick a needle full of ketamine in his thigh and then paddle out to sea and drown himself? It's not me Titus Creed should be examining but Brad, to get inside his head. But that's never going to happen, is it?"

Caitlin was shaking her head at the outburst. "I get it. But, you're here, Brad is gone, and you have to be here for Jack as well as yourself, so for the love of God, just go tomorrow and see this guy. And, if after that you feel it's not the right thing then okay, we'll think of something else."

CHAPTER THIRTEEN

The next morning Anna sat in the curve of the Mercedes' leather seat, looking out to where the waves were crashing against the base of the cliffs as the driver transported her into the restless energy of the city.

She'd put on jeans, sneakers and a black shirt, and had applied a lot of makeup, wanting to look well enough to ride under the therapist's radar. As she climbed out on the street corner she rehearsed the words and phrases she was going to use to project the grieving widow in control of her emotions, despite the tragedy of her husband's suicide.

She was definitely going to refer to it as suicide, even though the word felt like sandpaper in her throat. Best say it as it was, showing she wasn't afraid to speak the truth.

When she stepped out of the elevator onto the eighteenth floor of a new high-rise on Battery, she was surprised to find his suite occupied the entire floor under the banner of "Creed Therapies". She entered a light and bright, wood and glass complex of offices, with a central reception that wouldn't have been out of place in a Scandi design magazine.

A receptionist wearing oversize wire-framed glasses took her name, and guided her down a long hallway lined with black and white photos of fjords and forests, to the end, where a door stood open.

The view was the first thing that struck her. She could see down to the water. Scanning along the wharves she located the old Pier 23 restaurant where she and Brad had often gone after work, to chill out, drink cocktails, and eat crab linguine. Those days were long since gone, but the place was still there, the same, despite all the wharf reconstruction.

"Dr. Jones?"

She tore her gaze away from the glass to find a man with swept back salt and pepper hair, wearing a white shirt and blue jeans, getting up from a taupe linen sofa. He had an athletic build, and his sleeves were rolled up to the elbow. He was neither tall nor short, and if she had to guess she'd say he played tennis. She'd no idea where she'd pulled that thought from, but if you put him on court he looked like he'd play a strong game.

He held out his hand and gave her a firm handshake. "Titus Creed."

He was unremarkable except for his eyes. They were hazel, flecked with black dots. As he looked at her it was as if he was looking directly into her very core. She flinched at the intrusion. "Sorry," she said, snatching back her hand.

"Nothing to be sorry for. My deepest condolences." His voice was deep, measured. She wondered how many times he'd had to say that to his clients.

The receptionist left, closing the door behind her. Titus offered her the sofa he'd been sitting on and moved to a chestnut leather armchair on the opposite side of a long, low glass coffee table.

The first half hour he asked questions, which Anna batted back to him, keeping the responses short and to the point. "How do you feel?" / "Tired" was pretty much how it rolled.

She sensed she was making enough progress to be able to cut the session short and leave, having given it a good go for Caitlin's sake.

"Okay, Anna, let's cut to the chase. You don't want to be here, do you?"

That caught her off guard. Here she'd been expressing small darts of controlled emotion, and he was shifting the bull's-eye target, and now calling her Anna instead of Dr. Jones.

"Frankly no," she said. "I came here because my friend said I need this, but I don't. I'm quite capable of navigating the murky depths of grief, and coming out the other side on my own."

He didn't respond. They sat in silence. She felt it awkward to get up and leave on that note, so she waited for him to say something. Nothing. She caught his eye. The stare was like some laser, so she quickly moved her attention to a large jade plant next to his desk.

The minutes ticked by. She found herself beginning to relax in the quiet, and his observing her no longer annoyed her.

"So you hypnotize people," she said, the flame of curiosity finally sparking from the ashes of her mind.

It was the first time since Brad had gone that it'd resurfaced. Normally it fueled her days, powering her through mining the latest cyberdata and research, to find meaning and patterns.

He smiled. "Not all people, only my clients, and only with their permission. It's deep work that can help them understand more about themselves, and find clarity in perplexing issues."

"Do you think I need it?"

"We're a ways off getting to that point since so far I've only learnt that you're tired, stressed and busy sorting out all your late husband's affairs, while trying to get your and your son's life back on track," he said, referring to his notes.

She had to admit this guy was good. It was the dry, sardonic way he delivered the few observations he'd amassed over the last forty minutes.

It propelled her to get up from the sofa, reach across with her hand outstretched. It was now or never. "Can we start again?"

He took it. Time to share the thing that felt worse than death itself.

"I'm Anna Jones. Ever since Brad, committed suicide I keep getting flashes of a kind of shadow person in my head that chills me to the bone, and I want you to find a way to help me get rid of it."

CHAPTER FOURTEEN

When she stepped out into the street from Creed, the last thing she wanted to do was go home. Caitlin would have dropped Jack at school on her way back to Napa. She was angry at herself for revealing the dark shadow form that had now set up home somewhere along her mind's horizon. It was, as Titus had suggested, possibly to do with the nature of Brad's death.

"Suicide leads to a lot of unanswered questions for those left behind," he'd said.

At the end of their session he'd talked of a potential path forward, using hypnotherapy.

She'd said she'd think about it.

She checked the Patek Philippe watch that Brad had given her for her thirtieth birthday. The forty-eight diamond encrusted bezel of the "Aquanaut" glittered in the sunshine. It was so showy it was only the second time she'd worn it. But when she'd got dressed that morning, it'd called "armor" to her from the backseat row of her jewelry safe.

The delicate rose gold hands hadn't made it past noon. She watched the second hand circumnavigating the dial, methodically ticking off more seconds of her existence. Had Brad done the same, knowing he'd got seven minutes to paddle out?

She shuddered and started walking in the direction of Union Square, to where she could sink into the comforting arms of retail therapy.

The red and white flags waving in the breeze up the street called to her. She walked in through heavy black doors, into the serene luxury shopping experience that was Gumps. This was the closest she felt to religion amongst the hushed, museum-style curation of exquisite *objets d'art* and artifacts. Notes of cardamon and lime flowers scented the air.

She ran her fingers over the surface of a Robert Kuo lacquered entry table. Silken and cool to the touch. A tall jade glass Lalique vase stood at its center, the price tag of $18k offering *"An invitation to a dreamlike walk in the under bush, the Mûres vase exhibits an abundance of berries jealously protected by intertwined brambles."*

"Anna?"

She turned to find Kristy Lyle on her way out of the store, carrying a small, ribboned Gumps bag. She was, as ever, immaculately turned out in a long camel coat and boots with her hair in a tightly wound bun. They exchanged air kisses. Definitely not what Anna needed right now.

"I'm so sorry about Brad."

"Thank you for your note. It was much appreciated."

It'd arrived two days after the beach. A gold embossed envelope with indigo lining, containing a woven linen notecard embossed with *Kristen Van Hoeveren Lyle*. When she'd opened it to read Kristy's handwritten note of deepest condolence, she wondered if there were a lot of those notes she wrote, since the edges were etched in black ink.

"It's so nice that Alicia is there for Jack."

"She's a nice girl, he's lucky."

Kristy smiled, warmed by the praise.

Anna thought back to how Brad had freaked out, bringing an evening of World War Three to the Jones' midweek supper when Jack had announced his new friendship with Alicia Lyle, who went to St. Mary's in the city.

"Absolutely no way are you going to be friends with that girl," he'd said, slamming his fist down on the hard oak of the table.

"Why? You'd like her."

"I don't care what she's like, you are never to see that girl again!" Brad's face had gone puce, like some pressure cooker had just gone off inside him.

Anna had reached out across the table to steady him, but he'd jumped to his feet.

"Brad, that was years ago. You can't punish a girl just because she's Scott Lyle's daughter."

"NO FUCKING WAY! DO YOU HEAR ME?"

Anna had leapt up and grabbed his arm, pulling him away from Jack. "For God's sake, Brad, calm down!"

"I won't fucking calm down."

"Dad? What the hell?"

"Promise me you will never see her again."

"But why?"

Brad was now making a face as if he'd been given a bucketful of Tabasco. "She's a FUCKING LYLE!"

"STOP SWEARING, BRAD!" she'd screamed.

He'd hurled the crystal tumbler holding his drink at the marble surround of the fireplace, shattering it into a thousand pieces.

"Take Gui and go to your room. I'll take care of this," she'd whispered to Jack.

Her son had headed upstairs, leaving her to deal with the fallout. Using the best of her psych tools, she talked her husband down.

The result was that she'd brokered Jack not seeing Alicia again. That way old business wounds could be redressed.

Later up in Jack's room, she'd spoken with her son. "Your dad had a rough time taking TopMatch to IPO, and it wasn't helped by Lyle Venture Partners who, even though they invested, made it very hard on us, especially him. Scott Lyle was tricky to deal with, but your dad got it all worked out in the end. I said I'd talk to you and get your agreement not to see her again."

"But, Mom, I like her."

"I get that, but for your dad's sake..." She'd kissed the top of his head, and went back to smooth the frayed edges of her husband's past.

Kristy Van Hoeveren Lyle had been having a trying morning before she'd bumped into Anna. The new housekeeper had failed to answer the door in time to receive the signed-for delivery that she needed for today's De Young Board Trustee luncheon. So she'd had to run to Gumps to buy a last-minute replacement birthday gift for Georgia Kleinhof. And that meant she'd had to skip her facial aesthetics appointment, which she'd had in the diary for weeks. To make matters worse a new wrinkle had appeared overnight, compounding the utter frustration of the day.

But all that had vanished when she saw Anna Jones walk in through the doors. She was almost relieved at Anna's widowhood, a spanner finally thrown into the untainted image of the Joneses.

Her mind flashed to that moment, before TopMatch and the Joneses had become anything. She and Scott had just finished their SF opera board dinner, upstairs on the balcony. They were on their way out through the bar, when Scott had been intercepted by Brad. He was touting for investment and of course targeted Scott. She'd been rather taken by the young, surfer-style looks of the budding CEO.

She'd told Candice all about him at tennis the next morning: "Who knew someone in tech would look so good?" she'd said, on her second serve. They laughed. It was nice to let loose. So much of the time she had to be all buttoned up, showing decorum and poise. But what was played on the tennis court, stayed on court.

She'd been less impressed when he'd introduced his colleague and girlfriend, Anna. Some sort of boho Brit who, with all her long blonde hair, was over-alluring, even in leggings and slouchy sweater. She'd noticed Scott's radar go up. Had to rein him in, get them moving on and out.

She smiled at Anna's new mantle of widowhood, and found herself almost skipping from the counter to where the waif-like form was standing staring at a big green vase.

"If you and Jack would like a break from everything, you'd be welcome to join us up at Tahoe next weekend," she said. Kristy liked Jack. He was good for Alicia. He calmed her headstrong ways. He was the only child to the Jones' fortune. It was new money, but these days that was more and more overlooked in SF society's upper echelons.

They'd also have a more relaxing time with him around, less intensity from Alicia was no bad thing.

And Brad. To think he'd taken his own life. That was a hard one for her not to disclose on the tennis court, but Scott had sworn her to secrecy. And all those juicy pieces being delivered in that daily ByteBeat column—well, that had all tongues wagging.

"Oh, thank you. How kind." Anna was taken aback by such benevolence. To think it was the Lyles who'd extended the first olive branch since Brad.

CHAPTER FIFTEEN

Having spent years avoiding anything north of the Golden Gate Bridge, Kobe now found himself sitting, once again, at a table at Stinson's Ranch cafe. The fog had cleared so he could now take in the ocean view that had people dropping millions to call their own. Wild, dark, heaving water as far as the eye could see.

Even with the sun out in a cloudless sky it was cold, but this time he'd come prepared and was wearing his newly acquired Nolkin triple-lined hoodie. Cap was on low, and for the first time he felt the flickering flame of celebrity inside himself.

A lot had gone down since he was last here. Three weeks of non-stop research, interviewing and distilling the salient pieces into eight bits a day. And, with his sky-rocketing subscriber base, there was huge pressure from his boss to keep them well fed.

Lana had been a rich vein. He'd still got a couple of anecdotes from her for tomorrow's column, but he needed more. He hadn't managed to penetrate the inner circle—Caitlin and Mark, Dwight. They'd stone-walled him. Not that he was surprised.

"Hey journalist extraordinaire," said Sam, appearing next him.

"Might have to drop the journo title, vibing more on the columnist hack side of things the way this story's shaping. What you got for me?"

She leaned in close to his ear. "Five K plus five hundred for me. Coroner's office," she whispered.

"What're you saying?"

She smiled. "That I've got news for you that'll send your column into the stratosphere."

Kobe ditched the coffee, took his new company debit card for a spin by the local Wells Fargo, and extracted 5,500 in fresh fifty-dollar bills from the teller.

Once in his car he separated the five hundred for Sam (he'd drop that by on his return to the city *if* her lead proved worthwhile). He then divided the remaining funds into two, so he could calibrate the reward based on the length of column inches this source spooled out.

He set his satnav to the pin she'd given him, and put his foot on the gas, heading north up Highway One. This whole cash for leads situation seemed to be getting out of hand. The old days— hell only a few weeks ago—he'd have a few twenties in his wallet. Now he had a fat envelope in each pocket of his hoodie. If he was stopped by the cops and searched they'd accuse him of peddling drugs.

To take the edge off, he told his phone to open Spotify and play Miles' Davis "Freddie Freeloader". A swell of soothing notes washed through the interior of the Toyota. The smooth ease of the playing never got old.

"Fifty yards take a left onto Platform Bridge Road," said the satnav, cutting in.

Davis resumed. Kobe took the turn and headed up an open, winding road, past horse ranches and fields dotted with canopies of Canyon Live Oak, and Pacific Madrone. If he had to move up here, then this would be his choice.

"You have reached your destination." Satnav had to have been reading his mind.

He slowed, glancing around for a driveway or dwelling. Nothing but post and rail fencing. He continued on.

"Make a U-turn."

He sighed, pulled over and began the art of the three point turn on the narrow road. He was reversing when he caught sight of an old pickup truck closing in on him in the rearview mirror.

He pulled back over and waited, until the driver drove alongside. A worn looking guy with a graying mustache was at the wheel. "You Kobe?"

"Yeah."

"Follow me."

The guy moved off at speed up the road. Half a mile up he slowed and turned into a narrow track. The moment the car hit the gravel, a cloud of dry dust shot up, obscuring Kobe's view.

He glimpsed the faint red of the guy's brakes just in time.

"Chip," said the guy, extending his hand. "Thought it best we meet out of the city limits."

Kobe nodded. "Sam said you've got something for me."

"You good for the money?"

Kobe patted his right pocket. "For the right information."

ByteBeat by Kobe Otieno

"TopMatch Founder's Drug-Fueled Swan Song"
(PHOTO—Drug vial and needle—Getty Images)

TopMatch founder Brad Jones' Stinson Beach death has been ruled as suicide by Marin County Coroner's office.

After administering a fatal dose of ketamine, Jones crossed a point of no return.

He made his last paddle out into the turbulent waters of the Pacific for one final ride.

Seven minutes later he fell from his $75k Satoshi longboard and drowned.

Since the 70s, ketamine has been a popular injectable, short-acting anesthetic.

Ketamine is no stranger to the tech elite of Silicon Valley, with stories of entrepreneurs microdosing in an effort to bolster their brain function.

"Brainstorming with Brad was an event that all of us looked forward to at TopMatch. He had an intense power of framing and simplifying complex problems, and honing in on the essential knowledge," recalled colleague, Lana Fernandez.

What appeared to be an addiction, however, would lead a turbulent storm in the wake of his death.

CHAPTER SIXTEEN

Dwight felt the cold snap of a marine wind blasting in through the open window of his Ferrari as he drove across the Golden Gate Bridge. He refused to put the window up though because he needed to feel the fresh air on his skin, reinforcing that he was alive and well.

Ever since he'd got the news about Brad, he'd gone into a thought spiral of his own, becoming obsessed by his own mortality. He had been out at the Wolf Studio in Atherton at an art show preview of a new Moroccan artist when Anna had called. He'd tried to ignore it, deciding to call her later, but she'd hit redial three times.

She'd been so upset he'd found it hard to understand what she was saying. He'd had to borrow someone else's phone while she talked so he could read the latest fuckery from Otieno. How in hell had the guy got the coroner's report?

ByteBeat used to be some small sidebar on the trials and tribulations of tech life in the valley. Now every employee at his own company had subscribed to the feeding trough.

So much for an intensely private life in his self-curated

bubble. Brad had popped it, leaving him now wide open to public scrutiny.

Why the hell had Brad ended it? How fucking selfish. Anger fizzed again. Dwight could feel it in his gut. His grip on the steering wheel tightened.

They'd been to a 49ers game only the week before. Brad had been his usual, future-thinking self, shooting the breeze on the latest AI plays, and fixating on 3D printing development. Nothing unusual. He and Anna were tight, always had been.

Why end a good life way before its time?

Besides, he'd done all the really tough stuff years ago. If Brad had been vulnerable, that would have been the time—the TopMatch pressure cooker. Brad at the helm of the boat, trying to keep it on course, navigating the turbulent seas of the online business to IPO.

He crested a winding hill, and eased up on the gas, allowing his mind to wander back to those intense months when he was working for LVP, under the tutelage of the man himself, Scott Lyle.

Scott had put him in at TopMatch the second LVP's investment had hit the account. "Ride herd on them. And keep close to Brad. He'll either make us a fortune or disrupt the deal with some left-field play."

With those words Dwight had begun the daily commute up the 101 to TopMatch's South Park offices. After LVP's corporate Sandhill Road campus, the stark, cold warehouse with its overpopulation of fresh out of college, sneaker-wearing geeks was like entering some twenty-four-hour web nursery.

Dwight had been working at LVP for two years before the TopMatch investment. He'd noticed how Scott liked to play rival companies off against each other, often investing secretly in one, publicly in the other. He was never privy to that piece of the LVP puzzle, but he knew the patterns, and TopMatch versus LoveLink bore all the signs of Lyle puppeteering the players.

A deer darted across the road. Dwight slammed on the brakes. Narrow miss. Echoed those old days of car-crash-style financing by LVP.

Anna showed Dwight straight through to Brad's study. Just being in the room was giving him chills, even with Gui thumping her tail on the hand-knotted Wavelength rug.

Looking around he could see that Anna had been busy since he'd last sat in one of the leather armchairs, talking shop with Brad, only a month ago. The top bookshelf that lined three of the walls was stripped. In front of the floor-to-ceiling window that overlooked the beach, the books stood in stacks, forming some kind of skyscraper downtown.

"Since this shit's coming out," she said, shaking her phone that was displaying the neon flash of the "ByteBeat" masthead on screen, "and Brad decided to end his own life, I am beginning to realize that I didn't know my husband as well as I thought."

She brought a glass of wine to her lips. "So." She put her hands on her hips, giving him a guns-at-dawn stare down. "Shoot."

He walked over and poured himself a large glass from the bottle that stood in its zero-chill jacket. He'd declined the offer earlier, but the way this was shaping up he was going to need it, and it wasn't even noon.

"First off, Brad worshipped the ground you walked on, Anna."

She raised an eyebrow, folded her arms across her chest. "I'm not a piece of goddamn porcelain. Jesus."

"You and I know that, A. You're tough as nails, but Brad saw you differently. I think all that shit you both went through, busting your asses to get the company through the other side... After that, when you'd made it big time, he wanted to make sure you and Jack got the best of him."

"Well, what was the worst of him?"

Dwight exhaled heavily, shifting in the armchair. He'd rather be anywhere right now than here. Even that colonoscopy he'd had the year before was preferable to this. "Business-wise, Brad was a straight shooter. Maverick, yes. Hot-headed about LoveLink, yes. But who wouldn't have been when that wily fucker Chomodsky was at the helm?"

He paused to drink more wine, feeling the unusual buzz of alcohol in his system this early in the day.

"Okay," said Anna. "That's the business end. So what about the non-business end?"

"Just, you know, the drug use at Burning Man. He'd always have a menu all written out in his head for us for the whole time up there. Ways to bring us up into ecstasy, with a soft landing at the end."

"Did you take ketamine up there?"

Dwight sighed. "A few years back, we did. Microdosed it. Small amounts though."

"You should have told me that before, Dwight!"

"I'm sorry. It was such a small factor in the cocktail of stuff we took. And it was years ago. We never touched it after that."

They were both silent.

"What else?"

"Nothing."

"C'mon, Dwight." She held up her phone. "It's only a

matter of time the way Otieno's digging. And I'd rather hear it from you."

He looked out at the fog bank, sitting out on the horizon in a long gray band, weighing up the chances. He owed her the truth.

CHAPTER SEVENTEEN

Anna came back from her run up the mountain sheened in sweat. Gui was panting hard from the sprint up the steep wooded trail that led to the peak and back.

She'd screamed at the top of her lungs from the summit, out across the swathe of Pacific, blowing the top off a volcanic rage that'd started when Dwight had finished his truth download.

Now she was back home, her body exhausted, she was ready to dig. Checking the clock she calculated that she had at least an hour before Jack came back from sailing out on the Bay with Alicia and her family.

Kicking off her trail runners, she went back to Brad's desk, flipped open his laptop, activating the big flatscreen monitor that he'd used as his window into a world of online sex sessions.

"He didn't think of it as cheating," Dwight had said, earlier. "It was at a distance. He never hooked up in person, ever. He told me that."

She'd written the damn paper on cybersex. Brad had read it, helped edit some of the parts that didn't ring right. For fuck's sake. It played a big part in her work.

"*Engaging in cybersex with individuals online leads to*

gratification of those desires and fantasies that one would otherwise resist in real life."

Their sex life hadn't been off the charts like the old days when they'd first met. It'd been the only time she'd agreed with LoveLink's Chomodsky on anything, when he'd stopped her one time in the stairwell: "Hey, Anna, you had a lucky break with that Paris trip."

"It's good when a campaign pays off."

"How are you and Brad?"

It was an odd question considering they were little more than acquaintances.

"Fine thanks."

"Must be hard working together and dating."

"It's no problem."

"Mostly work I guess."

"That's the nature of the start-up beast."

He didn't reply so she began to climb the stairs.

"Anna."

She paused and turned.

He was standing watching her. "I'd triple your salary, give you carte blanche to build a community team ten times the size of the one you've got now, and there'd be a stack of fully-vested stock options, if you came to work with us."

She recoiled. "Why the hell would I ever do that?"

"Because I'm gonna build and take LoveLink to IPO, crushing TopMatch in the process. Then you can cash out and be on the winning side."

The way he smiled at her made her skin crawl.

"Never in a million years. As I've already said, Brad and I are in this together."

He scowled. "Your loss then. Carry on fucking each other like rabbits for all I care."

And that's what they'd done. Fucked like rabbits until she'd finally fallen pregnant. It'd taken a while, much longer than they'd thought.

Then the miracle of Jack had happened, and yes, sex had then naturally taken a back seat. They'd tried to rekindle the fire to create another baby, but when it didn't work, they'd settled into a once a week, then once a month coupling in the bedroom, mainly on a weekend evening after enjoying some fine wine.

That was what marriage did—dampen the lust, leaving a more tender, stable platform for expression. Well, that was what she'd thought about her own marriage. She'd written as much in her last book.

She entered the password, and watched Brad's desktop fill with reams of icons and apps.

People who have cybersex addiction are most likely to be addicted because of the anonymity the internet offers, its convenience, and also the escape.

She could hear herself saying that over and over again at the countless seminars she'd run over the years. Why did he need to escape?

Her hand shook as she searched his files for "AMERACAL". He'd buried it deep in an array of files containing 3D code.

Inside the file lay a few screen grabs. The dates ranged from a couple of years back, to a few days before the beach.

Best to bite the bullet. She selected them all, took a deep breath, and clicked "open". A spread of photos popped up, making her stomach heave. A young woman with ash blonde hair posed in various positions—mainly legs wide, her hairless pussy gaping at the camera.

She grabbed the garbage from underneath the desk and vomited. Wiping her mouth, she pulled all the photos into the trash and hit "empty".

She got up and carried the bin into the kitchen to wash it

out. The slideshow was replaying in her mind. Several studies she'd read focused on the AAA engine that drove online affairs: accessibility, anonymity, affordability.

Accessibility? Brad often boasted he could have been a top hacker if he'd chosen the dark side. Anonymity? After all these years, she felt she barely knew her own husband. Affordability? Brad had more than enough damn money to buy a Vegas brothel if he'd so desired.

She put her head under the cold tap, letting the water stream over, as she tried to get a grip on the fact her marriage had been some crumbling edifice and not the rock-solid foundation she'd thought. She wrapped her hair in a towel, and took the trash can back to Brad's study.

"Mom, we're back!" shouted Jack from the entrance hall.

Gui leapt up and ran out. Anna pulled the towel from her hair, just as Jack, Alicia and Scott walked in.

"Wow, looks like you've run a marathon," said Jack.

They, on the other hand, looked like they'd just stepped out of some Tommy Hilfiger ad for the perfect all-American family.

"Thought Gui needed a run," she said. "How was sailing?"

"Real cool. Alicia and I are going out back if that's okay?"

She shrugged.

Scott said, "Ten minutes, then we've got to head back. Got an opera to attend this evening."

The two teenagers walked out, Gui in tow.

"Thanks for taking him out for the day. It's a big help," she said.

"We had a good time," said Scott. He walked over to the skyscraper stacks of books and picked up a dog-eared copy of Ayn Rand's *Atlas Shrugged*.

"I can still recall your email response when I'd asked for thoughts on this."

"The Lyle bible."

He laughed. "I still do it with every start-up we invest in. A box of books when the deal's signed. A good way to lay the ground rules of objectivism. I still get reviews, but I have to admit yours was and still remains the best. And I quote: 'I hated this book with the fire of a thousand suns. If you like books that are slow, preachy, and based on faulty logic and a poor understanding of basic humanity, then this is a great book for you. I've noted it came forth into the world in 1949 and has evidently been appealing to narcissists ever since. Sincerely, Anna.'"

For the first time in a long while she smiled. "So, you still believe that you exist for your own sake? That the pursuit of your own happiness is your highest moral purpose?"

He shrugged. "That's how and why I've built my life."

CHAPTER EIGHTEEN

The sun was setting across the vineyard as they sat on the terrace eating dessert. After a barbecue supper, cooked by Mark, Caitlin told the kids they could go off and watch a movie in the cinema room.

She found herself taken aback by the news that both Anna and Jack were headed to the Lyle estate on Lake Tahoe. While she was aware of the strong dynamic between Jack and Alicia, the idea of Anna spending time with Scott and Kristy came as a genuine shock. It seemed that time had indeed marched on, reshaping dynamics and relationships in ways she hadn't anticipated.

In the TopMatch early days she'd had to listen to several rants from Anna about Scott making sly passes at her. But in retrospect that was how it was back in those days—god knows she'd dealt with enough of those herself—hot-blooded clients wanting more than just a software package. She'd held them at bay, and so had Anna. And when TopMatch had gone public, Anna had moved on, out of the firing line.

It was all water under the bridge now.

She looked across the table at Mark. He was even more

attractive than when they'd first met. He'd stuck to the same workout he'd always done. Some men aged like a fine vintage, others didn't. She'd picked well.

And they both liked each other enough to ensure they both reached orgasm before quitting to go to sleep. Bedroom manners mattered. She'd been surprised to hear how Marsha, a mom from school, always ended up finishing things herself with a vibrator in her closet. That would never be the case with her and Mark.

"What do you think, Cait? Should Anna try and make contact with the woman?"

They were both now looking at her.

"Whatever for?"

"In case she's thinking of approaching ByteBeat," said Mark, refilling their glasses.

"Maybe she's no clue who Brad was. He'd have used a pseudonym. You know that, Anna, you wrote a paper on it. You don't want to put the cat amongst the pigeons."

"Part of me wants to find out what he said to her," said Anna. "Maybe he told her why he was going to end it all."

Caitlin needed to put an end to this kind of thinking of Anna's. She was going to have to move on, rise above it all the horror of the Brad they all thought they knew, somehow...

"We've ring-fenced Otieno—Dwight, me, and Mark. He'll never get into the inner circle. There's only a finite amount of theories he can spin up from his sources, so it'll tail off soon, and he'll move on to the next hot story."

"I get it, you know I do," said Anna. "It's the unanswered 'why' that keeps me awake at night. And if Brad's relationship with that woman does come to the light of day, we've got to protect the Jones Foundation. I've already put a call in to the lawyer to move Brad's name off of it altogether."

Mark whistled in air through his teeth. "That's a big move. You sure you want to do that now? Might be a red flag."

"Better we get ahead of the situation rather than behind it."

They sat in silence. Caitlin hated to see her best friend's eyes filling with tears again. She passed her a fresh linen napkin. "It's so tough for you right now. Titus can help you. Give it another go, please," she said, thinking back to the *I've been once, no need to go again* conversation they'd had shortly after Anna's visit.

Mark wore a thoughtful expression. Caitlin could almost see the gears turning in his mind. She knew he had his suspicions about Brad, about the secrets he might have been hiding. Unlike her, Mark hadn't been surprised by the latest revelations. Brad had been a tech guy, after all, someone who lived as much in the virtual world as he did in the real one. Mark was convinced that there were more skeletons in Brad's closet, more trails that could lead to further heartache for Anna.

Caitlin shuddered at the thought. She hoped, for everyone's sake, that Mark was wrong, that Brad had been smart enough to cover his tracks.

Anna took a deep breath. "I'll make an appointment when I'm back from Tahoe. I have to be in the city anyway next week. I've decided to get back to work."

Caitlin and Mark exchanged a look, a silent communication they had perfected since Brad's death. It was a look that said, "Here we go again, another Jones bombshell." Dealing with their own teenage kids suddenly felt like a walk in the park compared to the emotional rollercoaster they were on with Anna. It was amazing how someone else's drama could eclipse the day-to-day issues in your own life, how it could put everything into perspective. Even Caitlin had found herself relaxing more into her family dynamics, grateful for the relative simplicity of her own life.

"Are you sure that's wise? You're processing a lot right now," said Caitlin, draining her glass.

Tomorrow, she and Mark were definitely not going to be drinking. They had to ignore the siren call of alcohol that'd lured them to open at least a bottle every evening since Brad had gone.

"I need to get off the twenty-four-seven grief track somehow, before I go insane. I need to operate back in my cyberpsych mindset. First off, I'm in at Xomftov to counsel the CEO on his online sex proclivities. Feel I'll be coming at it with a fresh perspective."

"Jesus!" said Caitlin. "You won't be impartial, A."

She shrugged. "I figure it'll help me process Brad's addiction in a clinical way."

"You'll be muddying the waters if you do that."

All three of their phones pinged. Caitlin's heart sank. It could mean only one thing.

ByteBeat by Kobe Otieno

"Did SWS trigger TopMatch founder's slide into oblivion?"

(PHOTO—Brad Jones rings the opening bell at the New York Stock Exchange—New York Times, October 17th 2002)

When Jones rang the NYSE opening bell at TopMatch's initial public offering (IPO) it triggered a $400 million case of SWS—Sudden Wealth Syndrome—for all TopMatch employees.

Worst hit was Jones, whose $225 million pay packet hit a home run that had him ditching the one-bedroom rental apartment on Steiner that he and his wife co-habited, in favor of a five-acre beachfront "tear down" at Stinson.

Dr. Jones went on to hypothesize on her husband's acute case of the syndrome in her 82,000-word doctoral thesis, "Sudden Wealth Syndrome and Identity".

Isolation—"For the first eighteen months after we moved to Marin, he'd often go out for hours hiking or surfing, often from dawn until dusk. He'd come home and go straight to work on the house build, distancing himself from our marriage and impending fatherhood."

Insomnia—"Brad suffered chronic insomnia, resulting in clinical exhaustion that led to a three-month residential stay in a Sedona sleep clinic."

Excessive spending 1—"The moment the money hit the bank he had a charity come in and clear every item we owned including all our clothes. I'd been up in Napa visiting friends. When I returned home there was nothing left in the apartment, except our passports. He said we had to do this to fully upgrade into our new post-economic world."

Excessive spending 2—"Brad went crazy, overspending on everything that went into our $30 million Stinson house build. If there was a more expensive type of flooring, he'd take it. He obsessed over designing a double-helix bladder-molded glass staircase as a centerpiece for the house, spending over a million dollars alone on its creation. His perfectionism drove him and everyone on the project into despair."

At $25 million, Dr. Jones was able to report that, unlike her husband, she only suffered mild symptoms.

CHAPTER NINETEEN

The tennis lesson was finally over. Alicia ditched her racket and ran off the lakeside court, along the gravel path to the main house. The sun was already high in a piercingly blue sky. Tahoe's ice-melt cobalt waters lapped at the edge of the Lyle compound. The last of the snow still clung to the very tops of the mountains, sending a crisp reminder of a long hard winter across the lake.

Up ahead she could see her parents sitting out on the front deck, still at the breakfast table, drinking coffee and talking with their friends. She didn't care if she never saw the Weizmanns ever again. They were so nosy and loud about everything, including her. The way that witch Leila had gone on about her being too young for a boyfriend last night at dinner was way out of line. Alicia had wanted to slap her, and that feeling hadn't faded yet.

Worse still, they'd brought their son along. Twelve-year-old Daniel. That was what sucked about being the youngest. You got ditched by your parents and had to host any younger kids of the friends who they invited up. If only she'd been first or second born, then she'd already be at college like Mitzy and Frank, getting on with her own life.

Shit, Joel Weizmann had seen her. Put his hand up to wave her over. A smarmy old man in his wraparound shades with his gray hair all smoothed back. He'd want her to come over and sit right next to him, he'd put his arm across the back of her chair and ask her how the game went, and did she think Daniel had the makings of a tennis star. She knew this because the same had happened the year before, and she hadn't forgotten.

Pretending not to see him she took off across the freshly mown lawn to the kitchen entrance of the vast granite building that had been in her family since the days of the pioneers. Her great-great grandfather Tyler Van Hoeveren had made good in the gold rush, and fallen in love with the mountains.

She took the narrow stone staff staircase up to her room to make sure she didn't bump into the Lindbergs who'd been up half the night arguing. Their oldest son, who was meant to be joining his dad's NY bank when he graduated, had just told them he wanted to pursue an acting career in L.A. Her room was next door, and even with a two-foot wall between them she still heard most of it. Marriage. She was definitely not going up the aisle in her early twenties like her mom did. Even if it was Jack, he'd have to wait. That way, they'd argue less than her parents, and the Lindbergs.

She picked her cell up from the winged-eagle Navajo totem nightstand her mom had installed in her room when she was born. At home she was enveloped in the French style of Versailles, her bedroom loaded with Louis XV furniture. Here it was all about the land and its history.

She'd learned the truth at school when she was ten. The Navajos were in Arizona and Utah.

That'd been a showdown dinner—her versus the rest of the family on a "do you know how bad our ancestors were?" debate.

Her mom had gone all defensive on the Van Hoeverens. If she'd been magicked back in time, Alicia just knew her mom would have been a shotgun-toting bastard like Great-great grandpa Tyler.

Her brother and sister both said they didn't really care what had happened back then because it was theirs now, and their dad claimed to "only live in the present" and that "you had to live for your own sake", whatever that meant.

"Shit," she said, seeing a text sent an hour ago by Jack. She checked the time: ten minutes and they'd be here.

After a quick shower she threw on the new Brandy Melville shorts and top that'd arrived the day before after a hasty online shop. No time to dry her long hair, or do her eyes. She was lucky though, she had dark brown, bordering on onyx, hair so her brows and eyelashes helped sculpt her features even without mascara and brow gel.

Her heart was beating faster; that was the effect Jack had on her. It had to be love.

She checked herself using her phone camera and headed back down the stairs, using the laundry as her exit to the driveway. Her dad's pointer, Rand, was lying on the front stoop in a patch of sunlight. He came running out after her, weaving through the cool canopy of sugar pines that lined the driveway.

She could hear the thwack of tennis balls as Daniel was being put through his paces by the ball feeder. Seriously, the coach her mom had got for the season this year was lazy. She could see him standing at the side of the court, checking his cell, while his wimpy client tried to keep up with the stream of balls. Two hundred bucks an hour. The guy should be fired. But she wasn't going to raise the alarm, because she'd negotiated herself a deal with him to say she'd scored better than she had, so she'd get to go to Florida with her friends.

That was the kicker in her family, everything was

conditional on performance. You got an ice cream if you did ten laps of the pool, a piece of heirloom jewelry if you got straight As. She was trained just like Rand, who right now was walking at heel alongside.

Seconds later Jack's mom's black SUV Porsche came driving through the gates, up to the security lodge, where the guard stood doing what he was paid to do. The passenger door opened and Jack jumped down, along with Gui.

Anna arched her back away from the leather seat. It'd been a long drive, and she was still hungover from the late night at Caitlin and Mark's. She listened to the "where to go from here" briefing by the guard.

"Have a good day, ma'am," he said, with a salute.

Anyone would think she'd just entered the White House.

Jack and Alicia had already moved off out of sight with the dogs in tow, so she drove slowly along with both windows down, enjoying a moment of peace and fresh mountain air.

She'd never stayed right on the lake before. They'd always taken a place up at Palisades Tahoe so they could ski or bike straight out. She rounded a huge granite boulder. *Fuck.* The house was an ode to Wild West pioneering on a grand scale. The timber house looked as if someone had taken a log cabin and made it a hundred times bigger. The stone porch alone looked like a giant could enter comfortably without having to duck.

She rolled up to the main entrance where a butler in white, monogrammed polo shirt and knife-edge chinos stood waiting. "Dr. Jones, welcome to Ravenwood," he said, opening her door.

"Good to be here."

"I'm Frost. Anything you need to make your stay more comfortable, just let me know."

"Thank you, Frost." She took her cell from the cup holder and slid out onto the smooth slate entrance circle.

"The Lyles are eager to see you. May I show you through to the terrace straight away, or shall I wait while you freshen up?"

"I'm good thanks."

He smiled. "Please follow me." He led her through a vaulted entrance hall into a wide hallway lined with oil portraits of what had to be ancestors, pioneering their way through history, vanquishing everything in their path to untold riches. No sudden wealth syndrome here. This was the Van Hoeveren dynasty: she could tell by how they all had the high cheekbones that Kristy and Alicia had inherited.

Stepping out onto the sun-filled terrace was like stepping out into a kingdom of the natural world. Slate led to a carpet of lush lawn, which led directly to the water's edge, beyond which the water stretched to a far shore that looked like a scene from a Grimm's fairy tale.

She was so entranced that she hadn't noticed the large table full of people off to the far side.

"Anna, welcome!"

She turned to find Kristy on her way over, arms open.

Now the people came into sharp focus over Kristy's shoulder. So much for a quiet family weekend away. She could see the unmistakable fluff of platinum hair that could only mean one thing. She was going to have to spend it with the Weizmanns.

CHAPTER TWENTY

The Southwest plane touched down on the rain-slicked runway at Eugene, Oregon. Kobe walked into the terminal, picked up his Jeep Compass rental and drove out onto the freeway, satnav set for the hills.

The muscles on his face bunched up, pulling his skin wide and high into a grin. A quick validation in the rearview mirror revealed his newly detailed teeth, blindingly white from the treatment he'd had a couple of days before.

Who would have ever guessed that call from Sam would have set his career on a rocket trajectory? He wasn't one to believe in luck, more a kind of destiny, where the signals on his true path had finally aligned. He was making not just national but international news with his commentary on the Joneses.

When he'd pitched flying up to Oregon to delve deeper into Brad Jones' upbringing, he'd been surprised his boss had immediately agreed. Where there was normally pushback, there was none. How times had changed.

The wipers moved rhythmically, sweeping the windshield clear of the pelting rain. One of the main reasons he'd got the Jeep was the blurb on the rental app: "You can easily navigate harsh weather conditions or rough terrain with this rugged four-wheel drive". An hour in and he was climbing a rough track strewn with rocks and boulders, like some storm channel from the Rockies. He checked the map, not trusting the satnav's "In one mile, take a left onto Bear Ridge Road", but sure as hell he was on target.

The word "bear" had him contemplating a possible interaction with the largest wildlife form in this neck of the woods, the grizzly. That visual overload, along with the pain of the laser on his teeth had resulted in a nightmare of epic proportions. He'd woken at 3am in a sweat in his room, hadn't bothered to go back to sleep since he had to be at the airport by six. He'd passed the time researching life in the wilds of Oregon.

Now armed with a partial knowledge of where he was headed, he knew that the grizzly has a distinctive shoulder hump coupled with short, round ears, while its counterpart, the black bear enjoyed having large, pointed ears.

Twenty minutes later, after laboring the Jeep up a steep incline that even a goat would take a pass on, he emerged out of the treeline.

"You have reached your destination," announced the satnav.

"Sure as hell have," he said. Up ahead, two pine posts had been driven into the ground, supporting a battered wooden sign. It looked like something out of the old days of the Wild West. He squinted through the windshield, trying to make sense of the faded, hand-painted words that swirled across its surface.

It wasn't named just Aragorn, commune since the 70s, it read *"Kingdom of Aragorn"*. He'd been transported straight to Middle-earth.

He moved the Jeep forward, crossing from rough gravel to a dirt track, overgrown with weeds a foot tall in some places, their thorns scratching the paintwork. He'd got this far, though. Nothing was going to get him to turn back.

The land widened into a large meadow, a carpet of weeds and grass that stretched to the edge of the forest. Beyond lay a view across green mountains. He reached a collection of broken-down cabins, roofs fallen in, walls covered in a creeping array of vines. A utopian dream gone sour.

Cutting the engine, he lowered the window and did a cursory check for anything moving around outside. With the added flair of sounding the horn a couple of times, he opened the driver's side door and stepped out, his new Amiri claret sneakers sinking into the wet dirt and grass. Inhaling the pine-scented, cool air, he closed his eyes for a moment.

Here he stood at the heart of Aragorn, a self-sufficient hippie commune formed in 1969 by Shehan Summerhorn. Opening his eyes again, looking around the rain-soaked vista, he tried to imagine the place at the height of its popularity.

He still couldn't get his head around the ideology of this kind of place. And the rain, man, did it ever stop? He zipped up the raincoat he'd found buried at the back of his closet and got on with the job of photographing the place where Brad Jones was raised.

As soon as he'd got enough material, he drove out, back down into "civilization and its discontents" to meet with an old Aragornian (if there was such a thing), who had made the wise decision to leave it before things had melted down.

Four hours later, in the chain-built comfort of the Hampton Inn, Eugene, he ordered an ice-cold Peroni and crafted his column.

CHAPTER TWENTY-ONE

Scott opened the throttle on his vintage Chris-Craft. The nose of the boat lifted and surged, slicing through Tahoe's clear, frigid waters, leaving an immaculate V-shaped wake. A perfect execution of power to weight ratio.

He'd bought the boat from a private sale at the William Randolph Hearst estate thirty years ago. It was a trophy buy, not something he'd particularly wanted at the time, but he knew of another interested party, who had been boasting its merits during a Bohemian Club dinner. The guy was so full of shit that Scott put in a silent bid he knew the guy couldn't afford, and the boat became his. It cost a fortune to maintain, like many things in his life, but it had become one of his most prized possessions.

A bank of dark clouds was gathering at the far end of the lake, and the wind had freshened. Time to head back before the lake began to swell and chop with an incoming storm. The kids in the back were laughing at the thrill of the speed, while Anna sat like some warrior statue in the swiveling co-captain's chair next to him, her head held steady, looking forward.

"You good?" he shouted, over the roar of the engine.

She turned and smiled, startling him with the openness of

her face. In all the years he'd known her, she'd been a closed book, like some hardcover mystery novel. But now her blue eyes were wide, and she was smiling in a way that made him feel good. Hell, not just good, but fucking alive in a way that he hadn't felt in years. All in an instant. Just like that. He didn't need to say anything else, but let that feeling expand like the horizon before him.

It was Kristy who'd invited her up, along with Jack. He could tell his wife was doing it to fulfill her benevolent duties to society. She was also hooked on gloating over someone else's misfortunes. It made her ride high and mighty, just like this weekend. Invite them up, give them gin and sympathy and stir the ashes of grief.

Lunch had been a drag. Avery, that harpy of Magnus's, was still going on about their son not joining the family firm. How Magnus put up with her all these years beat him. She was so self-obsessed she gave little room for any other conversation, even cutting in over Leila, which was a miracle.

Hence the boat trip, which had dovetailed nicely with Magnus and Joel's tennis game. Alicia, Jack and Anna had been eager to escape.

Anna wasn't used to being inside the doors of upper crust American society. She met many of them at various charity events. They were the ones who appeared annually in print in the *Social Register*—the black address book of the USA's old money elite, many with ancestors dating back to the Mayflower. She'd found a copy in her bedside drawer back at the house. Whether Kristy had put it there on purpose as a reminder of her breeding, she didn't care. Being new money, she and Brad would never have made the cut.

As the boat headed up the West Shore, she thought back to her first encounter with the grandeur of the Van Hoeveren Lyles.

She'd been at her desk in the TopMatch office. It was early days with her and Brad, and the company was struggling with the next round of financing. Josef had come over asking her to go to the boardroom. She'd left the community plan she'd been working on and went in to find Brad seated at the far end, talking to a finely suited man. A wave of expensive, cedar cologne came across the table as he looked up, directly at her.

Brad had said, "Anna, you remember Scott, don't you?"

Scott got up, his eyes locked on her as he shook her hand. "Good to see you again, Anna," he said. "I've been hearing how pivotal you've been in building TopMatch's community."

"I've got a great team."

"Scott's dropped by. He's interested in hearing about our plans," said Brad.

"LVP are doing a round-up of potential new portfolio investments. I like to drop in to get the raw facts, firsthand, no ceremony," said Scott.

"Anna, give Scott a brief three-sixty of your department and the wonders that it achieves," said Brad.

It took an hour and she felt she'd been run through the wringer. Scott had some mental checklist he'd created, and until all his questions were answered the meeting wasn't over. He was direct, and if he didn't think she'd expanded enough on her answer he told her so. It was like a courtroom cross-examination of strategy, implementation and results.

He watched her the whole time, his arms on the desk, fingers steepled, didn't take any notes, but he retained every fact and figure she gave him, because he'd repeat things back to her verbatim, further down the conversation.

Later that evening Brad had taken a call from Dwight at LVP.

"LVP wants to start preliminary due diligence on TopMatch," Brad said, after. "And that's not all. You and I have been invited to the Lyles' cocktail party this Friday. Hillsborough Carohill Estate, 5pm sharp. Dressed to kill."

That Friday they'd crested the brow of an oak-lined drive, onto a plateau where a French chateau sat looking across the hills to the Pacific.

"Fuck," said Brad, from the wheel of the BMW they'd borrowed from Nathan.

Her own awe stopped her from doing anything but silently agreeing. The turrets, wrought-iron balustraded windows, a colonnaded row of arched glass doors, every room in the house illuminated—pure Disney.

A uniformed valet team stood on duty at the front steps. Brad pulled up, their doors were opened and Anna took a helping hand to climb up out of the low-slung seat. She adjusted her dress and straightened up to her new height of 5 foot 9 inches with the shoe adjustment.

"Hell, you look good enough to eat," said Brad, taking her arm.

"This place is like Versailles," she whispered, her stiletto heels hitting the polished marble floor of the paneled and mirrored entrance hall. A sweeping staircase led up to an open gallery, above which a glass roof radiated the remains of the day.

A waiter in a white jacket and crisp high collared shirt offered them champagne. The din of voices echoed through the cavernous space. They passed through to a drawing room, where cliques of men in navy blazers, stood chatting to women in chic cocktail suits. The age range spanned at least three generations, the summit being a tiny silver-haired lady seated on a Louis XV chair at one of the open windows. She looked to be at least ninety. Anna noted the vintage Chanel suit she wore and the heavy pearl necklace, and had to remind herself that all this was authentically real.

"Hey, welcome."

She turned to see Scott exiting from a small group at the marble fireplace, above which hung an enormous oil portrait of Kristy standing on the sweeping staircase in a royal blue silk evening dress, her hair drawn back into a tight chignon. Her eye had been painted so that it tracked to whoever's gaze was upon her.

Scott shook Brad's hand, Anna held out hers, but Scott bypassed the gesture and leaned in to kiss on either cheek.

"Beautiful," he whispered, so that only she could hear.

She pulled back, feeling color rise in her cheeks—part affront, part shock. He seemed amused by her reaction.

"Thanks for inviting us. You've got a beautiful home here," said Brad, oblivious.

"You're welcome. This place was built for entertaining. Kristy's great grandfather believed that money should show itself, and created at the time the largest house west of the Mississippi." He turned to Anna. "Not quite in the league though of places you've got back home."

"I think you'll find yours in far better repair."

He laughed out loud at her response. People turned to see what was so funny. She could feel them looking at her and Brad with interest. The whispers began to circulate and stir; they were new blood.

Scott introduced them to the group he'd been with, by declaring TopMatch a company to watch, and that Anna and Brad were the leading lights.

"Scott's very charmed by you," said Kristy, later in the powder room.

Anna had emerged from the toilet to find her at the mirror,

reapplying lipstick. She glanced around nervously—no one else was there.

"He's interested in TopMatch. Brad's really excited that LVP's looking at coming on board." She turned on the tap to wash her hands, keeping her head down so that she didn't have to look at Kristy's face.

"I know my husband. He wouldn't laugh like he did if you didn't amuse him."

She glanced up, Kristy had moved away from the mirror, and stepped closer. "Understand though, he's mine."

Anna stood up, in their heels they were eye to eye. "Mrs. Lyle, let me make it perfectly clear that I have no interest in your husband whatsoever aside from in a professional capacity with TopMatch." She was clenching her fists, her newly painted nails digging into her palms.

"Don't let your naivety blind you, Anna."

CHAPTER TWENTY-TWO

It was nearly dark when Anna climbed out of the slate walled shower and took a VHL monogrammed bath sheet from the heated towel rack. For the first time since Brad had gone, she'd felt the rush of life, out on the water this afternoon, in the cool wind.

She'd been relieved Scott had suggested the boat ride. Anything to get away from the table held hostage by Avery.

He'd taken them up the west shore, past lakeside mansions, Tahoe City, granite rock shores and sandy beaches, all the way to the county line. To her surprise he'd been easy company, his brooding intensity gone as he pointed out landmarks, giving anecdotal stories of his years spent at the lake.

Jack and Alicia had been happy in the back, arguing over the next song to play over the boat's inbuilt surround-sound system. Jack had his arm around Alicia most of the trip, her head resting on his shoulder. Seeing them like that reminded Anna of what she'd had with Brad.

They'd got back just as sheets of rain came sweeping in. She checked the bedside clock: only half an hour until supper. Picking up her cell, she sent a quick update to Caitlin, then set about her wardrobe for tonight's casual attire, which in reality was anything but casual, judging by lunch, when both Leila and Avery wore designer suits.

She put on an ivory silk shirt and black jeans, pairing them with the vintage Bulgari diamond pendant necklace Brad had given her when his SWS symptoms were in full swing, before the slowdown to a birthday/holidays gift rotation.

Sitting at the dressing table she applied her makeup. In the background she glimpsed the super king-size bed with its Frette linen and goose down comforter. Her hand ceased its foundation brushstrokes. She turned on the tan leather stool. Bed stretched like a snow-covered desert across the room. She was alone. No more arguing over which side of the bed to sleep on when she and Brad traveled. Nothing but her and space. Time and space, until she too was gone.

A shiver ran up her spine, mind tracking to the hamster wheel of the suicide. She'd mapped it so clearly in her head that it ran like a video on repeat. The vial of ketamine and needle grabbed from his desk after his morning coffee. The surfboard from the garage. The run out onto the beach with Gui. The vial's contents sucked into the needle. The needle piercing his skin. His thumb on plunger, driving the ketamine into his body. The final paddle out. The loss of consciousness. The fall into the water. The water flooding his lungs.

Someone was knocking on the door. Next moment it opened and Jack walked in. He'd showered and changed into the Helmut Lang cargo pants and charcoal shirt she'd bought him a few months back. They'd been stashed, still in their gift boxing under his bed. Until now. Grief had made him grow up overnight. Her boy was gone; in his place stood a tall, young man.

"Checking you're okay, Mom," he said, as Gui leapt on the bed, wagging her tail.

"I'm fine." Thank God he couldn't read her thoughts. "That was nice out on the boat."

"Yeah. Fun. Scott said he'd take us out again tomorrow if we want. So long as the storm's passed."

She smiled. "I'm in."

"Kristy said we're eating now, then we're gonna watch a movie. You guys have got some special dinner going on."

"Wishing I was dining with you."

He nodded. "Avery is something else. She stopped me on the stairs threatening me if I messed up with Alicia."

The bitch.

"Ignore her. She's an A-type mother-raptor with an outsize obsession with family dynastic succession disorder."

He grinned, walked over and gave her a hug. "Love you, Mom."

By 7pm she was standing in the bar being passed a freshly shaken Martini by Frost, who stood on duty behind a polished silver-topped counter branded with a gold plaque "VH—1876". Behind him, on etched glass shelving stood lines of spirits and mixers that would put a five-star hotel to shame. Everything about the room was hushed luxury, like the Ralph Lauren store she frequented on Union Square. Deep leather chairs, heavy plaid curtains drawn against the storm outside. They could be anywhere right now—New York, London, Paris.

"So, Anna, tell me about your doctoring—what's the latest in the cyberpsych world?"

Magnus Lindberg was standing next to her. He was tall, much of his hair had receded and she could tell that, unlike his wife, he liked to wine and dine well. The oversize shirt he was wearing couldn't disguise the belly beneath.

"A new study just came out on how sexting's associated with depression, anxiety, sleep problems, and compulsive sexual behaviors." She said it to shock him somehow, expecting him to choke back on the double Old-Fashioned he was nursing over a giant cube of ice stamped with the LVH logo.

"Interesting, can you enlighten me some more?"

"Latest research shows fifty percent of adults reporting to have sent a sext, many of them revealing they enjoy consensual sexting. They feel empowered and that it builds self-confidence."

"Do go on."

"But most interesting were the participants who had only ever sent, but never received sexts either in reply or out of the blue. They were the ones who reported more depression, anxiety, and sleep problems than the other groups."

"No shit. You send something out and you get no reply. That..."

"That would what, Magnus?" Avery had appeared at his side, holding a vodka on the rocks, wearing a crimson silk cocktail dress. So much for casual supper.

"It'd suck. What's the word again? You'd be..."

"Ghosted," said Anna, sensing a marital unease about to erupt. "Love your dress."

Avery smiled. She was back on home turf. "Carolina Herrera. Latest collection. She was a great friend of my late mother. I was practically brought up going to her shows..."

Magnus slipped away leaving Anna getting a full download on Avery and Carolina's incredible bond.

Dinner finally got underway an hour later. Anna sat down feeling light-headed from drinking two martinis. She'd normally only have one, but the second had been already prepared and served to her by Frost before she could say no.

She was seated between Scott and Magnus at a round table in a covered heated porch off the far side of the house—the "orangery" as Kristy had called it.

The chef was serving them an appetizer of Seared Diver

Scallops in White Wine, which had Leila sounding like she was headed to an orgasm, when everyone's cell phones pinged in unison. Joel was the first to surreptitiously glance at his, a frown quickly appearing. Leila did the same, eyebrows shooting up. Avery followed suit and took a sharp intake of breath, looking across directly at Anna.

Anna's blood ran cold. She moved her hand to retrieve her cell that she'd stashed behind her back.

ByteBeat by your roving columnist, Kobe Otieno
"Prince of the Kingdom of Aragorn"
(PHOTO—Brad Jones, aged 4, Aragorn Commune, Oregon. Copyright Ellis Janko)

Our star of the column, Brad Jones, was raised in the now defunct ARAGORN COMMUNE, in the hills outside Eugene, Oregon. The arcs in his early life and those of Aragorn Elessar, the fictional *Lord of the Rings* character, have some surprising parallels:

Aragorn lost his father to the orcs in only his second year. Jones lost his father, Hank Jones, in a lumbering accident when he was two years old.

Aragorn's mother Gilraen took him to Rivendell, where he was fostered by Elrond. Jones' mother Tania took him to Aragorn where he was fostered by an entire commune.

Aragorn's identity was concealed, and he was known only by the name "Estel" throughout his childhood years. Brad's name was changed to Lynx Elessar.

After discovering his true calling, Aragorn took his leave of Elrond and traveled the wilds of Middle-earth. After figuring out there was more to life than a community existence, Brad enrolled himself in school, and took the daily bus to Eugene, where he reverted to Brad Jones. He excelled in his studies and won a scholarship to Stanford.

Soon after, Aragorn met Gandalf, and the two developed a close friendship and alliance. He then began a series of great ventures throughout Middle-earth. At Stanford Brad formed a close friendship with the late Stanford MBA professor, Kendall Gomez, who was instrumental in helping Brad get "Finback", his first online venture, off the ground. Six months in, the start-up failed, but that was par for the course in the early days of the dot.com gold rush. Jones then moved on to form three more start-ups before hitting the jackpot with TopMatch.com.

After a great victory over the Corsairs of Umbar, Aragorn traveled away into the east. After TopMatch's IPO, Jones moved north of the Golden Gate Bridge to Stinson.

Aragorn declared his love for Arwen and gave her the Ring of Barahir. Jones declared his love for TopMatch colleague Anna Hartley and gave her a six-figure ring from Cartier.

CHAPTER TWENTY-THREE

Dr. Jones was enigmatic. That was the word Titus had been searching for since she'd arrived. She'd called for an appointment late the night before, using the VIP emergency number that rang straight through to his cell. It had been a jumbled rant about Otieno's fucking column that appeared to know more about her dead husband than she did, and some uptight New York socialite whose vacuous personality was too much for any sane person to digest.

He'd juggled his other patients around to accommodate her, which had not been easy. His assistant had declared no joy with moving Arlo Cronin, CEO of Quorum. Arlo was great at harmonizing people's gut biomes, along with his own, but the holistic, hippy-esque vibe stopped right there. The guy was a Harvard alumni, top level narcissist. Asking him to move his time on the couch to accommodate an emergency patient had set off an expletive-ridden "don't you know who I am" tirade. Titus had to switch tactics and let him sound off into an hour-long phone therapy session, which the last thing he'd needed at 7am.

Man, if he was to write a book on half the stuff his clients dealt him in therapy, no one would believe it was true. And these were the brains behind AI. They'd all become human doings, fueled by the addled, twisted tech minds that passed through his offices.

He didn't often drink coffee, but the lack of meditation and the latest Cronin madness had him reach for a double espresso from the last of the independent Italian cafes in Downtown SF.

The buzz was helping him to zone in on Dr. Jones. "Anna!" he said.

She jolted at the abrupt interruption. Better. He took another sip of coffee. "How did you feel when you heard about Brad's father?"

"Brad told me he didn't have a dad, had no idea who he was, and that his mom had raised him up at some long defunct Oregon commune. Said he never knew the name of the place."

"And your feelings?"

"Feelings? Pissed off that Brad withheld the truth. God knows why he covered it up. You'd think Brad would have wanted Jack to know his lineage. Betrayed by untruth. That's how I am feeling. And then I am even more pissed off that the whole world knows. Private life. I mean how the fuck did I not know anything about his childhood?"

"And his mother?"

"Died long before we met. She was, according to what Brad told me, living in a cabin up in the woods."

Titus watched her face contorting through the flashes of anger that came volleying in on the tide of memory. She kept her fingers knit tightly together as if holding on to some invisible lifeline.

"Why wouldn't he tell me he was the one who enrolled himself in school? He always had his mom on some kind of pedestal whenever he spoke about her. I guess I'll have to wait for the next ByteBeat to tell me and the world more of what I don't know about my own husband."

She yawned. He could see she was exhausted, but the floodgates had finally opened on her therapy session. She'd set off driving before dawn to be here, leaving her son and dog with these socialite friends to follow her home the next day.

"Scott offered to get the helicopter to drop me back but I refused. If I have to listen to any more opinions from others about my situation, I will punch someone," she said with heat before adding quickly, "Not you. You're being paid to listen and ask the right questions so I can get it all out there and somehow, maybe, make sense of this new world."

"How about your childhood, Anna?" he said, checking his watch. They were already an hour in.

"Normal upbringing in the north of England. I didn't know my dad—he was in construction. He and Mom got divorced when I was three. He went to work in Spain and died there a year or so later. Mom was a schoolteacher, remarried. I had two stepsisters, who I never really knew, as they were with their mum most of the time. I went south to London straight out of school, found a bedsit and got some temporary work in an ad agency. Mom passed away of breast cancer when I was twenty-two. I quit my job, bought a round-the-world ticket, and the rest is history."

She paused, reached for the glass of water on the side table and took a long gulp. Sensing a need for a break, he continued with his notes, analyzing the impact of her childhood.

Suddenly, she jumped up and marched to the window. He looked up, watching as she gazed intensely over the city, her hands clenching and unclenching at her sides. Her body was tense, rigid with emotion. Taking a deep breath, she turned back to face him.

"Why do you think Brad was fucking another woman online?"

CHAPTER TWENTY-FOUR

The Sikorsky UH-60 Black Hawk touched down at the Mill Valley heliport. Jack gave Alicia a hug as he jumped down onto the tarmac. Flying down from the mountains, over California wilderness had given him a buzz that was almost, but not quite, the one he'd gotten when he'd shot the tube surfing off Maui the year before.

He knew he and his mom were wealthy, but the Lyles were on some other level. They used this helicopter like a car. "We're dropping you first, me after. Mom's already called in that I'll miss first part of class. It's okay, Miss DeFalto understands," Alicia had said earlier over breakfast, out on the terrace back at the lake.

The chef had made them both not just pancakes, but fresh crepes. Jack had eaten six, which he realized hadn't been the best idea when they'd gone up in the air, but he'd gotten over it fast as adrenaline and wonder had cut in when they'd swooped in low over a fast river run valley.

His mom would have loved that.

When she'd called him the night before she sounded more normal mom than the crazy one after that column shit that everyone at the Lyles' was talking about. He'd told her none of it mattered, that Dad was gone, and it'd all happened so long ago, who cared? But she wasn't the only one, especially Avery who he'd like to have punched. Alicia'd said she was always like that, even worse at home in New York.

He knew the Weizmanns. They came out to their Stinson place most weekends, and he'd seen Daniel on the beach a few times with friends, playing with drones. The dad, Joel, gave him the creeps, though. He was one of those older dads—there were a few of them in his year at school, the ones who kept in shape, drove open-top sports cars, and had much younger wives. They tried to look younger than they really were, but their tanned wrinkly skin was a dead giveaway. He didn't like the way Joel had come over to watch him, Alicia and Daniel playing tennis.

He'd stood at the net, arms folded, hair smoothed back like a wet seal, watching them from behind dark wraparound shades. You couldn't see where he was looking, but Jack knew he only had eyes on Alicia.

"Let's talk at lunch break," said Alicia, as he followed Scott out down the steps to the landing pad.

He grinned and she grinned back. That was one thing that was way better with his dad not around anymore: he didn't have to pretend he wasn't seeing Alicia.

Scott's driver was waiting next to a black Range Rover. Rand hopped up into the open trunk and Gui followed. The Sikorsky lifted off. Jack waved at Alicia.

"I'll drive, Gabino. You take a cab back to the city," said Scott.

The driver nodded and moved off towards the gate, already on his cell.

"Hop in," said Scott, climbing into the driver's seat.

Jack had only been alone with Scott a few times. He was intimidating to be with, especially since he was Alicia's dad. He was different to the others like Joel Weizmann. There was some kind of force field around him, like a superpower. He didn't do jokes, or goof around, like Jack's dad had done sometimes. When Scott Lyle spoke to you, it was like you were the only person on the planet, and you had to pay attention. Intense.

"Marin Academy's off Baker right?" said Scott, driving through the security gate.

"Yes. Thanks for dropping me."

"No problem. You set for class?"

"Double history."

"What's the topic?"

"Robert E. Lee surrendering the last major Confederate army to Ulysses S. Grant at Appomattox Courthouse."

"You enjoy it?"

Jack shrugged, unsure of what to say since he didn't really get why he had to know what happened back in 1865. The past was the past.

"You have to be taught the essentials of the knowledge discovered in the past, to equip you for the future. The only purpose of education is to teach you how to live your life, Jack. Developing your mind and equipping you to deal with reality. You're at the academy to be taught to think, to understand, to integrate, to prove. After that it's up to you to acquire further knowledge by your own effort."

Wow, heavy lecture. Does he do this with Alicia? "Still sucks though to have to learn it all."

Scott laughed the same way he'd done with his mom out on the lake over something she'd said. At least it made him sound more human. "You're smart. You'll make it work."

Jack wasn't sure he would. He had no idea what he was going to do when he was older. He wasn't a tech guy like his dad had been. Sure, he could navigate his way around using it all, but actually creating code that did cool shit was way out of his league. He didn't get that tech gene in the DNA mix. He'd got the sports one from his dad; and he'd got an aptitude for analyzing stuff from his mom.

The talk moved back to safer territory, to the upcoming soccer match that afternoon. Five minutes later Scott pulled into the drop-off line at the school gates. Jack could see Flynn's mom checking out who was in the car through her rearview mirror.

"Friend of yours?" said Scott, rolling to a stop at the curb.

Jack opened the door. "Yeah, Flynn Drexel."

"Drexel labs?"

Jack hauled his heavy backpack over his shoulder. "His grandfather was Gelder Drexel."

"Knew him well. He was a good man. I invested in his big pharma play."

"Cool," said Jack, not really knowing what it all meant.

Gui was whining in the back, wanting to get out.

"Better get going to Stinson."

A couple of moms at the gate were staring over at them, trying to figure out who was in the driver's seat.

"Thank you for Tahoe, the ride. I appreciate it," Jack said, remembering his best manners, as rehearsed with his mom over the years. He hadn't thought them very useful until now.

"Go learn how to live your life, Jack."

CHAPTER TWENTY-FIVE

Anna had written about confidants in a cyberpsych paper ten years before, just after she'd gone post-doctoral, and still felt the need to masochistically apply herself to an output of theory and report.

That phase had her burning the midnight oil for months, enduring the sharpened blade of perfectionism that kept slicing and dicing, until she'd published a slew of research to broadcast to the world. Fourteen papers in total. She'd have three on the go at the same time, in some sort of perverse internal race. As each one passed the finish post she'd felt a growing relief that somehow acted as a kind release.

It was only in retrospect that she realized it had all been some kind of guilt release for their sudden wealth. Where Brad had spent, she had worn the academic hair shirt in an effort to feel worthy.

Now, as she walked up the beach, she realized she had found a most extraordinary confidant in a most unlikely candidate. As they walked side by side, she went through her checklist of attributes:

An Active Listener. One who doesn't offer advice unless

you ask them for it. Empathy. Trusted. Nonjudgmental. Authentic. Self-Aware. Calm. Perceptive.

Damn, of all people, Scott Lyle was batting a hundred. She was now wondering if maybe, all those years ago, she'd misjudged him, been too harsh on how he drove his business.

Her mind flashed back to her first visit to the LVP offices. She'd been at her desk at TopMatch, eating a cookie to sate the hunger pangs from skipping lunch. Her desk phone rang. "Anna Hartley."

"Scott Lyle."

"Scott. How can I help?" she'd said, using a clipped business tone.

"I need you to give me optics on TopMatch performance this month and updated projections."

Why the hell was he asking her? "Brad and Dwight will be back Friday."

Silence on the other end.

"We both know you're capable of delivering before then. I'll send a car for you. 3pm."

The marching order dispatched, he'd hung up. She closed her eyes. The cookie was now sticking to the back of her throat, dry as dust.

He sent a black Mercedes, with a driver who operated in silence. It'd given her plenty of time to review the hastily printed projections, and for her mind to dart every other second to how uneasy Scott made her feel. She'd tried calling Brad, and Dwight, but all she'd got was voicemail.

The limo pulled up outside a long, low, two-story building. A discreet granite sign, carved with *Lyle Venture Partners* was set into a low brick wall, at the entrance to glass-fronted offices masked by deep beds of oaks, laurel and eugenia.

She took a deep breath and stepped out of the air-conditioned comfort into the blistering heat of the Valley.

Despite the sweltering temperature, a shiver ran down her spine. She was way out of her comfort zone. Being here. Alone. She silently cursed Brad for being away on his dog and pony show, then stepped into the grand marble atrium.

A guy who looked like he'd stepped out of a J.Crew shoot was sitting behind a glass desk. His crisp button-down white shirt was at odds with the "London Calling" T-shirt she'd thrown on that morning.

"Anna Hartley to see Scott Lyle," she announced. Go bold or go home.

He smiled. All perfect, gleaming white pearly teeth, like some young shark. "Hey, Anna, good to meet you," he said, getting up out of his leather aviator chair to shake her hand.

"Thanks."

"Mr. Lyle's expecting you." He escorted her into a long corridor lined with glass-fronted offices, all of them filled with more preppy LVP employees.

He stopped at the end, in front of a pair of antique Chinese doors. An intricate pattern of dragons had been carved into their surface, giving the impression that behind them lay some dynastic palace. Lifting a serpent-shaped iron knocker, he let it drop onto its back plate. She half expected an armor-clad guard to appear with the resulting thunk. Instead, the guy opened the door and stepped inside.

She followed him into an office that looked like it'd been raided from the Asian Art Museum. Ancient swords lay on display along one wall, their polished blades gleaming under spotlights. Opposite was a wall of sheet glass, looking out onto a bonsai-terraced walled garden, complete with koi pond. The floor was a dark ebony. On the far wall, a jade tiger statue sat on a black chest decorated with gold leaf.

At the room's center stood a lacquer desk, almost liquid in texture, a pool of pure midnight. Behind it, as if rising from its depths sat Scott. In place of a trident he held a phone to his ear, and was speaking in low tones. Like reception guy he was wearing a crisp white button-down shirt, but that was where the similarity stopped. J.Crew versus a fine Italian linen shirt, there was no contest. His sleeves were rolled up revealing deeply tanned, muscular arms.

He waved for her to take a seat on a low leather sofa in front of the sword display.

Reception guy withdrew, closing the door behind him. Scott continued his conversation, his eyes tracking her movements as she made herself busy getting the reports out, ready for his review. If she was swift and efficient she could be through and back in the car in thirty minutes tops, headed back to the safety of the city.

"Anna, good to see you." He took a seat opposite her, across the glass coffee table.

"Here are the latest traffic stats," she said, sliding the papers across to him.

He picked them up, giving them a cursory glance. "What do you think?"

She met his gaze. Intense.

"We're down twelve percent on target. LoveLink's ad campaign's sucking in new members and we're high and dry on anything but word-of-mouth since you've tightened the tap on our funding."

His nostrils flared, eyes burned with a momentary flash of anger at the jibe. He steepled his fingers. The vintage Patek Philippe on his wrist probably cost more than her and Brad's annual rent for their apartment.

He was now staring back at her with a poker face. She shifted, uneasy with the silence. Reaching into the folder she passed him a spreadsheet printout. "Now we're behind, this is what we need to get back on track."

He scanned the line items she'd put together. Each item had a hefty dollar amount next to it—an advertising campaign by state.

He stood up. "Bring everything with you. Follow me."

"Where?"

CHAPTER TWENTY-SIX

Anna put her foot in the stirrup and swung herself up into the saddle, while a stable hand held the pony's head. She collected the reins and urged the pony forward into the practice arena. Scott was already there speaking with his team captain.

Less than an hour before, she'd been in his office showing him the numbers. Now, she found herself at Menlo Circus Club, dressed in an LVP polo shirt, jodhpurs, and a helmet, preparing for her first-ever polo match. On a scale of one to ten for surreal experiences, this was a solid ten.

She could ride, had learned out in Australia, on the first leg of her around-the-world ticket. But this pony wasn't working ranch variety. It was all pent-up energy, like sitting on a revved-up Spitfire.

"Each time you get the ball, I'll give you the ad dollars for the state of your choosing," said Scott, handing her a mallet. "You get a goal, you get the full funding. Benicio here's going to give you the 101 on the rules."

"You have got to be kidding," she said.

"I don't kid. You play to win." He rode off, leaving her with the captain.

"First time?" Benicio's accent was syrup-thick Argentinian. She leaned in. "Yes."

"You ride?"

"Yes."

"Okay. You play hockey, golf?"

"Golf. Once."

"You use a broom on the floor?"

"Are you trying to be funny?"

"Non." He swept his mallet down. "Pico is fiery but steady. Rest your left hand on the neck to balance when you are standing up and hitting the ball, like this..."

Fifteen minutes later, Anna's head was a whirlwind of information. Game strategies, rules, and the four basic shots— off-side forward, off-side back, near-side forward, and near-side back—all vied for her attention.

She tightened her grip on the reins and long wooden mallet. Pico shifted beneath her, sensing her tension. She could feel the horse's energy, coiled and ready, but her mind was elsewhere.

She was here because Scott had made it clear that this was what it would take to secure the funding TopMatch desperately needed. A spark of anger ignited within her. She was a businesswoman, not a show pony.

She took a deep breath, trying to channel her anger into determination. She would play, but she wouldn't forget why she was here, and she wouldn't let Scott forget either.

"Which state?" said Scott, as they lined up for the first chukker. He was their attacking offensive player; she was assigned to back him up. Benicio and one of his grooms made up the defense, while the other team comprised of Menlo Circus Club riders whom Scott had paid to play. *The bastard,* she thought. *He was going to do this all along.*

"Texas."

"Ah, the Lone Star State. Why?"

"Nearly thirty million people."

The conversation stopped as the umpire threw the ball in. For a moment it was as if time stood still. She sat paralyzed, watching the game around her swirl up like some desert mirage. Ponies and riders became a blur of movement and thundering hooves. Pico snorted, all tight-sprung energy underneath her, waiting for a signal.

She gathered her reins, heart beating so loud she could hear it thundering in her ears.

The next seven and a half minutes were a blur of swinging mallets, abrupt changes in direction, and the thunder of hooves. Pico danced and zigzagged beneath her, pirouetting up and down the pitch with an energy that was electric. Anna clung to the saddle, her body jolted and jostled by the opposing team. Her mallet remained untouched by the ball, her attempts to swing thwarted by the sheer chaos of the game.

"Sticking on Texas?" said Scott, riding up alongside.

She glared at him, her fury rising like a tide. She dismounted from Pico. The pony's coat was slick with sweat and flecked with foam. Her own body ached from the exertion, but her anger was burning hotter than any physical discomfort. She took the reins of a fresh pony, Crow, for the second chukker.

She was mid-pitch when the ball came flying towards them. Two of the opposition came charging in. One of them bore down, bumping her out of the ball's path. But in that bump something changed. She finally allowed her weight to sink, and with it she found her balance.

Crow, sensing the change in the force, stopped head tossing. Her grip on the mallet tightened and she upped their tempo.

She saw Scott up ahead gain control of the ball and make a charge for the goal. This time she rode up, directly behind, blocking the opposition. He aimed and the ball hit home—the first goal.

Half-time was called. They were three-one down. She still hadn't touched the tiny ball. Trying to hit it from a fast-moving pony with her head eight feet off the ground, with a mallet that was over four feet long, all while opponents were charging at her from every direction, was hell on earth.

Her adrenaline was pumping like a stream engine as she mounted the next pony. He was a chestnut, all muscle and brawn. She rode over to where Scott was poised, ready to go. This time, there was no smirk, no flippant remark. He ignored her completely.

The umpire threw in and the third chukker got underway. Anna finally got the ball, kept her head down and made it halfway up the pitch before being run off. Texas, funded.

A couple more ball contacts, a goal by Scott and the third chukker was done.

The heat and dust had parched her throat. She drank a pint of lemonade straight down as she changed ponies.

"Two more states down. What's your pick?" said Scott, riding up.

"Florida and Alaska."

He frowned. "I get Florida, but you'd take Alaska over somewhere like New York?"

She took the reins of the next pony and climbed up into the saddle. "Then you don't know our customer base."

Without waiting for a reply she cantered out to her position on the pitch. This was the final chukker. She leaned forward, her lips up close to the pony's ear.

"I'm expecting great things of you," she whispered.

The umpire threw in. This pony was like a terrier, following Anna's cue to ride off any opposition who had possession of the ball.

Finally, her mallet met the ball with a satisfying crack, the impact resonating through her like a gunshot. She leaned into the pony's powerful stride, trusting its relentless gallop as they pursued the ball towards the goal.

Scott tore past her, his voice a harsh bark. "Pass it NOW!" Not a chance.

Seconds later, a stick came crashing down on hers, hooking around it, wrenching it away from the ball. Lightning fast another stick came flying in to sight and smacked the ball.

"You bastard!" she shouted at the rider, who was still hooked to her stick.

Out of the corner of her eye she could see Scott on track towards the goal. That was meant to be her.

With a swift twist, she freed her mallet and rose in the saddle, her body taut and focused like a jockey closing in on the finish line. She urged her pony forward, matching Scott's pace, her eyes locked onto the ball. With a deft lean to the right, she pulled alongside him.

In one fluid motion, she raised the mallet high, the sun glinting off the polished wood, and brought it down with a powerful backhand swing. The full force of her strike connected with the ball, sending it soaring up off the pitch like a missile locked onto its target. It hurtled through the air, slamming into the back of the net.

Her hair was still wet as she sat down at the linen clad table on the verandah. She smelled of the ladies' locker room essentials—mint-scented shampoo, conditioner, and body lotion. All trace of makeup was gone. There was no replacing it as she hadn't been prepared for this kind of afternoon.

Scott sat opposite in a fresh, pressed blue linen shirt, open at the neck, unreadable behind his black sunglasses. He passed her the menu.

The sun was on its way down, cutting a swathe of bright orange light across the grass pitch, to where they were positioned, a little distance from a table occupied by a couple of elderly, well-dressed couples. She felt out of place in her T-shirt and jeans.

The game was still replaying in her muscles and mind's eye.

"I'll take a vodka tonic," said Scott, as the waiter appeared.

"Ma'am?"

She paused. Wine was probably the wisest choice, but glancing across the table at the person who was now forcing her to dine with him because he claimed to still have more to discuss on TopMatch, she needed a stronger hit. "A margarita please."

"Blended or on the rocks, ma'am?"

"On the rocks, thanks."

"Salt?"

"Please."

A chasm of silence ensued when the waiter left. She focused on the menu choices, while silently cursing Brad for not picking up her call from the locker room. She was way out of her depth here.

"Under that delicate English rose veneer there lies an unexpected killer instinct," said Scott, when the drinks were set down. He was raising his glass, holding it midway across the linen. This was the first time he'd brought up her taking the ball off him to score the goal. Even now she couldn't tell if this was praise, some kind of veiled threat, or a line in the sand.

She clinked her glass and took a long draw from its tart, icy contents. "We needed the ad dollars."

"And you won them."

"Fair and square."

"Indeed."

"I don't get it, though," she said, feeling the tequila's fire.

"What?"

"You invest in TopMatch to make money. You put in Dwight as an ace to get us through IPO. We're on track, and then you turn down the funding tap to a trickle, forcing Dwight and Brad to head east to raise more funds."

He sat back, put his glass down, resting his elbows on the arms of the chair, steepling his fingers. "Roll the red carpet out with too much ease and the company forgets that in reality it's digital vaporware getting traction on the grit track to monetization."

"That's your Tao? You really think we don't know that we're still on the grit track?"

He removed his sunglasses. He was staring at her, unreadable. "You think Brad's got what it takes to play in the big league?"

"Of course I do."

"Is that because he's your boyfriend?"

"No. It's because he knows how to build something out of the ether. He's got a brilliant mind and is one of the best software architects around." She gritted her teeth. "You know that too, otherwise you would never have invested."

"Have you ever thought there's another reason why I invested?" His stare was unflinching.

"Like what."

"You."

A punch to her gut.

"I'm not for sale." She recoiled, spitting out the words.

He smiled. "Everyone has their price."

She pushed her chair back. Time to get out, get far, far away.

"If you leave now I'll withdraw all investment."

She gripped the table. "That's bribery."

"It's negotiation. You. Or, I take down TopMatch, brick by brick. Everything Brad, you and your merry band built up."

She pulled out her phone.

"Call him if you like. It'll hurt. He and Dwight have just been turned down by Riverwave."

"You fucker, you set them up?"

He shrugged. "But you are their knight in shining armor because you just secured the funding TopMatch needs to meet payroll, and get the ad dollars rolling."

"I am not some chattel."

He raised an eyebrow. "It's an easy deal. I want you for one night."

"Like some whore." She was shaking, fury rising. "I'll tell your wife."

He narrowed his eyes. "It would be your word against mine. And who's she going to believe? A young, ambitious English girl, or her husband?"

Anna felt sweat bead and trickle down her back. One night to save a company, to keep it on track to untold riches. To the life she and Brad dreamed of...

She sat back down. She could almost hear Scott purring at the satisfaction of him getting his way. Picking up the icy glass, she drained the last of the margarita, and locked eyes with him. Any woman could see he was attractive, many would jump at the chance to be with such a man. She placed the empty glass back down on the table.

"Even if you were the last man on earth, I would never, will never, sleep with you. If you choose to keep funding TopMatch do it because you know you will make money. But let me make one thing clear, I'm not for sale."

Blinded by her own resolve she got up and marched off the verandah lightning fast. Anyone watching would have said she was a blur of motion, a vanishing specter into the twilight.

In reality the second she rounded the corner of the building she sprinted down the drive, out onto Park Lane, and across the road into a school soccer field.

Adrenaline was pumping through her. What the fuck had she just done? Had she just brought down TopMatch? Brad, the team, all out of work because she didn't say yes?

A screech of tires gave away Scott's ire. She caught sight of his Porsche swinging out of the entrance and roaring off up the street.

Fingers trembling she redialed Brad's number. It went straight to voicemail. He had to be in the air right now.

"Brad, call me, it's urgent," she said, hanging up.

CHAPTER TWENTY-SEVEN

THREE MONTHS BEFORE BRAD'S DEATH

Brad waited for the familiar slowing of Anna's breath as she fell into a deep sleep. They'd been up later than usual, both hooked on the latest HBO drama, and had binge-watched the final two episodes. There weren't many shows that held the two of them together in rapt attention.

He rolled out of bed and padded out onto the landing, checking in on Jack as he headed for the stairs. He found him lying on his back, laptop open on his chest, AirPods in ears. The machine was still in game mode. The player was sound asleep. In a well-honed move Brad removed all the equipment and put it on the nightstand.

Stopping off in the kitchen, he selected a craft beer from the drinks fridge. As he cracked the top off the can, he felt the anticipation. He took a long draw, allowing the cool nectar to slip down his throat. This was his time. Alone in the quiet darkness of the house.

He closed his office door, pushing the lock across. Hushed silence. He'd escaped reality, and was now cocooned on the other side of the book-lined walls. His notebook lay open on the desk, the pen uncapped, lying in the spine, where he'd left it earlier that evening. Either side of it a newly spun web of diagrams was mapped out, marked up with arrows, handwritten code and ideas. He closed it and dropped it into a drawer. In the same move he grabbed a pair of gray glasses and put them on.

Another slug of beer and he woke up his laptop. The surround monitor activated above his desk bathing him in a sapphire haze.

He flexed his fingers and, with the skill of a concert pianist, he scaled together complex keyboard strokes, into a concerto of passwords, which accessed the web address via a VPN.

She was there waiting, lying on a bed of black satin sheets, scowling into the camera. "You're late," she snarled.

"Sorry."

She planted her stiletto clad feet on the fur rug and stood up. His dick twitched in response. She was wearing the leather pantsuit he'd requested. It molded to her every curve, the front zip pulled down just far enough to show the creamy swelling flesh of her tits.

"You like it?" she said, running her long nails down her body.

He nodded and adjusted his shorts.

"You want to talk?"

"No."

The anonymity of their exchange gave him the buzz of absolution he craved. Glass and ether between them.

He watched as she teased with her eyes and mouth, tossing her long hair side to side in a platinum curtain. Every move she made acted like an eraser on his everyday life. The past disappeared into oblivion, all blood and thought fused into one piercing shaft of lust. Blinding lust.

He licked his lips as she unzipped, peeling herself out of the suit, until she stood naked, filling the screen with luxurious, supple skin. She ran the tips of her ruby nails around each nipple, squeezing them until they glowed red and hard.

His hand went to his groin, to the hardened prick that had lain dormant for a month. As her hands traveled down, he stood up, dropping his shorts so that she could see what she was doing to him.

She smiled, her own hands now moving inside the labia of her hairless pussy.

"Why won't you let me see you?" she said.

He shook his head, his other hand going up subconsciously to check the gray glasses were firmly in place with their "blackout" activation to anyone seeing him on screen.

She moved to the bed, spreading her legs wide. The track changed to a slower, more rhythmic song as she rubbed her clitoris and put her fingers deep inside her.

He could feel his breath shortening to a pant, his pupils dilated behind the dark lenses as he pushed and pulled at his cock, imagining himself inside her glistening wet pussy.

Stars exploded in his mind's eye, disappearing at light speed, as he fell into the deep velvet folds of a black hole.

The moment was over. He cut the connection, needing neither comfort nor companionship in the aftermath.

"You okay?" said Anna, walking into the bathroom the next morning, where he was brushing his teeth.

He nodded and spat out a white stream into the flow of cold water from the polished chrome faucet.

She went over to the toilet, and sat down. Years of marriage had whittled away private communion with ablutions. "Thought you'd be out by now."

"Decided to skip the surf. Gonna take Jack out instead for

an early ride." He caught his own reflection in the mirror. Jaw was taut. He could feel his teeth clamped together inside, caging in the rising guilt. Now he wished he'd fought the fatigue and gone out to ride the waves early like he normally did.

"Nice," she said. "Better than him gaming to kick off his weekend. You see the latest report on microtransactions? A player on Diablo Immortal blew a hundred thousand dollars buying everything the game offered. We're talking deep commerce buried in every facet of the game. All those small wins giving constant, gradual progress are now screwed over with commercialization. Fulfillment's flushed away."

"Jack knows the pitfalls."

"I'll be reminding him anyway. Nothing like reinforcement."

Even without makeup his wife looked good. As she lined up next to him at the mirror, pulling a headband on to start her "daily face excavation", as she put it, he felt that familiar pull to watch her. Just as he had back at TopMatch, when they were first together. A magnetic force of attraction.

Life before her had been a casual array of on/off girlfriends who complained that he had too little time for them. Then Anna had arrived on the scene and blown away the competition. The way they played and worked together was the kind of relationship that left him in no doubt that she was the one. The keeper. And now?

"I'll fire up the coffee machine," he said, making a swift exit.

The bike clinked, clunked and whirred beneath Brad as man and machine ascended the steep, rocky trail to Mount Tam's mighty summit. Jack was up ahead, working his way through the gears of the new carbon Santa Cruz Blur bike they'd given him for his birthday, its superlight frame with technology made for swift upward momentum.

The sweat was beading out of Brad's pores. A cool breeze wicked it away through the PriCross bike suit. Dwight had discovered the brand on a trip to Switzerland, and had FaceTimed him from a mountain chalet: "Dude, we gotta invest in this shit. Custom tailored perfection."

That was it. A five hundred K investment, and he had his own PriCross suit. Worth every damn cent.

The fresh scent of pine and wild thyme filled the air as the tires crunched and crushed the mountain's skin, every pedal making a clean bite into nature. The physical exertion and resulting endorphin rush had done the trick; equilibrium was restored.

He'd take Anna out for dinner later. That new sushi place over in Mill Valley. They'd drink sake and shoot the breeze. He wanted to hear her latest research on AI and the human impact. She'd been burning the midnight oil and was due to deliver a lecture on it at UCLA the following week.

When she was in that research mode, he knew to leave her well alone, until it was done. Just like all those years ago when her paper output mania was in full flow.

"Dad!" Jack had stopped and was hissing his name in a long whisper, holding up a gloved hand, signaling stealth approach.

Brad hopped off his bike, lifted it up and carried it upwards to where Jack was now crouching low behind a rock. "What we got?" he said, moving in low.

Jack pointed up the tree shrouded slope to a low branch of cypress where a tawny mountain lion was resting up from the heat of the day. The black tipped ears twitched, its golden eyes were fixed on their location. Jack started taking a video with his cell.

"Puma," Brad whispered.

"Cool. We okay here?"

"Sure. It's just scoping us out."

"How d'you know?"

"Where I grew up we had a mom and cubs on the other side of the mountain. We left them in peace, they left us in peace."

They sat watching in silence. The minutes ticked by. The puma emerged from the canopy of trees, taking with it a young deer that neither Brad nor Jack had even seen.

CHAPTER TWENTY-EIGHT

2019

Kobe sat back in his latest gift-to-self. The warmth of the soft leather of the vintage Eames soothed the aching muscles in his back. It'd been a long day at the keyboard and on the phone. Now he was officially an influencer with a following north of three million, he was being approached by everyone from fashion, tech and food.

The invitations had come pouring in too. Guest speaker, VIP access, invitation-only preview—the roped-off events of the rich. He was access all areas.

The evening sun bathed his new apartment with its Golden Gate view. A swift move. Only the week before at a VIP event, he'd met a private equity guy who was going to Tokyo on a six-month assignment. He'd been given the keys at the weekend. Nominal rent and a promise to send him first drafts of ByteBeat.

He raised his crystal tumbler of vodka and ice, offering a silent toast to Brad Jones. The man who'd given him the wings of success.

Success, though, came with a price—the need to constantly feed the media beast with juicy enough bites to keep column momentum and expansion.

He'd thoroughly mined the rich vein of Oregon, excavating quips and quotes from locals, who'd cemented themselves back into the daily humdrum of urban life, and then a few who'd remained in the woods and mountains. It was hard to devise what was truth or fiction, but he'd used it all anyway since Brad himself wasn't there to refute the memories or claims.

Whenever that whisper of impartial, verified truth came whispering from the high and mighty journalist on his shoulder, he reasoned with himself that this was just the way the news went down these days.

He took another sip, appreciating the cold peppery hit to his palate. No more bottom-shelf booze from Walgreens. This one was from the gods, a cobalt blue bottle with the silvered letters of Skyy giving a pleasing ambience to the experience.

What he needed right now was a new angle; something crisp and fresh. Even Sam had gone quiet on the cafe intelligence, and the others down at Quorum. Now he was making news it was him being talked about in the booths and at the counters.

The mellow notes of a saxophone vibrated across the room and out through the open balcony window. He could feel their flow resonating through this body, broadcasting a complexity that piqued every sense. This heightened state lifted his mind to a bird's-eye view of the situation—of the curious life of Brad Jones.

The crux. Why? Why did he end his life when he had everything that most people dreamed of—wealth, health, power, family? What had led him to a watery grave? Oregon was a place he'd escaped from on his own terms. He'd graduated first class from Stanford. He was a maverick start-up genius who created one of the biggest, most profitable online dating sites in the world. He'd gone on to invest in and build more tech companies, amassing further wealth—more than could be spent in a hundred lifetimes. He'd met the woman of his dreams at TopMatch, and they'd ridden the dot.com wave together, moving on to BigData, cloud computing, and AI.

Why would you end it all?

He let the question sit in its majesty as story's beginning and ending. It didn't add up.

He stepped out onto the balcony, into the cool of the evening. The hum of traffic and a city of 800,000 people, few of them having access to all areas. And when you had that, did you stray?

That was it, the thing that had so far escaped his mindset. He'd been thinking of Brad as the man who had it all. But when you had it all did you want more? Did you crave something different?

CHAPTER TWENTY-NINE

Trouser suits—neutrals and black, paired with Loci Reed Nine trainers. Anna was back in her cyberpsych uniform of choice, sitting comfortably in the boardroom, while opposite, squirming in his seat, sat their CEO and lately, online porn aficionado, Jason Lwang.

She'd run through the shame-based thinking and online disinhibition, and felt like she was making some headway by giving him the hardline stats on sextech use. It was the first time he looked as if he was properly listening.

It had been a difficult conversation so far. She could tell he was hiding something bigger. Impact on business and his role hadn't moved the dial, neither had office etiquette and sexual antics.

"Okay, Jason. Let's cut to the chase. We've been in here nearly two hours already, and I'm sensing there's more that you want to say..."

She waited, watching his eyes dart right to left. Silence.

"Let's be honest. I'm sure you know I've recently been widowed. What you're doing could lead you down a road where you compromise everything you're working towards—financial success, a real relationship, a family."

He frowned. "Your husband did stuff like this?"

Damn. She was letting emotion in. "No. What I mean is you're young. You've got the whole world waiting for you to get Xomftov out there. Don't screw it up."

"I get that. You're right about it all, except..."

"Except what?"

"I want a relationship with someone but I don't have time. I have to be here eighteen hours a day to keep everything on track. Investors are breathing down my neck to get the product out, I've got a heavy churn in engineering, and the burn rate's up."

He stopped. His shoulders slumped, and he let out a long sigh.

She softened. All the huff and puff of the CEO had vanished. Before her sat a deflated man. "Okay. Let's set some rules of engagement. First off, you cannot get your fix from your office, or anywhere else on company premises. And no one is effective at their job working eighteen hours a day. I will send you the stats on that. Go home at a reasonable time, get some rest and think about going outside. Get some fresh air, get into nature, go and interact with people other than your colleagues. Get a life, Jason..."

The door to the boardroom opened, and to her surprise Scott Lyle came striding in. Charcoal suit, sapphire blue shirt, tanned. He brought with him the familiar scent of Oud Wood that carried the ghost of Brad.

Jason leapt out of his chair as if he'd been electrocuted.

"Scott?" she said, closing her notebook. *What the hell are you doing here?* was what she wanted to say.

"Mr. Lyle," said Jason, shaking his hand as if operating a water pump.

"Thought I'd drop by to see how the product roadmap's doing."

Typical. In all the years he still hadn't changed tactics. That casual dropping by the office, unannounced, meant he was on the cusp of investing.

"Anna." He turned, fixing his eyes on hers. "It's a nice surprise to see you here."

Her mind raced to their walk on the beach, to Tahoe, to the boat ride. Had she mentioned Xomftov? No. She was sure of it.

In a surprise move he leaned in and kissed her French-style on both cheeks, his skin lightly grazing hers. The touch quickened her pulse. Flustered, she picked up her notebook. "Your timing's good. Jason and I have just finished our meeting. I'll leave you to discuss." She checked her watch. "I'll schedule a follow-up call," she said to Jason.

And with a swift turn she made a hasty exit.

Wait time twelve minutes. Where was an Uber when you needed one? Her appointment with Titus was in ten. She was about to start walking when she noticed Scott's Range Rover at the curb.

"Gabino?" she said, tapping on the window.

"Mrs. Jones," he said, lowering it.

"I have an appointment downtown in ten minutes. Would you be able to help me out please?"

He smiled. "Sure. Hop in the back. Mr. Lyle will be pleased I can be of service." He set off up Third, navigating the traffic with the skill of a rally driver. "Pine and Battery you said?"

"Yes, right on the corner, Embarcadero side."

"You got it."

"Can I ask you a question, Gabino?"

"Sure. Fire away."

"Did Scott know I was at Xomftov?"

He looked at her through the driver's mirror, his dark glasses giving nothing away. "He knows most things, Mrs. Jones. That's the way he does business."

"That I know. But did he specifically know I was there?"

"All he said to me was to take him up to Xomftov when I picked him up first thing. Nothing more."

"Thanks."

Titus was ready to pick up where they'd left off, heading into deeper discussion on Brad's virtual infidelity. Instead, Anna came in wanting to unpick her present conundrum with Scott Lyle. Titus found himself writing, *Out of the frying pan and into the fire* at the top of his notepad.

The subject of Scott Lyle was a familiar one that had peppered the angst-ridden minds of many a tech executive who had sat on his couch. The man was a narcissist by all accounts, who wielded the sword of power and money. Few liked him, many respected him. It never went beyond those two subjects. He'd never had anyone who had arrived with an emotional connection issue with the man. Most would say he was incapable of emotion.

"Weird, huh?" she said, from where she'd chosen to sit opposite, cross-legged with her trainers kicked off. "One moment we're walking on the beach and he's acting as a confidant. Next, he's arriving at Xomftov unannounced."

Titus probed, making notes, watching her every move as she recounted how Jack and Alicia had bonded, how that had led to the Lyles taking her under their wing. Guarded but positive, with an undertone...

After several breathing exercises he asked her to close her eyes and think back to their earlier encounters.

He watched her face contort from exertion and pain as she

told him how Scott had propositioned her. How she'd told Brad, and that he had been ready to confront Scott but stopped, as the funding had come straight through with an added bonus sum for a national ad campaign. It had been an empty threat from a man who couldn't and never would have her.

"And after that?"

"New York. I was there on a girls' weekend with Caitlin, but Sunday, when I was about to fly back, I got a call from Scott saying he wanted me to stay on another day and help out with due diligence on a new tech company there. We were so locked in with LVP at this point, getting us to go public, that I didn't have a choice. Had to go out and buy a suit. Took a cab from our three-star hotel in the Meat Packing district to The Plaza. He was sitting in the lobby, talking on his cell."

"How did he look?" said Titus, wanting her to immerse herself more deeply in the memory.

"His hair was wet. Looked like he'd just stepped out of the shower. Usual outfit—navy sports jacket, pale blue button-down shirt. Nice he could be so leisurely, unlike me who'd had to rush across town with a lunatic cab driver. Waved me over, signaled the waiter, like he was directing air traffic."

She paused. Titus watched her eyes moving beneath her lids, a mind in the motion of recollection.

"What did Brad say about Scott asking you to do this?"

"He told me to see it as an opportunity, saying it showed how much Scott respected my opinion."

"Go on with the Plaza."

"It was all business. He gave me a folder on the company. Workbox. At the time they were new in the online recruitment space, but they had some cool tech. He was looking at going in early with them. I told him I knew nothing about recruitment, but he countered that I knew the TopMatch community inside out, so I knew what makes people tick. People matching with people. People matching with jobs. He was right. It's a similar kind of setup.

"I left the hotel in a limo, headed to a grungy office for a day with Scott drilling and digging into every aspect of Workbox's existence. I got sideswiped to a corner with some tech guy who had not been home in a couple of nights because of site issues. He took me through the interface, membership database and content plan."

She wrinkled her nose in disgust. "Had my work cut out as they didn't have a clue about community, customer experience, engagement and retention. They had a solid piece of tech, that was all. Didn't leave until after six, when it was already dark outside. I told Scott it was grueling and that I couldn't believe he actually enjoyed the process of finding companies to invest in. His limo pulled up, and I had a flight to catch. He gave me his limo. Not sure how he got back to his hotel. Once I landed back at SFO I got a text from him: 'You asked me earlier why I actually enjoy the process of finding companies to invest in. It's the game. The chase to get in there before anyone else.'"

CHAPTER THIRTY

The fog was rolling in over the pine-forested slopes from the ocean. Scott sat on the stone balustraded terrace of his home, drinking a two-fingered measure of Kentucky's finest—Woodford Reserve Wheat Whiskey. He was oblivious to the cinnamon and cedar wood notes because all his powers of sensibility were focused on the cell held to his ear. Magnus was on the other end. It was nearly midnight in New York and he was slurring his words, making it hard to fathom what he was saying.

This was not the moment that he'd been savoring when he'd gone into Xomftov earlier. When he'd seen the cyberpsych herself in action. When he'd gotten close enough to graze her silken cheeks with his lips. He knew she'd asked Gabino if he'd known she was there. And, yes, she was the damn reason he was there. He couldn't give a shit about the company. It was small fry to what he invested in these days. What he wanted was to see her again. That beach walk had him wanting more, much more.

He'd planned to sit out and savor the memory of her orchid

scent, the lilt of her accent, and the ice blue of her eyes. His guard was down and he, for once, was allowing himself the pleasure of the want.

Magnus had put a stop to that because a complaint had just come in from a woman in PR at the company.

"Your lawyer's going to take care of it," said Scott. "You gotta chill out."

"I know that, man, but it's, you know, what else will they find out?"

He listened to the deep inhale and exhale of Magnus smoking one of his banned-by-Avery cigarettes while he hid out on his roof deck, out of her sight, smell and hearing.

"The other stuff..."

"You're getting paranoid. Keep quiet, keep your head down, and make sure you tell Avery before it's out."

"She's going to kill me."

"Hang tight." Scott ended the call.

As much as he'd told Magnus not to worry, it had triggered the past. He refilled his glass from the bottle that stood on the glass coffee table and let the steel trap door of memory lift an inch, transporting him back to the beginning of the new millennium...

The 2000s

The sky was a hard-edged, crystal-cut blue, contrasting with the green like some Hockney retrospective on Californian life. Scott adjusted his black Pebble Beach golf cap stamped with its iconic lone cypress, so that the glare of the sun didn't affect his shot.

A strong wind was whipping the top of a Pacific swell.

White foaming crests were crashing against the dark protruding rocks below the cliff. He could taste salt in the air.

Gripping the third iron tight in his kid leather gloved hands, he set up his shot for the 106-yard, par three seventh hole. Many would be distracted by the sheer beauty of the location—crafted, contoured man-made landscape of light and shade. The white sand bunkers set in manicured greens against a backdrop of wild, untainted ocean. A legendary hole. But for him, whose youth had been honed at the nearby private Carmel Academy boarding school, this was home turf.

He adjusted his foot position, took one more look at his ball's destination, and took the shot.

Magnus was leaning on his club, breathing heavily. "Hell, you're on your A-game today."

Scott glanced at him. "You should quit smoking. It'd do you good."

Magnus laughed. "Yeah, yeah. It's definitely a more compelling reason than Avery nagging me every time I step out onto the penthouse roof to light up and contemplate Central Park."

"She still on your case about that?"

Magnus nodded. "But I like those moments. Just me, a small fire, fanning the embers of my true nature."

Scott admired his straight shot, the ball having sailed effortlessly over a challenging kidney-shaped bunker, landing cleanly on the green.

They headed back to the golf cart.

"You're up next, Wingman," he said, taking the silver hip flask from his friend, who was at the wheel. He took a swig, the smooth burn of the single malt Glenfiddich a welcome sensation.

Wing yawned. "Jet lag's a bitch," he said. "Even whiskey

can't take the edge off that fifteen-hour time difference between here and Hong Kong."

"You came straight from landing at SFO?"

Wing yawned again, leaning back in the cart. "Yeah, any sleep on the journey down the peninsula was nixed by a long call with my second-in-command. Had to put a deal back on track."

Scott clapped him on the shoulder. "Well, you're here now. Let's make the most of it."

As Wing pushed down on the pedal, and started cruising along the cliff edge, Scott felt a rush of youth return. He was with his two best friends from school days. This was their time.

"You got us taken care of tonight?" said Magnus, leaning in between them from the back seat.

Scott held up his hand. They high-fived.

"Shit man, moments like this are pure gold. Three Musketeers gathered again," continued Magnus, leaning back, spreading his arms wide across the back seat.

Eighteen holes played, Scott victorious, they ate club sandwiches washed down with beer over at the tennis club next to the pool. It was a quiet day since it was midweek. Just a few older socialites eating cob salads, wearing sun visors to keep the rays off the latest work they'd had done, sipping ice tea, and gossiping. Scott had to pass a table of their coven on his way to the bathroom. One of them clawed onto his arm as he tried a brief "hello ladies" keeping forward motion.

"Scott, now tell me how are Kristy and the kids? We haven't seen them in a while." Nancy Fulton, doyenne and heiress to a zipper fortune, had him gripped. Gold and bones. Both felt cold and hard against his skin.

"Doing well thanks, Nancy. Kids are doing great. Kristy's busy on the steering committee for the Beaux Arts Ball."

There were murmurs of "oh my" satisfaction, a collective

purr around the table at the news of their social echelon continuing on its age-old traditions. A smiled formed across Nancy's thin lips at her victorious gain of information.

He slipped his free hand in his pocket and drew his brand-new Motorola flip phone like a loaded gun. "Sorry, ladies, I've got a call to make."

All eyes darted to this wondrous piece of new technology. He flipped it open with a sleight of hand.

"Business must be good," said Nancy.

He grinned. "Hitting home runs on a daily basis, Nancy." With that, he turned and strode fast towards the bathroom.

He could hear Nancy continuing her broadcast. "Kristy's mother was so worried he'd squander her fortune when they got married."

Bitch. Would he never escape the fucking judgment? He may have needed the Van Hoeveren fortune to get launched, but now it was his show.

Scott stepped out onto the glass and steel deck of his family beach house, the cool Pacific night air a contrast to the warmth of the fire pit. He looked out at the expansive view, the ocean a dark, restless mass under the moonlight. The sashimi feast prepared by Kibo had been topflight, and now, as they moved from beers to sake and finally to bourbon, the night was taking on a familiar, exhilarating edge.

Magnus was hunched over the glass frame of a photo, meticulously chopping and forming rails of coke. The image beneath his hands showed Scott skydiving over the Nevada desert, a moment of pure adrenaline and freedom captured in time. Scott watched as Magnus worked, anticipation building within him.

Wing was by the Bang & Olufsen player, stacking CDs into the sleek, modern device set into the wall.

The opening notes of their theme tune, "Riders on the Storm", filled the air. Magnus joined in alongside Morrison, his voice booming out the lyrics with a raw, primal energy. Scott pulled his wallet from his back pocket, rolling up a hundred-dollar bill with practiced ease. He leaned over the glass frame, the white powder disappearing up into his nasal cavity, leaving a sharp, acrid trail that he quickly countered with a slug of bourbon. Ignition.

The other two followed suit, their jaws working side to side as the conversation up-ticked and amplified.

"AGM time, guys," said Wing.

"Yeah, tally time!" roared Magnus, beating his chest like a five-hundred-pound gorilla.

Scott refilled their glasses and took a seat at the fire. He steepled his fingers, rubbing his nose over the tips to remove a few specks of coke. He'd been damned excited about this whole event, them all being together again, and what he'd had planned for later. But she'd taken that edge off, declined his favorable offer, ruined his tallying...

"Hey, bro, you with us?" Magnus clapped him on the shoulder, jolting him.

"Let's get to it. Wing, you're up first," Scott replied, looking over the flames at *Time* magazine's "Asia Pacific Entrepreneur of the Year".

Wing took a deep breath and exhaled. "It has been a strong year for Victoria Peak Ventures. We have made twenty-three investments, mainly mainland China and Taiwan. And, an outlier in..." Dramatic pause. "...Finland."

He looked at the others. Magnus was smirking. Scott raised an eyebrow.

"Give us the tally, Wing," said Magnus, taking another swig of bourbon.

"China sixteen for sixteen. Taiwan five for seven. Finland one for one."

"Sweet sixteen. You fucking rock, you motherfucker!" said Magnus high-fiving him.

"Taiwan?" said Scott.

Wing shook his head. "Chip manufacturing company. Other one was a small outfit, three web programmers with a real estate play. No women, no dice in either deal."

"You gotta tell me about Finland, man. That's a first," said Magnus.

"Eco Finnish fashion house going online. All hand-knit wool designer pieces. Bricks and mortar place but with a global client base. Eager to expand."

Scott held up his hand. "Cut to it."

He looked at Wing, noting the rare smile spreading across his friend's lips. Wing, the future heir to the Chun dynasty, was a man of serious demeanor ninety-nine percent of the time. But here, in this moment, Scott saw that one percent of pure hedonism that Wing allowed himself.

"Deal was sealed in Pallas-Yllästunturi National Park. Flew in by helicopter, snow mobile out to this remote luxe chalet I found. Marjatta Koskinen, CEO. Five ten, thirty. Cold as the snow outside. Hated to fuck for the deal, but once she saw no way out she went dominatrix. Tied me up with some reindeer hide strips she cut up from a rug in the place. Three thousand dollar rug. Got the bill for it after. Worth the investment. A woman after my own heart. I even gave her another point in the deal for her top performance."

He saw Magnus adjust his chinos. Hard-on at the shared information.

"Your first CEO prima nocta," said Scott, casting his mind back over the years.

If he remembered correctly Magnus had that one in Texas four years back, the CEO of some oil company. She'd been pushing forty. He'd had a couple himself. The graphics company in San Diego, that medical start-up last year. Neither of them memorable though, like this Finnish bitch.

"Next year I'm expanding horizons. Doing due diligence on a geothermal company in Iceland, run by two women scientists," said Wing.

"Seeing the Northern Lights every which way. Like your thinking," said Magnus, turning to Scott. "Hey, did we ever work out how a CEO scores?"

Scott got to his feet and picked up the already empty Jack Daniels bottle. "Chop out some more lines. I'll get the book."

He returned moments later with a fresh bottle and his old school copy of Herman Melville's *Moby Dick*. Opening the last page he revealed the wickets and gates of their tallies over the years.

First entry at Carmel Academy, when they'd been smoking weed under the bleachers. First entry "CA—SL 5. ML 4. WC 2." All of the girls were virgins back then. Pure prima nocta, poached from the beach and tennis club, and neighboring all-girls' school.

The college years still showed Scott and Magnus vying for first place. They'd had to change the rules based on the fact that virgins were few and far between at college. Instead it'd been a tally of one-night stands that had to be of girls they'd never met before, and would not meet after.

Once they headed into the workplace, mastering the art of the deal, Scott had proposed new rules—prima nocta could only happen when investing in a company. You held back the investment capital until a woman had been thrown in to sweeten the deal.

The three of them had competed hard over the years, upping their acquisition strategy to get skin in the game. In later years, Wing was blazing ahead in the tally because he had deep pockets, and had honed his gameplay skills at the gambling tables of Kowloon.

"CEO scores same as a virgin. Double points," said Scott, entering Wing's tally using his new Montblanc pen bearing his initials that Kristy had given him at Christmas. The moment he'd opened the box he knew that it was to be kept for one purpose only.

"Based on your latest numbers, further boosted by the CEO, you are thirty-eight ahead. Magnus, what's yours?"

Magnus snorted his newly chopped line, leaning back in his chair as he gazed up at the night sky. Scott could see the contentment in his friend's eyes, the rare moment of peace that Magnus found only in their company, the two people who truly understood him.

Avery saw only the polished exterior: the New York hotshot, the perfect husband and family man who brought in over thirty million a year. She saw the provider of the Central Park penthouse, the Hamptons summer house, and the ski lodge in Vail. But she was clueless about the man beneath the surface, the man who had upped his inheritance a hundredfold since their marriage.

"Twelve New York start-ups, three in Toronto, two in Bermuda." He leaned in. "Bagged four data scientists in that mix. Let me tell you, they are not what they seem. All that analytical shit rips off in the sack and they go like steam trains!" He thrust his pelvis back and forth.

"You still going large?" said Wing, screwing up his face.

"Sure am, dude. Not one of them under two twenty-five. Hey, I should get double points for that."

Scott leaned across for the mirror and bill. Took a hit.

"You should get therapy for that," Wing said.

Magnus held his hands up and squeezed two imaginary melons. "I like a lot to hold on to."

Scott laughed. He always wondered why his friend had picked Avery, the socialite X-ray, to be his loving wife, when what he really craved was flesh-laden women—the bigger the better. Even Kristy said Avery was like a skeleton, and she was a woman who lived by the "you can never be too thin" mantra. Seriously, both needed more meat on their bones. He preferred more athletic, like Anna. Damn, he had to stop thinking about that bitch.

"Had some mighty fine rides this year. One in Toronto though was a doozy. It was slim pickings with only two women to choose from. None of them was a looker, so went by weight. Cost me eighty fucking grand as she was general counsel. Took her over her desk. Should have seen her. Pantyhose round her ankles, gray skirt hiked to her waist. Man, she was pissed and dry as dust. Like gettin' into Fort Knox. Dick got chaffed, nearly broke off in there it was so tight."

Scott snorted with laughter. Wing joined him. Magnus sure knew how to tell a tale. He penned the tally, checked his watch. "Okay, shooting fast here as company is on its way. Twelve West Coast, one Paris, Amsterdam and London. Fifteen total there plus the three tonight, two of which are my gift to you both since I'm hosting this year."

He drew the gates and wickets under his name, slammed the book shut.

"Dude, you know you gotta give us more than that," said Magnus.

Scott got to his feet. Normally he'd spin out a story or two, whetting appetites for what was to come. But everything felt tainted because the gift he'd set for himself tonight had said no. And now second best was going to be served, from an online insurance site that LVP were backing.

"We are waiting for the salient details," chimed in Wing.

He paced, metering out the story runway. "You know my particular tastes."

He paused to watch the others lean in, excitement glinting in their eyes. His phone rang out. He checked the LED screen: GABINO. "They're here."

CHAPTER THIRTY-ONE

Investing in a tech company was an art form, one that Scott practiced and honed every day. Like a military strategist, he employed a range of weapons each probing business plans and financials, before blowing holes in the entrepreneurial visions that had been laid out before him. But his main weapon was his mind—his acute insight and intellect that he prided on bringing into the arena after his lieutenants had paved the way in.

The odds of finding a winner in the frenzy of start-ups that were springing up in every warehouse and apartment block in the Bay Area was somewhere between a crapshoot and a poker game, but he could slice through the bullshit on a PowerPoint slide based on amateur numbers, and find the nugget of an idea that, with some LVP alchemy, would be pure disruption and gold.

The Bay Area, the epicenter of the dot.com boom, commanded most of LVP's resources, but Scott had cast a wider net, cultivating a global network of researchers and associates.

Lifting the lid on any new prospect was what gave him the kick. His disposition made life easier on any emotional baggage that founders tried to dump on him as strike price on the deal got underway. The real high came later, when investment dollars were held in a kind of escrow of his own making, and he took prima nocta.

Normally this would be celebrated in the privacy of his office at Sandhill Road, but since he was entertaining Magnus and Wing, he'd made an exception, choosing the beach house, where they were guaranteed discretion.

Gabino, dressed in an immaculate dark suit, white shirt, narrow black tie, led the way across the decking to where the three musketeers were waiting.

None of the women were smiling.

Gabino brought out a silver tray laden with a glass ice bucket containing a bottle of vintage Dom Perignon and crystal flutes. He disappeared into the kitchen, where he was to be on guard until the night was over.

Small talk got underway. It had been carefully orchestrated, mapped out in the deal that Scott had made with each of the women. If someone was passing by on their boat, they'd look up and think it was a cool place to be having a cocktail party, nothing more.

He listened as his friends held court, entertaining the women with war stories of adventures in the VC world, of deals gone wrong, of boardroom battles won. He topped up glasses, kept the music running hot, and waited for the moment to strike.

CHAPTER THIRTY-TWO

2019

Anna was grateful she had finally agreed to join Caitlin. They had chosen the hardest trail, the one that ascended from Stinson and stretched across the skyline. Two hours of sweat and exertion, running in the mid-morning sun, proved to be the perfect antidote to a sleepless night and a mind full of turmoil.

The night before, when Caitlin had said she was getting up early and coming down from Napa for this very run, Anna had flat-out refused. She had insisted she needed some time alone. But Caitlin, being Caitlin, had persisted.

"You should quit your sales job and become one of those tough love therapists," said Anna, bending over, hands on thighs to catch her breath when they'd reached the end of the trail.

Caitlin laughed as she stretched a hamstring. "That'd drive me mad. I love doing this to help you. But God, just imagine a stranger running at this pace, listening to what I've got to say."

"You've made more sense to me than Titus has. He just asks questions, digging in and opening up memories that, frankly, I'd rather keep a lid on."

"He's doing a good job so far, A. He's got you opening up."

Suddenly, anger surged within Anna. One second she felt

an exhausted calm, the next a seething, teeth-clenching rage. She lashed out, kicking hard at a nearby cypress trunk. The sharp pain of impact made her recoil.

Caitlin placed a comforting hand on her shoulder. "Let it all go, A. It's okay."

But it didn't feel okay. It felt like she was being torn open from the inside. "Sorry, Cait."

"Do not apologize."

"Thanks. I guess I'm..." For once she couldn't find the words.

"You're letting go."

Anna wiped a stray tear away with the back of her hand.

"How about we go stuff ourselves with pancakes at Ranch? God knows we deserve it," said Caitlin.

"I'm a mess."

"No you're not. Just keep your sunglasses on and no one will be any the wiser."

Now, more than ever, Kobe needed to hide in plain sight. The baseball cap was pulled so low that it obscured most of his vision, allowing him to see only the decking and chairs as he walked into the Ranch Cafe. The new apartment location in North Beach had proven to be a strategic goldmine—it had taken him a mere twenty-one minutes to reach Stinson, park, and position himself in the same vicinity as Anna Jones.

His new Tesla had sped along the freeway and coastal road, eating up the miles with a swift efficiency that bordered on the miraculous. He had reasoned that even if he were caught speeding, a traffic ticket would be a small price to pay for the opportunity at hand. Fortunately, the gods of motoring and journalism seemed to be on his side. He had made it to the cafe in record time, without a single hitch.

Sam, ever the reliable source, led him straight over to the table she had reserved for him. "Took your time," she hissed in his ear as they approached the table. "You're lucky they've decided on a second coffee."

The table was perfectly situated for his needs—discreet and tucked away, yet close enough to Mrs. Jones and her closest friend, Caitlin Rivera, to be useful. A planter filled with wild grasses provided a natural barrier between them, offering a semblance of privacy while still allowing him to eavesdrop. He strategically positioned himself so that his back was to Mrs. Jones, in the closest chair to her.

As he settled into his seat, he couldn't help but steal a glance at them. He had written so much about Mrs. Jones, delving into her life and connections, that seeing her in person felt surreal. She'd now stepped off the page and into his reality. She was dressed in designer athletic wear, her hair pulled back into a sleek ponytail, eyes hidden behind dark glasses. Her friend was similarly attired, both of them exuding wealth and privilege. He took in the expensive jewelry, the high-end watches, and casual elegance that seemed to come naturally to them. It was a stark reminder of the rarefied world they inhabited.

He hit the record button on his cell phone and angled the microphone in their direction, hoping it would pick up something useful.

If only he could turn down the sound of the ocean. The constant roar of the waves was white noise, threatening to drown out the conversation. He strained his ears, trying to tune in.

Just as he was starting to catch snippets of their conversation, Sam approached his table with a tray of food.

"Here you go," she said, placing a plate of pancakes and a mug of coffee in front of him.

He looked up. "Sam, really? Now?" he said, trying to keep his voice low.

She smiled. "Hey, you can't eavesdrop on an empty stomach."

"You're interrupting a crucial moment here."

She leaned in, her voice dropping to a conspiratorial whisper. "Well, you can't exactly blend in if you're not eating."

As she walked away, he leaned in again, trying to pick up where the conversation had left off.

"Brad was always so..." Anna's voice trailed off.

"If I could go back, I would..." Her friend's voice was softer, even harder to hear over the ocean's roar.

He moved his head into the grass barrier, the blades brushing past his face.

"Imagine, if anyone ever found out about..." Anna's voice was now tinged with worry.

This was it—this was the moment he had been waiting for.

Someone scraped a chair back from a neighboring table. Damn.

"...with AMERACAL..." Anna's voice was barely audible, but Kobe's heart leapt in his chest.

Later, as he pulled away from the Ranch Cafe and reached the Stinson Beach town limits, he rolled down the window and punched the air with his fist. The 250 bucks he had withdrawn from the local ATM was a small price to pay for that one word —AMERACAL.

CHAPTER THIRTY-THREE

Jack sat staring at the clock on the wall above the classroom door. Three minutes until the bell went. Lunch time. He was starving. He'd done the math paper. Finished it ten minutes ago. Checked it through. And now all there was to do was wait.

Time moved slowly when you watched it, second by second. More than lunch though, he wanted to see if Alicia had replied. Whether she could go with him to the Ross party at the weekend.

His life was somehow completely wrapped up in Alicia these days. He guessed he was probably in love with her. He wasn't going to tell her that. Game play was to keep your cards close to your chest.

He fell into a daydream—the helicopter ride back from Tahoe. They were flying low when the classroom door opened.

"Ah, Jack, there you are," said Mrs. Monroe.

Why the hell was the principal after him? His stomach flipped and twisted itself into a knot. The classroom erupted into whispers.

"What's going on?"

"Why's the principal here?"

"What's going down in Jonesland this time?"

The murmurs grew louder as she drew up alongside his desk.

"Mom? Is she okay?" he whispered, feeling the weight of his classmates' stares.

"She's all good, Jack," Mrs. Monroe reassured him. "She'll be here shortly and will explain."

His mind raced as he followed her out of the room. What could possibly be so important that his mom needed to come to the school?

Mrs. Monroe led him straight outside to the curb, just as his mom came racing into the parking lot. She pulled alongside. Jack opened the passenger door and climbed in. Gui leaned over from the back seat and started licking his ear.

"Thank you, Mrs. Monroe. I'm sure you'll understand when I say that I'm taking Jack out of school for the rest of the day."

"Of course, Mrs. Jones. If there is anything you need from us at the academy, we are here for you. Think of us as extended family."

He closed the door and his mom tire-squealed out of the parking lot. She was still in the workout gear she'd been wearing when she'd dropped him off. Her face was etched with panic.

"You've got to tell me what's going on, Mom."

She handed him her phone without a word. Jack looked down at the screen, his grip tightening as he read its contents.

ByteBeat by Kobe Otieno

"Hidden Lynx"

(PHOTO—Ameracal. Copyright Ameracal)

From founding one of the world's most successful online dating platforms, our man of the moment, Brad Jones, found an online match of his own with Ameracal.

Through a web of innovative and nefarious connections, access was gained to Ameracal's hidden pleasure den, where Jones spent lavishly to indulge his fantasies.

In an exclusive interview, a disgruntled former employee has blown the whistle on Ameracal, exposing Brad Jones as a man driven by lust.

Jones quickly became their most valued client. The scale of his indulgences ensured that his name held significant weight within the establishment.

"He would send drawings of costumes. Leather. Sometimes latex. Jones paid top dollar for our premium AI partner."

If you're hooked up online with an AI robot are you technically cheating on your partner?

Was Mr. Jones unfaithful to Mrs. Jones?

What does sex with AI do to a human's psyche? Does it drive you to an existentialist crisis resulting in suicide?

Jack felt as if someone had ripped away the very foundation of his life. He was falling through space into a deep black abyss. How the hell was he going to live this down?

"Your father was a fucking asshole," said his mom, with such uncharacteristic vehemence that it made him jump. "Gui and I were out running the ridge when that rancid piece of shit story came through. How the hell that Otieno got his hands on that information confounds me. I'm so sorry."

"Did you know?"

"I didn't until after he'd died. I found a file on his laptop. So stupid and ignorant of him. I deleted it. Thought that was it, until this," she said, her voice trembling with anger and sadness.

Jack had never seen his mom worked up like this. She was driving fifty in a thirty. "Mom, you gotta slow down!"

She took her foot off the gas. "God, sorry. I am better than this. You are the last person I should be talking with about this. He was your dad."

Jack remained silent, his mind a whirlwind. Their world had been fractured beyond repair by his asshole of a dad, and they were left to pick up the pieces.

CHAPTER THIRTY-FOUR

Two days later, Anna found herself airborne, the vast expanse of desert and mountains unfolding beneath her like a tapestry from the passenger seat of Scott's helicopter. With every beat of the rotor blades, she felt a sense of lightness, as if the weight of the world was being lifted from her shoulders. The helicopter whisked them down over the rugged beauty of Nevada, heading towards the breathtaking landscapes of Utah.

As she gazed out at the panorama below, she quietly thanked Alicia for stepping in to help Jack navigate the horror of Brad's latest revelation. Now, she found herself thanking Scott for his wise counsel, urging her to get away for a day and escape the viperous tongues of Marin's gossip mill.

He, of all people, had been first to offer help, bringing Alicia up straight after tennis to be with Jack. They'd sat out on the deck drinking wine, while he'd listened to her download on Brad's secret life.

She looked across to where he was sitting, reading an incoming message on his cell. The cream linen trousers and navy shirt were tailored but casual. His hair was pushed back by the sunglasses he had propped on top of his head. In side profile he was classically chiseled. Strong jaw. Textbook good looking, even after all these years.

Sensing her scrutiny, he looked up at her. A frown vanished, replaced by the intense look he favored. Piercing eyes that reminded her of wolves hunting.

"Do you ever really relax?" she said.

"You saw me on the water at Tahoe."

She laughed. "For an hour I think you did. But seriously, do you ever just chill out, do nothing. Contemplate the universe?"

"I've created my own universe. Keeps me busy."

"Well then, thank you for taking the time to do this today." She looked back out of the window, watching the clouds cast fleeting shadows over the earth below. The landmass stretched as far as the horizon. Oceanless dry rock, sand and soil. Perspective. That was what she was in danger of losing through all that had happened. The world out here was little changed in the past weeks, whereas hers had gone through a seismic shift.

The thought brought her a hint of inner peace. She felt her pulse slow and her mind expand into the wonders of the planet.

"We're coming up on it," announced the pilot.

Scott's gaze gravitated toward her. "You ready?" he said.

"For what?" she said.

They were climbing up the side of a steeply forested mountain, flying low over the canopy. Seconds later they crested the summit.

"Oh my God," she said, her jaw dropping.

The pilot angled them in over an amphitheater of towering garnet, magenta, and terracotta colored rock formations. Thousands of spires, pinnacles and mazes mapped out below. The terrain was expansive. Sculptured geology on such a scale that it took her breath away.

"It's like an ancient city."

"Nature's city," said Scott.

A sudden bolt of pure joy shot through her and she found herself gripping Scott's arm.

For the next half hour, they were lost in the wonder, until finally the pilot lifted them up and away to land on a pad in the middle of a desolate, barren valley.

The second Anna stepped out onto the concrete she was greeted by the blasting inferno of the desert.

A uniformed driver in an immaculate white golf shirt and khaki shorts, stood waiting for them by a Jeep.

Minutes later he drove off the dirt track into a large courtyard, shaded overhead by red canvas, through which the light slatted onto a rough-hewn concrete slab of wall.

"Where are we?"

"You'll see."

A woman in white shirt and black trousers opened the door of the Jeep. "Welcome." She led them up wide steps into a cool, shadowy expanse of concrete where a sparse, spare luxury enveloped the massive space. A large rectangular pool of water lay in stark contrast to the backdrop of the desert. Alongside sat a few strategically placed, low neutral-toned toned chairs and sculpted wood tables.

The place smelled of sagebrush and cedarwood. They walked through the hush to a private dining room, where a floor-to-ceiling window gave them a view out over the Colorado Plateau.

"Wow. This place is stunning..." Her voice trailed off. The waiter filled their glasses with a chilled rosé wine.

"A toast to a lighter mindset," said Scott, raising his glass.

They clinked and she took a long sip, relaxing into a sense of peace she hadn't felt in weeks. "To think only a few hours ago I was dropping Jack at school. And now I'm here, looking at this. Thank you."

"You're welcome," he said, clinking her glass once more.

By the time Anna got up to visit the bathroom she was moving across the floor in a kind of swaying sashay. The five-course menu had been a grazing feast across tenderloin, white truffle and wild field greens. Each course had been paired with a wine that made each dish sing an extra octave.

She checked her phone and saw a WhatsApp missed call, followed by a "Where are you?" message from Caitlin.

The lulling effects of the meal had her guard down. She selected a slew of shots from the helicopter and sent them with an "off-planet day courtesy of the Lyles" message.

"I bet your family love coming here," she said, sitting back at the table.

"They would if I brought them here, but I don't."

She looked at him, surprised. "Why not?"

"I'm only ever here alone. A stopover coast to coast. Solitude at its core."

"And now?"

"I wanted to share it with you." He looked at her. That poker face.

"So Kristy doesn't know about..."

"This. No. Bryce Canyon. Yes. And I'd prefer it stays that way. Alicia too. And Jack."

"Okay. So..."

"A short trip to the canyon and back."

The waiter brought the Sauternes wine to pair with the Marble Canyon Chocolate dessert.

"Let me level with you," said Scott, swirling the cold golden wine around his glass. "I live a controlled, focused existence that revolves around power, competition and money. But what drives me is beauty. The art of the deal embodies this. And where we are now is a perfect representation of beauty. One that I have no intention of sharing with anyone but you, because I think you are the only one who can appreciate it like I do."

172

"Do you really believe that?"

"You're as driven as me. I know that. I saw it in the way you played that polo game to save the company. The way you built TopMatch. It was never Brad's visions that saw it through to success. We are a lot more alike than you would admit, Anna."

She stared into her glass. He was telling her a truth, something she'd never considered before, about what drove her, what made her tick.

"But above all, Anna, you are beauty."

CHAPTER THIRTY-FIVE

A blood-curdling scream came volleying down the hallway. Loni had been in practice eight years and had never heard a sound like it before. It chilled her to the bone. She leapt up from her desk and ran out, heading to the source of the disturbance in Titus' office. Another therapist and the receptionist were hot on her heels.

She entered the room to find a woman reclined on the chaise longue, presenting as if heavily sedated or experiencing a psychotic episode. Titus was assessing her vital signs.

"Loni, stay here," he said, signaling the others to leave.

She sat down in a side chair and checked Titus' notes. The name at the top read "Dr. Anna Jones". Looking at the woman on the couch and the woman she'd seen a few weeks before on the front page of the SF *Chronicle* with her TopMatch founding husband, she'd have said they were two different women. The one in the photograph had projected an alluring confidence that only the very rich possessed. The one in the room was reminding her of Edvard Munch's *Scream*.

Dr. Jones was now mumbling. Titus was leaning in to try and make out what she was saying.

"Sleep just a bit... Brad... So tired..."

Then she was still again.

"Anna, where are you now?" said Titus.

Long Pause.

"Dark. I can't see. Lifting. Someone's lifting me. Heavy."

Loni began documenting the session, adhering to Titus' rigorous standards for note-taking, which he had ingrained in all therapists at Creed Therapies. "Digital recording captures only so much. Being present in the room allows you to pick up on subtleties and impressions that a computer might miss. Record everything you perceive, not just the words," was what he'd told them all.

He'd check in the beginning, over the first few months after you'd joined Creed, going through all the case notes. The five senses were what he was looking for—sight, sound, smell, taste, and touch. Leave one out and you'd be asked why.

Dr. Jones was still again. Loni couldn't quite make out if she'd actually fallen asleep. But Titus kept talking, asking her where she was, what she was doing.

Suddenly her fingers twitched again. She began to shift uncomfortably on the recliner, pain etched on her face. "Get the hell away from me!" she screamed.

"Anna. You're okay. You're with us in a safe place. Let's explore this memory together," said Titus, signaling to Loni to fetch more Kleenex.

"It's dark, so dark," Dr. Jones continued.

Loni crossed quickly to the walnut cabinet and retrieved a fresh box of Kleenex. She ripped the top open and handed it to him.

"I see. And you're not alone, are you?" Titus said.

"No. There are hands... and lips. They're... they're touching me, grabbing me. Like they're... feeding on me."

"I'm right here with you, Anna. You're safe. Can you tell me what you're doing?"

"I want to fight them off. My arms, my legs... they're so heavy. I can't move them."

"I understand. It's okay, Anna. Let's take a step back if we need to. You're in control here. What happens next? Only if you're ready to share."

She paused. It gave Loni time to catch up, her therapeutic instincts on high alert. She noted the shallow, rapid breaths, the tremors, the way Anna's fingers were clawing at the leather upholstery. The word "feeding" was making her own skin crawl.

When Anna spoke again, her words came out in a staccato rhythm. "The hands... they're moving lower, parting my legs. They... they've gone inside me."

Tears were now streaming down her face. "A body... it's on top of mine. It's forcing into me."

Loni noted the raw emotion in Anna's voice, and, despite her years of training, she felt her hand tremble as she wrote, the words turning into an almost illegible scrawl across the page.

"You're safe now, Anna. That's in the past. Can you tell me who was there?"

Dr. Jones started to squirm, frantically punching at the air at some invisible assailant.

"Brad," she said, suddenly going limp and slumping back.

Silence. The dam had broken and the tears came gushing out.

"Thank you for sharing that, Anna," Titus said, softly. "You're safe now. Brad can't hurt you anymore. Whenever you're ready, we'll slowly bring you back to the present."

He turned to Loni, signaling her to leave. Clutching her notes, she hurried from the room, closing the door shut behind her.

Out in the corridor, she pressed her back against the wall,

taking a deep breath. The intensity of the session had left her rattled. Dr. Jones' raw, unfiltered trauma was replaying in her mind like some horrifying film loop.

Caitlin handed Anna the flat white that she'd purchased from Blue Bottle, which was handily on the corner of the building that housed Creed Therapies. That was what was so great about cosmopolitan cities like San Francisco—she could always find places of delight that satisfied highly-curated needs like her own. The appointment had gone on much longer than expected. She'd phoned into the receptionist a couple of times to check on whether Anna was nearly done, but both times she'd been told, "Dr. Jones is still in a hypnotherapy session."

So she'd had way more caffeine than she was used to.

To say she was shocked was an understatement. Anna had gone in on a high. That mystery trip with Scott had done her the world of good.

Two hours later, this harrowing revelation. She felt like going up in the elevator and punching Titus Creed for reducing her dearest friend to a shivering wreck.

"Drink a little. You need it," she said, wrapping an arm around Anna's shoulders and steering her out of public view.

Instead of getting the valet to bring the car out, she took the keys off him and headed straight to it, helping Anna into the passenger seat before running round to hop in the driver's side. The sooner they were out of the city the better.

She shuddered to think what else could surface. Brad was a monster. If this was the tip of the iceberg, it would destroy Anna and Jack.

CHAPTER THIRTY-SIX

ByteBeat was now syndicated across the globe through Tidal Media, making Kobe a cool five-million-dollar paycheck in one day. Suddenly those eight bits of news a day didn't seem so onerous to mine and mold into the daily ByteBeat. It was the AI angle that had launched him into the public eye.

He unwrapped the package, which the Knightlink delivery driver had just handed to him at the door. He now had a custom-tailored single-breasted blazer and trousers in his hands.

Moments later, he'd put on the suit. His reflection in the mirror was that of a made man. He turned left, right. The suit fitted like a glove. They'd got the tailoring perfect.

He liked the bare-chest reveal between the two lapels. That was exactly how he was going to wear it later that evening at the Asian Art museum annual gala.

First though, he needed to work on the day's column. The AI track had been a pleasant detour from the Brad Jones story. Ameracal had opened the door for new topics and gossip. Leak this, leak that.

He was pretty much out of juicy morsels on the Jones saga. But, where one well had run dry, another had spawned.

He hung up the suit and headed to the kitchen to get the Daily Quorum that had arrived on the doorstep prompt at his new wake-up time of 6am. Normally he'd have slugged it straight down, but he'd been up late partying, and a hangover had demanded a triple shot of caffeine before he could do his new daily run route down to the Embarcadero and back.

Checking his email he was surprised to find a slew of emails from various wealth management companies, inviting him to do business with them. Everything happened in a nanosecond these days. One sniff of news that someone had made a fast buck and the sharks came circling.

That got him thinking... why not a piece on sudden wealth syndrome? A neat, concise eight-bit ByteBeat that'd be a nice sidebar to the AI track. He'd throw in a quote from Dr. Anna Jones, expert on the subject. That'd be a nice touch.

An easy column day now lay ahead. Since the sun was out, he ditched the laptop and went to sit out on the balcony with a paperback novel. In an effort to get into the mind of a genuine Pulitzer Prize winner, and somehow let that magic rub off on him, he was rereading Steinbeck's *The Grapes of Wrath*. The dust bowl era search for the promised land in California was epic, and he was soon drawn deeply into its themes of thwarted desire (he knew that all too well) and powerlessness (much easier to digest when you had some power yourself).

He got so lost in the story that he forgot time and space. The hours ticked by, and when he'd finished, he found himself exhausted, wrung out by both the drama and the caliber of prose. He jumped up and got to his desk, flexed his fingers, and started typing.

Kobe was getting high on the elixir of wealth surrounding him, observing the gathering of San Francisco's elite as he stood, holding a glass of Cristal champagne. He'd delivered the column in record time. Rubbing shoulders with this crowd was heady intoxication. You could hear the mixture of drawl and clip in their privileged accents, and you could just smell the money on them, oozing out of every pore.

"Capri? Yes, we'll be there in June."

Of course you will. He took another sip and moved on to the next bronze object in the case: "Arrowhead, 300BC."

"We're joining Teddy Moffet's yacht this year. Cannes to Marrakech. It'll be quite the party..."

He might have five mil in the bank, but these people were post-economic. Many of them had no doubt inherited—gold rush, railroad, banking, pan-Pacific trade. Oldest fortunes on the West Coast.

"That's some suit," said a voice behind him.

He turned to find himself looking at one of the doyennes of society herself, Kristy Van Hoeveren Lyle. He'd seen her in the press over the years. She presented an unchanging image, an almost ageless caricature of an heiress—her red hair swept into a tight chignon, clad in a Parisian peacock blue cocktail dress, and adorned with an original South Sea pearl choker that would have required an army of divers to scour countless oysters.

When he'd been bored by his day job, he'd enjoyed reading the society column in the *Examiner*. He'd even looked at back issues to fuel his curiosity about their rarefied lives, and now here in the flesh was the lady who, once upon a time, was "launched into society like a luxury liner at San Francisco's Cotillion Ball".

"It would seem that we both read the same memo," he quipped, since they were wearing the same color blue.

She laughed. "Makes a change from the norm here. I'm Kristy."

"Kobe," he said, shaking her hand.

"ByteBeat?"

"The very same."

She raised a perfectly arched eyebrow. "My, you've kept us all awash with gossip and intrigue of late."

He reached for his cell phone, that was humming softly in an inner pocket, and checked the screen. Fernando, an informant he couldn't ignore.

"Hell, I'm sorry I've gotta to take this. Please excuse me," he said, with a small bow of his head.

Kristy reached into her evening purse and pulled out an orchid-edged calling card. "Here. Call me. This conversation has only just begun. We should have lunch."

He took the thick, engraved card. "*Kristen Van Hoeveren Lyle*" and her cell number. That was it. Hell, that was an "in", right at the top.

He made his way swiftly out onto the steps passing Scott Lyle on his way in. The way the guy walked and looked, you'd think he owned the museum.

"Hey, Fernando, what you got for me?" Kobe said, taking the call.

CHAPTER THIRTY-SEVEN

The column dropped like a depth-charger into the abyss of midnight. The ping woke Anna. She'd forgotten to silence her phone. Reaching out, she fumbled her fingers across the unfamiliar terrain of the bedside table in the guest room at Caitlin and Mark's, sending the phone plummeting onto the polished oak floor.

Part of her wanted to leave it there until morning, so she could have a chance of sleep, but the all-too-familiar dread that ping brought had her getting out of bed.

She picked the device up, turning it in her hands, so that she could see the screen. It took a moment to adjust to the bright light, before the stark, black type came into focus.

ByteBeat by star columnist, Kobe Otieno
"Creed jumps into the valley of death"
(PHOTO—Titus Creed. Copyright Creed Therapies)

Silicon Valley's top shrink takes own life and jumps from the deck of his offices in Downtown SF, plummeting forty floors to his death, after the office closed for the day at 8pm.

Is this what three decades of listening to the addled minds of the tech world's elite leads to?

Creed was known as a leader in the field of hypnotherapy. He succeeded in hypnotizing the notoriously outspoken data giant Tryon DeGroot, which he described as "hard as taking down a bull elephant".

Over the course of his nearly 35-year research career, Creed wrote and co-authored hundreds of scientific papers and twelve books including *Silicon Valley Behavioral Theory* (Denton Simms, 2010).

Creed began his practice in the Mission District, in a small rented space during the burgeoning dot.com boom, specializing in counseling the "SWS"—kids in their mid-twenties with sudden wealth syndrome, helping them adjust to their newfound riches.

After the dot.com crash, he shifted his focus to counseling those affected by the wave of suicides triggered by the sudden loss of fortunes that had been made virtually overnight only months before.

Dr. Anna Jones was seen leaving his practice after a hypnotherapy session earlier the day before his leap into oblivion.

"The screaming was terrible. It was like someone was being murdered in there," said a patient in reception (anon.), at the time of Dr. Jones' hypnosis treatment.

Impossible. She had to be hallucinating, or maybe it was another nightmare. Her heart was hammering as she switched on the light. She read the column again, her hand now shaking. No, not Titus. She'd only just seen him. How could he possibly have ended his own life?

Nausea swilled in her stomach as she recalled their last

session. For her, so much pain, but Titus, he'd been nothing but his professional self through the whole hypnosis.

And now he was gone and that bastard Otieno was dragging her in. Again.

She put on the Roaring Bear toweling robe and headed out, along the hallway and onto the deck. The familiar pitter-patter of paws came in her wake as Gui came trotting out of where Jack was sleeping.

Out in the cool night air, she looked up at the blue-black sky, the half moon's watery gleam, the stars shining their millennia-old light.

"Come on, Gui. Let's go," she said, taking the steps down to the vineyard.

She trudged along the row of vines, the hem of her robe damp with dew, her slippers sodden. The night was cool and quiet. Gui darted ahead, picking up rabbit scents, oblivious to the turmoil that was churning inside her.

Titus Creed is dead. The words echoed in her mind, hollow and disbelievingly. She'd seen him just yesterday, sat across from her in his leather chair, the tick of the clock counting out the seconds of her life as he helped her mine her subconscious. He'd been his usual calm self, no hint of despair, no whisper of a farewell.

She hugged the robe tighter around her, as if the thick fabric could ward off the chill that seeped into her bones. The column had been brutal. A leap from the fortieth-floor window, the thud of his body hitting the pavement. She shuddered, the images playing out in her mind like a grotesque slideshow.

Otieno had a knack for making even tragedy seem sordid. And now he was dragging her into it, painting her as some sort of key player. She could see the raised eyebrows, the whispered speculations. *Dr. Anna Jones, the last client. The one who'd screamed*. She felt a surge of hot, bitter anger. Damn him for making this about her.

Gui paused up ahead, nose lifted to the breeze, before darting off again. Anna followed, her steps slow and heavy. She thought about Titus' family. Did he have one? She realized that she knew next to nothing about his personal life.

As she moved upwards, the valley spread out before her, a patchwork of shadows under the moonlight. Despite the beautiful vista she felt a prickle of unease, the sense that something was off.

Two deaths, both unexpected, both violent. Brad, and now Titus. Both men she'd trusted, both men she'd confided in. It was too much to be a coincidence. She shook her head trying to dislodge the thought. She was being ridiculous, letting Otieno's insinuations get to her.

But the doubt lingered. She needed answers. Not just for herself, but for Jack. She'd put her research mindset to work, start digging. She already knew the worst; nothing could top that.

When she and Gui finally made their way back to the house, the first light of dawn was casting a soft glow over the vineyard. As she approached, she saw Caitlin, her face illuminated by the harsh blue light of her phone. She knew.

"Oh my God, Anna!" she cried, seeing her coming up the steps. "We've been worried sick. We read the column. About Titus."

The roar of a dirt bike cut through the air as Mark came racing around the corner. He braked hard when he saw her, and cut the engine. "I was just headed out to find you," he said, jumping off. "You okay, A?"

Anna pulled her robe tighter around her, suddenly feeling the chill of the morning air. "I'm sorry, I didn't mean to worry you. I just had to get out, find space to think."

"So tragic. I can't imagine what that poor man was going through to do that," said Caitlin, holding up her phone. "I'm so sorry."

"I can't believe it. When I saw him he seemed fine. There was no hint that he was... that he would..." Anna trailed off, unable to finish the sentence.

Caitlin put her arm around her. "And Otieno mentioning you. He can't just get away with this."

CHAPTER THIRTY-EIGHT

Kristy tasted the sweet, salty sweat as she screamed out in orgasm on the emperor-size bed in the North Beach apartment. The release was so extreme she entered oblivion. Being nailed like this was exactly what she needed.

She'd kind of put all the ideas of lust and physical peak into a neat box of "the past". But now, heart rate up to a tango, she felt she'd gone through a radical rebirth.

Kobe pumped into her one more time before stars and stripes blurred his vision and he convulsed at the peak. He swore he could feel the hot blast of semen literally explode out of the end of his dick like some firehose.

Here he was fucking one of San Francisco's scion heiresses like she was a Vegas hooker. Not that he'd done either before, but in his head he was already writing the comparison. Another first was that he'd never been with a woman older than him before. And this one had a good couple of decades on him. But, man, she needed to be tasted and savored.

They'd had lunch down at Galant on Washington Square, in a corner booth, where they'd sparred and laughed over a bottle of cabernet and a three-course French meal. When they'd first sat down she'd got a big castle wall up between them, but one glass in, the drawbridge had come down. She was quick-witted, and one hell of an off-the-record gossip.

He'd soaked it all up like a sponge, filling in the massive potholes he had in the inner workings and rankings of the SF social scene.

And then the laws of attraction had come weighing in. He wanted to touch that porcelain veneer of hers, to undo the tight bun and run his hands through her auburn hair. It was a polar opposite magnetic attraction that had them skipping dessert and heading back to his place for an intense afternoon of sex, and surprisingly laughter, since they'd melded on a humor wavelength that neither party had felt in so long.

They finally came up for air at 5pm. Kristy sent him out of his own bedroom while she re-attired herself from the stripper scene mounds of clothing littering the floor.

With her hair pinned back in place, Kristy slipped her Manolos back on and walked out into the open-plan sitting area. Kobe was sitting in an olive-green velvet armchair near the window, head bent, deep in concentration.

She put her French manicured hands onto his smooth warm shoulders and looked down at where the pen was hitting the paper of a leather notebook. The slant of ink across the page reminded her of her grandfather's writing. She hadn't thought of him in a long while, despite his portrait, astride a horse, overlooking Half Dome at Yosemite, looming down from its place amongst the ancestors on the main staircase at Carohill.

"If you and I pooled our sources, imagine the in-depth level and angle of stories we could spin up," she whispered into his ear, accompanying it by a playful bite on the lobe.

He didn't look up, instead he grabbed her by the wrist and pulled her to him, so that she fell into his lap.

CHAPTER THIRTY-NINE

Anna punched in the alarm code, silencing the Sentinel system, as Jack kicked off his sneakers and ran out onto the beach, Gui hot on his heels.

She exhaled deeply, the sudden silence a balm to the past few days. The familiar scent of her home wrapped around her—the salt of the ocean mixed with the subtle tones of her "Belgian Linen" room diffusers.

Rest was the last thing on her mind now they were home. She was ready to roll up her sleeves, to dissect Brad's office piece by piece. But first, she needed a moment to gather her thoughts and check in with Jack. There'd been no opportunity up at Roaring Bear with everyone around, and all the way home he'd had his headphones on listening to music.

She'd ordered sushi for dinner, a small comfort amidst the chaos.

As they sat down at the kitchen table, Jack looked at her. "Sushi, Mom? It feels like you're trying to make things normal, like when Dad was here. But they're not, are they?"

"We have to make an attempt at normal. And I know it's your favorite."

He sighed, picking up a piece of Californian roll with his chopsticks. "Yeah, but it's not going to change what's happening, is it?"

"No. But it might make us feel a bit better, even if it's just for a brief moment in time."

He took a whole lump of wasabi and started mixing it into the soy sauce. "I just don't get it. First Dad, and now this doctor. It's like we're cursed."

She reached out, laying her hand on his arm. "We are not cursed. Dr. Creed's death came out of the blue. That had to have been something he was dealing with. Nothing to do with us."

He dipped a piece of sushi in the soy and stuffed it in his mouth. A second later she saw the hit of wasabi make his eyes water.

"But Dad. Why?"

"I don't know. But I'm going to find out."

"Then I want in. Let me help."

"Okay. You can help me go through some more of his things later, once I've got more of a handle of what we've got to go through."

He looked at her. "Fine, Mom. But if you find anything, you have to tell me. No more secrets."

To kick things off she went down the spiral staircase off the back of Brad's office, to his cellar, where she selected a bottle of his favorite vintage Duckhorn Vineyards Merlot from the extensive racks. It felt like a fitting tribute. She poured it into a hand blown over-sized glass, filling it to near the brim. She had no intention of wasting time coming down for a refill. With a firm grip around the stem she headed up to take a seat in the

Herman Miller Aeron chair at the command center of Brad Jones' empire.

She raised her glass to a black and white photo of them on their wedding day, both of them radiant against a backdrop of redwood trees. They'd waited until Jack was born before getting married. She'd wanted to really enjoy the day rather than wallowing through it heavily pregnant.

She warmed up going through Brad's desk drawers, no longer looking for traces of drug addiction or suicide notes, but for something else.

The wine warmed and softened her movements as she methodically emptied the desk.

As she sorted through, she wondered how many hours he'd spent in here. More than anywhere else since they'd moved in.

Her back ached from sitting. She stood up and wandered over to the Downtown skyscraper book stacks next to the window.

Her eyes traveled to the black tower block of Moleskine Medium Hardcover Ruled Notebooks, each secured shut by an elastic band. Tech entrepreneur's written recording platform of choice.

She picked the top one. March 2015. Complex lines of coding, written in black ink, with notes about the software's overall architecture goals. Pages and pages. She dropped it to the floor and picked up the next one. August 2010. More of the same.

She reached for her glass and sat down cross-legged on the rug. Next one. She flicked through. Code, code, code until she came across a page in the middle of the book. One line across both pages:

"Pay off Tony Q." written in red pen. Tony Q.? Why did that ring a bell? She looked up, her gaze focusing on Brad's chair, almost picturing him sitting there, watching her, angry that she was invading his world. The room seemed to grow colder, the silence heavier, as if Brad's presence still lingered, disapproving of her intrusion.

Not Tony Quan, the old IT guy at LVP? Had to be. Who else had that name?

Shaking off the chill, she picked up her cell phone and opened the LinkedIn app, heading straight to the settings to search in private mode. She navigated to: "Tony Quan, IT Director, SalesPort Inc." The photo looked like him, just older, with gray hair now, but the same rectangular wire-framed glasses.

Why ever would Brad have paid him off?

CHAPTER FORTY

After drop-off the next morning, Anna continued her search, feeling like some one-woman forensic team, mining Brad's laptops, backup drives, and cloud accounts. All to a zero-sum game except for Tony Quan, on whom she'd done some more digging, and who was ignoring her emails, and calls to his office.

She couldn't just sit back and wait for him to decide he was ready to talk. No, she needed to hustle her way in. She headed out, driving over the Golden Gate Bridge, its iconic red towers standing sentinel against a blue sky. She then merged onto the 280, heading south into the heart of Silicon Valley.

The Cupertino parking lot of SalesPort was a sprawling expanse of asphalt and steel, the sun reflecting off the sea of cars with a blinding intensity. She stepped out of her car, and made her way towards the main entrance. The monolith glass and chrome building loomed above her.

The atrium was a cavernous space, reaching five floors up. Techies with lanyards dangling from their necks were clustered on glass walkways above. A few were picking up coffees at an in-house barista bar set under a cluster of olive trees that some enterprising architect must have drawn into the plans.

In places like this she couldn't help but marvel at the sheer audacity of it all—the way these companies had built empires on something as intangible as software, their marketing machines churning out digital ads and messaging to give weight to their ethereal products.

The days of walking straight into the thick of things were long gone. Security had become an intrinsic part of the tech world, data a heavyweight champion that needed constant protection. No more casual drop-ins and unchecked access. Now everything was locked down, guarded by layers of security and protocol.

She approached the reception desk, her steps echoing in the vast space. "Hi, I'm Dr. Anna Jones," she said to the young guy on reception, showing her driving license and business card.

The guy looked from her to the credentials, back to her, his eyes growing wide with recognition. She had dressed the part, donning head-to-toe Armani—a sleek ensemble consisting of a caramel silk shirt and cream palazzo pants. And, she'd applied a generous amount of bronzer to mask the toll that recent weeks had taken on her. The effect was polished and professional, a stark contrast to how she really felt right now.

"Hey, Dr. Jones. I'm excited to meet you," he said, leaping up from his chair, and extending his hand.

"Good to meet you too, Joe," she said, reading off his security badge.

"Are you here to do a talk?"

"Not exactly, more of a drop-in meeting."

His eyes lit up. "Any dating tips?"

She'd hoped he would ask this. If he hadn't, she would have had to resort to plan B, getting him to call Tony to come meet her, which was a long shot at best. She leaned in slightly, her voice taking on a conspiratorial tone. "You have a profile set up?"

He whipped out his phone, navigated to his dating app with a few quick taps, and handed the device to her. She scanned down the screen, looking at him intermittently as she did. This was her trademark icebreaker at lectures, a way to establish rapport and trust.

"Okay. You open for some feedback?" she asked.

"Sure am," he said, putting his shoulders back and chin out.

She turned the phone back to him, and scrolled through his profile photos. There was the shark-suited pose at a cocktail bar, the shirtless selfie, gym mirror pic of him sweating next to a weight machine, another in workout gear (again) with his arms wrapped around a spaniel, and a final selfie in San Francisco of him giving a thumbs up with the Bay Area Women's March in the background.

"Top line is that you're image warping, because what I'm seeing here, on screen, is nothing like what I'm seeing and reading on meeting you for the first time. You're a guy who comes to work in a lime green logo golf shirt and tan chinos, with stack heeled trainers. The arms I am looking at now, as opposed to the ones shown here at the gym, are not from the same guy. And neither is that torso."

"I did some doctoring. Used the MorphMe app to give me an edge. Everyone does it. You gotta put some sugar out there to get traction."

"It's giving more horns than halo. Now, is this your dog?"

"Belongs to my roommate."

"And are you really committed to women's rights?"

He shrugged. "I could be."

"Then you're both dogfishing—using your roommate's dog as bait to lure in potential dates—and wokefishing too—masquerading as holding progressive political views to attract potential partners."

"Ouch."

She handed back his phone. "You ready for some more?"

He took a deep breath. "Okay. Shoot."

"You are max, even with your trainers, five foot eight, not six foot. You can't lie about height. And your About Me section makes you sound thirsty, giving off the impression that you're desperate for sex. Any self-respecting, normal human being would run a mile, rather than hit the 'let's connect' button."

She watched the air leave him like a deflating party balloon. Maybe she'd been harsher than usual, must be the grief giving itself an anger outing. "Sorry. That was too harsh."

"No, I'm down with this. That's why I asked you."

"So you've had no bites?"

He shook his head.

"And what do you want out of it?"

"Someone to date, long term." He smiled, and when he did, she saw there was some kind of hope to get him off the starting blocks.

"Then be real about yourself. Honest. I can see you're a decent guy, holding down a good job. Say it how it is and show yourself for who you really are. Then you'll attract the right person."

"Hey, when you guys have finished up the psycho-dating babble, can I get a tag? I'm here to see Will Chase."

She turned to find a veteran VC type in a white shirt and Zegna slacks, gum chewing, behind her.

"Here you go," said Joe, handing her a security tag, without questioning who she was going in to see.

"Thanks, Joe. Let me know how you get on," she said, taking the tag.

"Fuck, you millennials are neurotic. You need to get out into the real world, kick the tires on a few," said the veteran VC, moving into her place.

Part of her wanted to run back and punch him so hard he choked on his gum.

CHAPTER FORTY-ONE

Anna made her way down to the basement, the nerve center of SalesPort, where the hum of servers and the cool breeze of air conditioning filled the long, white hallway lined with glass-fronted offices. This was the domain of IT support and infrastructure, the unseen backbone of the tech giant.

Tony Quan's office lay halfway down the corridor, his name displayed in the custom SalesPort typeface that adorned every sign and instruction in the building. Anna paused outside his door, taking a deep breath to steady her nerves. She knocked lightly, the sound echoing in the quiet hallway.

Tony looked up from his desk, a frown forming on his face, clearly annoyed at the disturbance. But as his eyes met Anna's through the glass, his expression shifted dramatically. It was as if he was looking at a ghost.

She didn't bother waiting for a "come in"; she just opened the door, strode in, closing it behind her. "By the look on your face I don't think we need a reintroduction, and I think you know why I'm here."

She sat down in the blue, standard-issue guest chair, scanning the room. It was a shrine to *Star Wars*—posters adorned the walls, collectible figurines lined the shelves, and a replica lightsaber stood proudly in the corner.

She raised an eyebrow, a faint smirk playing on her lips. "I like what you've done with the place," she said.

Tony cleared his throat, his voice barely above a whisper. "I'm so sorry about your husband. He was a good man."

Anna leaned forward, her eyes narrowing. "You know I'm here because he paid you off. And the property records indicate you bought a three-bedroom ranch-style home with a swimming pool in Los Gatos that same year. That must have been a big stretch on your Lyle Venture Partners salary of forty K."

Tiny beads of sweat formed along Tony's thinning hairline. His eyes darted around the room like a cornered rat, searching for an escape that wasn't there.

"It was a deal," he admitted, his voice shaking slightly. "Brad approached me with an offer I couldn't refuse."

Anna's gaze was unyielding. "Which was?"

Tony leaned across the desk, his voice dropping to a conspiratorial whisper. "If I tell you, you have to promise you will not expose me. Never say how you got it."

"Got what?" she said, recoiling on the whiff of his stale coffee breath.

He rubbed his face.

"Come on. It's an easy one for me right now to pick up the phone to the good old IRS and find out what was going on with you back then."

"Promise me."

He looked so scared, she relented.

"I promise. Buck stops here if you tell me everything you know."

His shoulders slumped in defeat. "It's complicated," he said, barely audible. "Brad needed something, and he wanted me to get it for him. He offered me enough money to change my life."

"How much money?"

"Five hundred thousand."

She gripped the arms of the chair. "What in hell did he want that was worth half a million dollars?"

Tony shifted uncomfortably in his chair, his gaze flicking nervously around the room before settling back on her. He took a deep breath as if he was about to dive underwater. "He asked me to make a copy of Scott Lyle's hard drive for him."

Her eyebrows shot up. "What? Why?"

Tony rubbed his hands together, his palms sweaty, his eyes darting around the room as if searching for an escape. "I don't know the specifics. Brad didn't tell me why he needed it. I didn't ask questions. But he offered me so much money to do it, I could finally buy a house for me and my family."

"How did you do it?"

"I set up a crash situ on Scott's laptop. Froze him out. He was livid, but he couldn't get it working again without IT help. That was me. I took it in, fixed it, copied the whole hard drive onto an external drive, and handed him back his laptop. I met Brad up at Crystal Springs off the 280, gave him the drive, he gave me the cash."

"What was on it?"

He shifted uncomfortably in his seat, his eyes avoiding hers. "Spreadsheets, business plans, financial projections. But a lot of it was password protected."

She tightened her grip on the arms of her seat. "You and I both know you're the kind of guy who could get past that. So, what else was on there?"

Tony squirmed. "I don't know. I tried, but I couldn't crack all the passwords. And I don't know what your husband did with the disk. Maybe he got what he wanted and destroyed it."

She stood up, her chair scraping against the floor. As she turned to leave, she paused, her hand on the door handle, and looked back at him. "Make sure if I call you again, you pick up the phone."

She exited and made her way quickly out to the parking lot, into the harsh light of day. Why Scott's hard drive? What was in there to make Brad pay Tony $500,000?

Once in the quiet of the car, she dug her phone out of her bag. As she unlocked the screen, a text message notification popped up. It was from Scott Lyle. Past and present collided in that instant. She dropped the phone as if it was red hot. It fell into the footwell.

Reaching down, she fumbled around and pulled it back up, opened the message:

> Lunch Friday in the mountains?

She leaned back against the headrest. Whatever Brad had been after on Scott's hard drive all those years ago had to be some kind of tech play. But what was it that was worth so much? And why resort to such desperate measures as bribing a mid-level IT manager?

But the one person she knew not to question on the matter was Scott himself, who, right now with his one-liner, had her right back in the present.

CHAPTER FORTY-TWO

"Mom. That tapping thing you're doing woke me up."

Anna glanced down, startled to find Jack silhouetted in the doorway of Brad's office, his PJs rumpled and his hair sticking up in every direction. He rubbed his eyes, still heavy with sleep. Gui slipped around him and came, tail wagging, to where she was balancing up a ladder.

"You are gonna have to tell me what's going on."

"Hey, I'm looking for something of your dad's—" she began, trying to keep her voice steady.

"No shit."

She had to admit she was going to let that go, because on the face of it, things were a little... messy. All the neat piles of books were now strewn across the floor.

Since she'd returned from the meeting with Tony Quan, she'd phoned Dwight, hoping for answers. But he'd dismissed it as most likely a business matter from years past. Brad wouldn't have been the first or last guy to do some industrial espionage to boost his portfolio.

But a gnawing unease had her flipping through each one of

Brad's books, convinced that he'd sliced out the pages to conceal the drive.

When that proved fruitless, she had turned her attention to the bookshelves themselves, running her fingers along each shelf, tapping for some hidden compartment. She was sure Brad had conspired with that Lake Shasta woodworker to create a secret compartment.

"It's just an old disk drive, but it has some important files on it..."

"Mom, you're tapping on shelves at two in the morning," he interjected, his voice tight with growing alarm.

"I know, but it's what might be behind them."

"Why would Dad hide a drive?"

"Like I said, it had some important things on it."

"Like what?"

She paused, looking from where Gui now sat at the foot of the ladder, tail thumping on the sea of books, to her son, whose eyes were now wide with fright at seeing her up there. Maybe she was going mad. Maybe Brad had taken the disk as a way to get ahead with some investments. She knew he'd spent a big chunk of their TopMatch money spread-betting across a slew of new start-ups.

She exhaled and started her descent. "You know what," she said, reaching the bottom and bending down to stroke the warm fur on Gui's head. "I think I should stop. This is grief calling. I'm sorry I woke you."

She looked up at Jack, her heart catching at the sight of his worried face. He was just a boy, her boy, and she was scaring him. She navigated the sea of scattered books, making her way to where he stood, and wrapped an arm around his shoulders.

"Let's go to the kitchen. I'll fix us some hot chocolate. It's not good for either of us to be up at this hour dwelling on the past."

Fifteen minutes later, after she'd gone into therapy mode with him to calm the situation, she kissed him goodnight and shut the door on his room. But instead of crossing the landing to her room, she took the stairs back down. The lure of Brad's office was a siren call she couldn't ignore. She had unfinished business.

To take the edge off she headed down to the cellar. Underground, hushed, low-lit and safe. The smell of musky fermentation and aging oak soothed her frayed nerves.

She scanned the racks for something different to the Duckhorn.

Her gaze landed on a bottle perched on the top rack. She pulled it out. Her fingers caressed a small, understated label—a simple pen and ink drawing of a bird in flight, the elegant serifed font spelling out SCREAMING EAGLE. A 2007 vintage Cabernet Sauvignon. California's most coveted wine, produced in minuscule quantities from a tiny vineyard in Oakville. She remembered Brad bidding on it in an online charity auction, hosted by Caitlin and Mark's school in Napa. It'd cost him eight thousand dollars.

The promise of the complexity within made her taste buds tingle. She carried it reverentially to the oak barrel tasting table, and began the slow process of cutting off the foil seal. She bit her lip in concentration as she wound in the corkscrew and pulled.

It popped out with a satisfying *toc*. She lifted it to her nose, inhaling the charcoal, licorice scent.

After pouring the deep, rich, red wine into a clean balloon glass, she swirled it around like Brad had taught her, releasing its unique aroma compounds, allowing them to attach to the oxygen in the air.

The velvet smooth wine slipped down her throat. Instant salve to the world outside. She took a seat on one of the high stools. If nothing else she could drink herself to death down here. Wouldn't be such a dreadful way to go, wallowing in vats of vintage wines that few on the planet could acquire.

Halfway through the bottle, the edges of her reality softened, blurring into a comforting haze. Jazz music floated through the air, courtesy of the state-of-the-art sound system Brad had insisted on installing throughout the house. She'd wondered what the point was of having it down here in the cellar as it was normally a grab-and-go zone, with the bottles headed up to the patio, kitchen or his office.

But now, as she sat on the leather-covered bar stool, staring into the candle she'd lit, she was grateful for his attention to detail in their home's construction. God knows how many hours he'd pored over plans with the architect, driving them both a little insane.

Even this cellar, this unseen part of the house. He'd spent days agonizing over its size, rack space and layout... a chill went down her spine. She looked up from the flame, eyes darting left and right scanning the room. If you wanted something hidden...

She jumped up, turned up the lights. They were still dim. The place was still a shadowy cellar. She flicked on her phone flashlight, and swept the beam across the racks. She knew this place was a fortress, poured from reinforced concrete to withstand earthquakes, shifting sands, and the relentless force of the ocean.

To give it an authentic vibe he'd acquired reclaimed bricks from an old warehouse in San Francisco to make it look just like the one they'd visited on their honeymoon in France.

She ran her fingers over the bricks, pressing on them, expecting one to pop open.

Got to think straight, be logical, channel Brad's methodical mind.

And then it struck her. The wines were meticulously

arranged by year and date, a testament to his obsessive organization. She remembered the first wooden crates arriving, being treated with the reverence of sacred artifacts. He had overseen their placement on the racks with more care than he'd shown for anything else, even his precious computers and servers.

She made her way to the far end of the cellar, where the dimmest corner held the holy grail of his collection. Shining the phone's flashlight over the dust-covered bottles, she inhaled the scent of must and old churches, the smell whispering secrets of the past.

One by one she removed them, placing them on the cellar floor, until the rack was empty. She leaned in, her fingers tracing the bricks behind. They were smooth to the touch, until halfway along when her fingertips snagged on one with a rough sandpaper surface.

She examined it in the beam of light, pushing and pulling at it, trying to coax it out, but the mortar was unyielding.

With the corkscrew she scratched and dug at the rough cement. It kept slipping and her hands ached, her knuckles were grazed and raw.

With a grunt of determination, she felt the brick shift. She wiggled it back and forth, until finally, like a stubborn tooth being extracted, it came out.

Reaching inside the dark recess, she wrapped her fingers around a cloth-covered object, about the size of a cigarette pack. She pulled it out and carried it over to the barrel table.

The soft cotton cloth carried the old TopMatch embroidered logo. She ran her fingers across its red lettering. He'd used one of the old company T-shirts.

She took a sip of wine, liquid courage burning its way down her throat. Time to reveal its contents.

Her fingers trembled as she unwrapped the T-shirt. The last

fold fell away, revealing an Iomega 750MB Zip disk. She stared at it, her heart pounding. Such a small, innocuous object, yet it held such secrets that Brad had felt the need to hide it away in the dark recesses of their cellar. A shiver of dread snaked up her spine.

CHAPTER FORTY-THREE

THE 2000S

Brad had been bracing himself for the call. It was the eleventh hour, and he was still on the cusp of getting the software to full release. QA had found so many anomalies in the first version, with nearly every sequence resulting in the yellow spinning wheel of death, that they'd rejected it only hours into testing. The sheer frustration at having to keep hard rebooting had them refusing to continue until the issues were fixed.

As Brad pushed through the glass doors of LVP, he was greeted by an unexpected sight: Scott, standing in the lobby, looking every inch the poster boy for some high-end luxury brand. Clad in a crisp white button-down, navy blazer, and perfectly pressed linen chinos, he was the epitome of polished and smooth.

Brad couldn't help but feel a twinge of envy mixed with a healthy dose of skepticism. Scott was almost too perfect, like a Ken doll come to life. They shook hands.

"Where's Dwight?" asked Brad, after the swift pleasantries.

"Busy on some financials. Let's grab a drink."

Scott led the way out to where his Porsche was parked. As Brad slid into the passenger seat, Scott lowered the roof.

Brad eyed the hand-stitched tan leather interior, the way the black dials and instruments were set into the curved dashboard. "Nice ride," he commented, trying to sound nonchalant.

Scott merged smoothly out onto Sand Hill Road. With the roof down, the world rushed in, the wind and sun sensations making Brad feel exhilarated. He wondered if perhaps things weren't as bad as he'd thought. Up until now all LVP communications had been channeled through Dwight. The way Dwight had painted the wrath that was going down at the mothership, that Scott was "pissed" about his TopMatch investment, didn't seem to hang right with the friendly vibe that Scott was giving out right now.

It didn't add up. Maybe Dwight was leveraging his own position and points in the deal by giving Brad such a hard ride, when in reality LVP were playing ball.

They pulled in through the gates of Menlo Circus Club. Brad smiled. This was somewhere you'd bring someone to impress. "Hey, this is the place you brought Anna," he said.

"I like to come here to decompress. You ride?"

The valet took the car and they headed up the front steps into the club.

"A wave, yeah. Horse, never. That's Anna's gig not mine."

Scott walked through, nodding at the staff who greeted him with a "Good to see you, Mr. Lyle."

He was clapped on the back by an older guy in a striped polo shirt and chinos. "Great game the other day, Scott," he said, in a light-hearted exchange.

A waiter intercepted them out on the deck. "Your table's ready for you, Mr. Lyle," she said, guiding them to the farthest edge, a little away from the others. It gave the best view across the grass to where a couple of polo players were practicing their shots.

"I'll take a Martini. Brad?"

He'd not normally drink a cocktail at a meeting, a beer at the most, but this didn't seem like the kind of place or time to be going light. "An Old Fashioned please."

Scott nodded. "Good choice."

The moment the waiter had left, Brad was expecting Scott to launch into status mode, instead, he talked of his family, and how he would eventually take enough downtime to cross the Atlantic by yacht.

They were two drinks in, and Brad relaxed into the moment. They were a couple of industry leaders shooting the breeze. He let go, spoke of Anna, their engagement, how they wanted kids, what they were planning post-IPO.

He was surprised how much detail Scott wanted, how carefully he listened. Maybe he'd read him wrong, and now he was so invested in TopMatch, he'd invested in the dream of what it would do for them all. He could see them becoming friends when it was all over and he and Anna crossed into the same league as all these people here.

"Okay. Let's get down to business," said Scott, steepling his fingers.

Brad talked fast, mapping out the final pieces and parts needed to get the matching software released. Scott waved his hand, as if swatting away a fly.

"That I know you can do. What I'm interested in is the money you still need to bank to get you over the finish line."

"If we hadn't hit so many roadblocks in the last release, we'd be right on track."

"But you're off track. What's the hit?"

Brad took another swig of Old Fashioned. If Scott was asking, then he was going to pad out the latest numbers that he and Josef had been sweating over.

"Burn's up with the additional engineering hires. We need

another two mil to get us over the line." Brad looked across the table.

Scott sat back, relaxed, yet his fixed stare was enough to say that camaraderie was gone.

"With that we can sprint to the finish," he said, the alcohol giving him a bump.

Scott didn't reply at first. The seconds of silence felt like hours. A chill set in.

"I'm guessing you didn't know LoveLink's got SEC approval and has set their date?"

It was like he'd pushed Brad under an ice-cold shower and turned the faucet on full. The shock momentarily shook him.

"They're going public in six weeks. Accelerated their whole plan to launch."

Fish when they're hooked out of the water and left to flail on deck, their mouths open, gills flapping, fighting to breathe, are powerless. That was exactly where Brad was at. He could hear Scott continuing with what he'd unearthed from the inside—the LoveLink assistant he had paid off in cash once a week for her loose lips. But the words were white noise.

The waiter landed another Old Fashioned in front of him. Scott motioned him to drink. The alcohol slowed the panic.

"We're fucked," said Brad, envisioning the unfolding horror. "We haven't the time or funding to beat them."

"If I told you there was a way, would you take it?"

"Of course I'd take it."

Scott leaned in and outlined a plan that made the hair on Brad's neck stand on end.

CHAPTER FORTY-FOUR

THE 2000S

Thursday night and Il Fornaio was heaving. Anna was relieved Mark had booked a booth at the back for the four of them. You could actually hear each other speak over the crowd.

Caitlin was blooming and her bump was finally showing. Anna wondered how she could hold down her high-powered job, and juggle impending motherhood. An ache ran through her whole being, and she willed herself to be in the same state soon.

Mark topped up their wine glasses with a robust pinot noir, while Caitlin stuck to San Pellegrino. They'd moved through a platter of antipasti and were awaiting their main course, and Brad. She'd no idea what was taking him so long. Ever since yesterday, his demeanor had changed. She'd tried to press for more details, but he'd been uncharacteristically cagey about it, saying he had some finance restructuring to work on.

Mark was talking about being headhunted for the nth time. His phone never seemed to stop ringing with offers of great stock options and pay if he moved to the latest XYZ company about to go stratospheric.

Over the top of the crowd Anna saw Brad's head appear in

213

through the door. Finally. Part of her wanted to haul him over the coals for being late. The other part of her knew what a knife-edge the company was on. She struggled to keep the site content fresh, and the messaging on target with the slashed budget. Every day she felt they were falling behind, into the wake of LoveLink's ride to go public. First move advantage was everything.

Brad slid into the booth next to her and made his apologies. He put his arm around her shoulders and gave her a hug, kissing the top of her head. She frowned at the way he did it, and prayed for the relaxed, free-wheeling guy she'd first encountered to return.

"We have news!" said Caitlin, eyes sparkling. She turned to Mark for their reveal.

"The Richthorns accepted our offer. We're on our way to the Silverado Trail!" he said, grinning from ear to ear.

Anna fixed a smile on her face, while inside she felt a stab of jealousy at their luck. They'd secured the home of their dreams —a huge, sprawling house with a pool, guest house and vines. She'd seen the photos, heard of their plans for how they wanted to update the place—which architect, designer and contractor they'd use. And they'd start their family there.

"Guys, that's awesome!" said Brad.

"We're so happy for you!" she managed to say.

They talked it through over the main course—the when and how it was going to happen, the salient details of how Caitlin was going to cash out in the next week with the Microsoft acquisition that Nathan had finally closed. In total they'd have over six million dollars to buy the perfect home and life together.

"Hey, let's get another bottle," said Brad, emptying his glass that he'd refilled only minutes before.

Anna flashed him a look. He shrugged. "Hey, we're celebrating. This is amazing news. They're paving the way!"

"Oh my God, do you think you'd move to Napa too?" said Caitlin, barely able to contain her excitement.

"Well hell, maybe," said Brad. "When we go to IPO, sky's the limit!"

This was all news to Anna. "We're still thinking of being next to the ocean. You know, Stinson, up that way." She looked at Brad as if he'd gone mad. Maybe he had.

Caitlin shrugged. "I know you're both beach people. Well, you'll not be too far away and we can look forward to weekends by the ocean, and you can come to see us in the country."

Mark signaled the waiter. "So much to celebrate. We definitely need more wine. And now you need to tell us about TopMatch. Sounds like you're moving fast there. Damn happy that you're going to whip LoveLink's ass. Those ads of theirs are everywhere. Can't believe they can get away with their sideswipes at you guys in them."

"We are going out guns blazing," continued Brad.

Anna's mind flew into overdrive, trying to imagine what made Brad sound so certain this was going to happen. "So financing's back on track?" she said.

"It is, and to celebrate, I'm taking you to Carmel for the weekend."

"What? We don't have time," she said, and was about to add *or money* when Caitlin chimed in.

"Oh my God, that's just what you both need! A getaway will do you the power of good."

"Recharge your batteries," added Mark.

"Where are you staying?"

"It's a surprise."

They departed from the TopMatch offices just after 2pm the next day to beat the traffic in the valley. Anna would have liked to think they were relaxed, but she was stressed to be leaving her team in flux, although Rain had taken over, insisting she could hold the fort. As for Brad, he was like a cat on a hot tin roof. He'd spent the morning reading his dev team the riot act to get the "fucking software watertight", and then a closed-door meeting with Dwight.

"You sure this is a good idea?" she said for the hundredth time.

He rested his hand on her knee. "We need to get away."

"I don't understand how you think that us going away will change anything from where we are today. If anything it's a risky move leaving everyone and swanning off to Carmel. Not great optics."

He moved his hand to the radio, flicked it on. K-Fog came blasting out. "Like I said, you need a break, I do too. I'm taking care of things. So, let's enjoy it."

She surprised herself by nodding off to sleep. She only awoke when he turned up a long drive just inside Carmel Valley to a grand French country-style chateau, set amongst towering pines and oaks. Horses grazed in rich grassy paddocks. Anna didn't know there could be anything so beautiful hidden here. In an instant all the pent-up anger she had for him taking her away evaporated.

"This is heaven," she said, stepping out onto the pea gravel driveway.

A uniformed concierge came out to greet them, loaded their luggage into a crested golf cart and whisked them to the Hermès House near the stables.

Stepping inside Anna gasped. It was a full-sized house with a grand gallery, huge, vaulted ceilings and deep, luxury furnishings. Out of the window she could see horses training on a practice track.

As soon as the concierge had finished his tour and left, Anna threw her arms around Brad. "Oh my God, this is incredible. I love it!"

He tensed slightly before molding to her, burying his face in her neck. He pulled her tight.

She arched her back to face him, to hold him in her sights.

"I love you, Anna," he said. "You know that."

She wrinkled her nose. "Of course I know that and I love you too."

He kissed her, long and slow. They undressed each other, made their way to the master suite and took their time, navigating each other's body as if for the first time. He entered her, taking long slow strokes, watching her intently. "I want to see you come," he said.

They took a bath together afterwards in the deep, claw-foot tub, drinking champagne and discussing what kind of beach house they wanted to build.

Two glasses in and Anna began to feel light-headed. "Maybe the water's too hot," she said, allowing Brad to help her out.

He wrapped her in one of the huge white fluffy Stonepine robes, and helped her to the bed. Everything around her blurred; her body felt leaden, her eyelids so heavy she just had to close them...

CHAPTER FORTY-FIVE

2019

Anna had abandoned any attempt at a methodical search, leaving a trail of discarded peripherals, modems, and tangled cables in her quest to find an old Iomega drive to play the disk. Their garage could have doubled as a tech museum, filled with relics of silicon and plastic.

It was in the very last box, tucked away at the back, that she found what she was looking for, nestled among a couple of old Zip drives.

With the prize in hand, she made her way to Brad's office, where the disk and the remnants of the bottle of Screaming Eagle awaited her.

She sat down at his desk, poured herself another glass, and began the finicky process of connecting the old drive to his laptop. The adapters, of course, were a nightmare—the tech world seemed to change its standards as often as fashion trends.

Thank God for YouTube and for geeks who laboriously uploaded solutions to issues like these. She drained the last of the wine as she watched a five-minute tutorial by some guy called Zafon, his soothing voice guiding her through the labyrinth of outdated technology.

It was way past 5am when she finally accessed the disk. Inside was the usual file tree index of yellow folders. She browsed through LVP financials, and projections. It was pretty dry stuff.

She hit on a backup email folder. It had to have been pruned down as there was only one folder in there "PN". She clicked it open. It was a batch of email threads. She opened the first one, her eyes scanning words that sharpened with each passing second. It was a decade-long exchange between Scott, Magnus, and a Wing Chun. The wine's numbing effect evaporated.

The emails were filled with a chilling banter about something they called "Prima Nocta"—a sickening tradition of claiming a female employee as a prize from each of the companies they'd invested in. The names were conspicuously absent, but the tally was there, a grim ledger of their conquests. Under Scott's name, she found a cryptic gate numbering system that sent a shiver down her spine.

Her blood ran cold. Each word left her breathless and reeling. The casual, almost gleeful tone of their messages was a stark contrast to the horrifying reality they described. Betrayal and disgust rose in her throat.

Her eyes fell on one of the entries labeled "TopMatch". No. Not possible. A woman in her company? She ran through the crew until she remembered Frederike in graphics who moved back to Germany not long after the IPO. The realization made her skin crawl.

"The Three Musketeers", as they sickeningly referred to themselves, were not just engaging in some harmless banter. They were systematically preying on innocent women, using their power and influence to satisfy their twisted desires. The horrifying truth hit her like a punch to the gut.

She had sat next to Magnus at Tahoe, shared meals and

laughter with him. She had thought he was decent, an upstanding pillar of the financial world. Not this. Not a monster hiding in plain sight.

She googled Wing Chun, and caught her breath. He was head of Victoria Peak Ventures, one of the heavyweights in Hong Kong. A recent photo came up of him and his dynastic family in their sprawling mansion high up on the Peak. It was hard to think the man in the photo, was the man who'd written the sickening banter in these emails.

She clicked on the final folder on the drive, labeled X. As it opened, she was greeted by hundreds of JPEG files, each meticulously named after various companies: Hedtech Ent, Sci View Systems, and more. With a sense of foreboding, she selected them all and launched them in desktop preview.

At first, the images were a confusing jumble of pink folds and glistening skin, reminiscent of some exotic flower or ripe fruit. It took her a moment to comprehend what she was seeing, fanned out onto the screen like a garden in bloom. Each and every one was a close-up pussy picture, someone's open vulva laid bare to the camera lens and its photographer.

She gripped the external mouse—Brad's preferred tool over the laptop pad—so tightly that her knuckles turned white.

Her eyes widened in horror as the full implication of the images sank in. The room seemed to tilt, and a wave of nausea washed over her. These weren't just pictures; they were evidence of something far more sinister and depraved. The names of the companies flashed through her mind, each one a chilling testament to the extent of the corruption.

Reeling, she pushed her chair away from the screen. The world she thought she knew was crumbling around her, revealing a dark underbelly that she could never have imagined. Why the hell hadn't Brad done something about this? Why hadn't he intervened and exposed these bastards instead of burying this in the cellar?

With a deep breath, she forced herself to roll her chair back up to the screen. She closed the preview window, banishing the horrifying images from sight—but their imprint remained seared into her mind. The scale of what she was uncovering was monstrous. This wasn't the work of one rogue individual; it was a coordinated effort by three men, wielding their wealth and power like weapons. They were holding women hostage, forcing them into a sickening bargain: submit or lose everything.

Her hand trembled as she grasped the mouse, scrolling through the seemingly endless list of JPEG files, until she reached T. Not one was labelled *TopMatch*.

Next, she opened a search window and typed in the company name. A cascade of documents appeared, mostly financial reports and projections. But towards the bottom of the list, she spotted a folder she must have overlooked earlier: *TopMatch_PN_Anna*.

PN—Prima Nocta. Her name staring back at her like a grim accusation. With a sense of dread, she double-clicked the folder, bracing herself. It was empty. The screen and room around her spun. A high-pitched buzzing invaded her ears. A tsunami of nausea came up and out of her mouth, spewing out onto the desk. She toppled off her chair, her head hitting the hardwood floor.

CHAPTER FORTY-SIX

The first thing Anna became aware of was the rough, warm sensation of a tongue on her cheek, accompanied by Gui's anxious whining. She opened her eyes to find she was floating on a sea of books.

Her head felt heavy as she tried to lift it from where she lay in a pool of her own vomit, the acrid smell assaulting her senses. She must have passed out, her body succumbing to the overwhelming shock of what was on that disk.

"It's okay, Gui," she said, stroking her head.

But it wasn't okay. Far from it. She needed the dog to calm down, to stop her from waking up Jack. If he found her like this, he would ask questions, and he would find out about the disk. And that could never happen.

She had to clean up this mess, had to hide the evidence. She couldn't let anyone know what she had uncovered, not until she herself understood the full extent of the horror.

She pulled the cable out of the laptop port, and picked up the drive. The weight of it in her hands was more than its physical manifestation. It was the explosive contents, the disk, carrying those bits and bytes, unveiling a pattern of repeated crime so abhorrent it made her blood run cold. And her name was on the TopMatch folder.

She would have known if Scott had done that to her. She would have known. She had seen him off at the polo club. The thought brought another wave of bile surging up her throat. She leaned over Brad's waste bin, her body convulsing as she retched into it, the hot vomit splashing against the metal base.

Maybe Scott had lied about the other women, all to keep up with some sick game he was playing with his friends. The photos could have been sourced from the web easily enough. God, she was trying to give him the benefit of the doubt, trying to reconcile the man she thought she knew with the monster lurking in the shadows of her discovery.

She wiped her mouth with the fabric that had been the disk's wrapper all these years. What the hell was she supposed to do next?

She locked the cellar door, got the mop and bucket from the utility room, and filled it to the brim with hot water mixed with Pine-Sol. The pungent scent of it filled the air. It was a grim cleanup job, made all the worse by the pounding headache that was rapidly developing. She was normally a light drinker—a cocktail here, a couple of glasses of wine there—but her recent habit had been anything but moderate. If she was going to think straight, she knew she had to quit.

As she mopped the floor, the repetitive motion provided a strange sense of comfort amidst the chaos. Each stroke of the mop felt like a small step towards regaining control, towards clearing her mind and preparing herself for whatever came next. The hangover was a brutal reminder of her recklessness.

With each passing minute, the room took shape again, the remnants of her breakdown slowly disappearing. But the real cleanup, the one that mattered most, was the one she had to do within herself.

She texted Juan, their handyman asking to come around as soon as possible that morning to remove Brad's bookshelf contents and drop them at the recycling center. She also asked him to do the same with the mess in the garage. She knew it was a big ask, for Juan to drop everything, but she'd offer him triple his hourly rate.

"Mom, is that you?" Jack was calling from the top of the stairs. She turned the tap off from rinsing out the bucket and mop. Gui, ever the eager escape artist, made a dash for the door, but Anna lunged forward, blocking the exit just in time.

"Yes, just sorting some washing out," she called back.

She couldn't go upstairs now, which had been her next stop, to get in the shower and get clean, and then to wash Gui off too. Damn.

"Just going to take Gui out for a short beach run," she shouted up.

"Okay."

She waited for his door to close, but he left it open and padded back to his bed.

There was only one thing for it. She opened the back door and she and Gui ran out onto the sand, the cold wind whipping her hair, stinging her cheeks.

They reached the water's edge, and Gui bounded into the freezing shallows, barking with pure joy at the unexpected early morning adventure. Anna stopped, her bare feet sinking into the damp sand.

Being this close to the water flooded her mind with twisted, concocted images of how Brad had slipped unconscious from his surfboard and drowned. She pictured his mouth opening, filling with salt water, and the water flooding into his lungs.

Her head throbbed, and tears welled up, blurring the horizon where the waves met the sky. They spilled over, becoming hot, salty rivers flowing down her cheeks. A lump formed at the back of her throat, making it hard to swallow. How could everything have come to this? How had her life taken such a drastic swerve, sliding into a nightmare of suicide and widowhood? And now Scott... How was she supposed to pick up the pieces, keep it together, and carry on?

She wiped away the tears with the back of her hand. Gui was paddling in the surf, cleansing herself from the office fallout. Taking a deep breath Anna ran in after her, diving in under the next wave, letting the icy water envelop her.

Even in the height of summer, it was a challenge for her to enter the water without a wetsuit. Now, clad only in her workout gear, the cold seeped into her bones, numbing her body and mind.

Gui paddled alongside, matching the rhythm of her strokes. The chill of the water provided clarity, a momentary respite from the thoughts running around her head like a freight train.

It was Jack's appearance on the shoreline that brought her back to reality. He was standing there in his PJs and school hoodie, waving and shouting, his voice carrying over the sound of the surf. "Mom! Mom!"

Hell, what was she doing out here? Another wave came rolling in. She grabbed Gui's collar and pulled her around.

"In, Gui," she said.

They caught the flow, coming to land back on shore.

"Sorry, just had to cool off from the run," she said, reaching his side, her breath coming in short gasps.

"What were you thinking, Mom?! You never go in there. What the hell was your plan? End up like Dad?"

Gui shook out her wet coat, spraying droplets of water, and nosed Jack's hand. Anna could feel the tears welling up again. She gritted her teeth, willing them back. "I'd never do that. I'm sorry, I just needed to chill out, to calm myself."

The wind was now blowing through the thin fabric of her

workout gear. She began to shiver, her teeth chattering. Suddenly, she felt the warmth of a hoodie being draped over her head. Jack helped her arms into the sleeves and then wrapped his arms around her, pulling her close.

"I will never leave you. I'm sorry," she said.

"I miss him, Mom, just as much as you."

They stood, tears now flowing, frozen in time, as the tide crept back in.

Gui whined softly, her eyes darting between Anna and Jack. Anna let go, linked her arm through Jack's. They turned and walked back towards the house.

"I think we could both do with pancakes," she said.

As they reached the back gate they were startled to see Scott standing there, looking as if he'd just rolled out of bed. His six o'clock shadow added a rugged edge to his usually polished appearance, and instead of his crisp office attire, he was dressed in blue jeans and a gray knit polo neck.

"Enough for three?"

He had to have been watching them out there. Oh God.

"Jack called me."

She turned to Jack who was brushing any traces of tears from his face. His eyes were red and swollen. She guessed hers were too. Bloodshot most likely as well from last night's excesses.

"I was worried," he said, as the three of them headed inside.

CHAPTER FORTY-SEVEN

THE 2000S

Anna had no idea where she was. A thin shaft of light was coming into the room from where their fitted closets lined the wall. Maybe she'd swapped sides with Brad? Although that was odd, because he liked the right, her the left. And they didn't have air con, and she could hear the unmistakable low drone of it at work, cooling the air.

She tried to lift her eyelids higher than the quarter mast they were at, but the effort was too much so she let them drop. Her jaw was too heavy to open, her tongue flaccid.

Her brain was a fog. Its cogs and wheels weren't turning at their usual pace upon waking, racking up the to-do list she needed to get done that day. Her body lay numb, an inert mass.

Christ, was this what burnout was like? Had she somehow tipped herself over the edge into the realm of chronic fatigue? She'd heard stories of people living in that state for months, even years. Overcooked before she was thirty, before she was married, had a baby.

"Hey, A, you awake?" Brad was stroking her hair. His voice was soft and deep.

She forced her eyes open. "Where..." was all she could manage.

"We're at Stonepine. Carmel. You've been asleep a long time. Must have needed the rest. Here..." He put another pillow under her head and helped her sip water through a straw. It was ice cold against her throat.

"What time?"

"It's way after noon."

His face was crumpled, as if he'd been crying, brow deeply furrowed, staring at her as if she really had died and miraculously come back to life.

The hot bath, champagne, acrid taste in her mouth, dizziness, him helping her into bed. It was all coming back.

"Sorry, I must be—"

"Exhaustion," he interjected. "But you're okay now, you're here with me. That's all that counts." He leaned in and kissed her forehead before laying his own against it. "I love you, babe."

Hearing him was balm to the thumping headache that came on like a shot out of the dark. Burning bile crept into her mouth. Oh God no. Her body convulsed, Brad leapt back, as a volcanic eruption of amber bile came spewing from her mouth, covering the white Egyptian cotton bedsheets.

Tears sprang up as she arched back and forth, emptying what felt like her very being. Brad held her head. "It'll be okay. I promise," he soothed.

Wrung out, she lay back against the pillow, while he removed the top sheet and duvet, bundling them up as he crossed to the bathroom. Seconds later he reappeared with a stack of clean towels bearing the Stonepine logo, and a facecloth that he'd passed under the tap.

"Here," he said, cleaning her up, helping her to another tiny sip of water, changing out her pillows for his.

"Thanks," she said, grateful for his concern and lightning

quick action. It made her love him even more than she already did, and she didn't think that was possible.

Now she'd been sick, although drained and exhausted, she felt somewhat better. "Must be something going around," she said, managing to smile for the first time.

"Yeah. Someone told me there's something going around South Park." He got up from where he'd been sitting on the edge of the bed and fetched the room service menu off the leather-topped desk. "Think you can eat? It'll help if you can."

He opened it and showed her the offering. The list was long and if she'd been well it'd have been hard to choose between the blueberry pancakes with maple syrup and Chantilly cream, and the full American breakfast, complete with grits and hash browns.

"Sourdough toast, butter and jam."

"You got it," he said, immediately lifting the phone receiver to summon room service.

Once relayed, he called reception and asked for the room to be serviced as soon as possible.

"I'm not sure I can move for them to come in," she said.

Instead of a reply he slid his hands under her, scooping her up into his strong arms.

"Ah," she said, nestling into his chest, as he carried her out into the vaulted sitting room, through to the other guest room.

The view from there was out to a paddock where a chestnut thoroughbred was grazing under the canopy of a large oak. Its coat gleamed in the dappled light. Brad opened the French windows so she could get a better view from where he'd propped her up on the fresh bed. She inhaled the fresh, warm air, listening to the horse methodically chomping its way through the green grass.

"Here. This'll help settle your stomach," he said, giving her two white pills and a glass of water.

She winced as she swallowed. Sharp pain. Someone was knocking on the outer door.

"I'll get it," he said.

———

A couple of hours later, after a further nap, Anna woke up to see the horse had been moved from the paddock. The sun was setting, bathing the landscape in a rich tangerine glow. The door was open to the sitting room. The familiar screech and whistle of their portable dial-up modem meant Brad was out there, no doubt catching up on work.

She wriggled to the edge of the bed, her body protesting with each movement. She swung her legs out, her toes sinking into the thick, cream wool rug. Inch by inch, she pushed herself to standing, her head swimming. The nausea was gone, but her body felt fragile, as if she were made of glass.

She shuffled into the bathroom, the cool tiles beneath her feet a stark contrast to the warmth of the rug. As she sat down on the toilet, she gritted her teeth against the sharp pain that shot through her. Bloody hell, she was sore. Then it hit her—the memory of her and Brad before the bath and champagne. They hadn't had sex like that in a while. Over the last few months, it had become a quick, almost clinical routine in their quest to make a baby. Maybe she was just out of practice.

Hobbling over to the sink, she caught sight of herself in the large, gilt-framed mirror and recoiled. Jesus Christ. Her eyes were puffy and bloodshot, her face pale and drawn. She turned on the tap, cupping her hands to splash cold water on her face, willing the swelling to vanish.

"Hey, you're up." Brad lingered in the doorway watching her.

"God, I look terrible," she moaned.

He guided her to the elaborate, deep-buttoned pale blue stool next to the claw-foot tub, positioned beneath another picture window that overlooked the rose garden. She watched him plug the drain and fill the tub, adding and mixing in the complimentary Hermès bubble bath. His movements were precise, almost ritualistic.

Once full, he helped her out of her robe, averting his eyes as she stepped in. Her lips twitched with amusement as she sank into the warm water. "Very gallant, but you have seen me naked before."

She thought he'd laugh, instead he busied himself checking which bottle was shampoo and which was conditioner. "Damn, why do they make these look the same?"

She took a deep breath and lowered her head below the surface. In an instant his hands had plunged in and lifted her back out.

"I'm not five years old!" she said, spluttering.

"I'm sorry," he said, his voice nearly cracking.

She wiped the water from her eyes. "Are you okay?"

A fleeting cloud scudded between them.

He nodded. "Yeah. Sorry, A. It's just the pressure. Engineers are slow without me there, and you're not well."

"I'm not that bad, you know. It'll pass. And of course your crew are slow, without you cracking the whip."

He leaned in and kissed her softly on the lips. "Let me wash your hair," he said.

The next morning, the familiar to-do list spooled inside Anna's head, waking her from a deep but restorative slumber. Brad was lying next to her, his head close to hers. She smiled.

"Keeping a watchful eye on me?" she said.

"Something like that. How're you feeling?"

"A lot better. Although now I'm thinking it's been such a waste of us coming here. We've not even seen any of Stonepine."

He stroked her face. "Can you be ready in a half hour?"

"For what?"

"A surprise."

Showered and dressed in jeans and a white linen shirt, sleeves rolled up, she headed outside to where Brad had been calling for her to hurry up.

Now she understood the rush. Brad was, for the first time ever, up in the saddle. His feet, clad in well-worn canvas high-tops, were wedged into gleaming silver stirrups that seemed far too heavy for his casual shoes. He was gripping the reins of a tall, midnight horse, sitting upright and rigid as if he'd been cast in stone.

Beside him, a weathered cowboy held the reins of two more horses—one a rich bay, the other an appaloosa with a coat as striking as a midnight sky speckled with stars.

"Wow," she said, heart leaping at the prospect that lay before her.

"Morning," said the cowboy, tipping his hat. "This here's Tokala, she's all ready for you." He offered her the reins of the appaloosa.

She looked up at Brad, towering above her. "A million thank yous. I know this is way out of your comfort zone."

He smiled. "You deserve it."

"Here," said the cowboy, ready to give her a leg up.

The second she hit the saddle she winced at the pain, biting her lip. But this was worth it.

"Brad says you know how to ride," he said, adjusting her stirrups.

"I can hold my own."

He laughed. "Tokala's like a Cadillac, a real smooth ride." Turning to Brad, he began his instruction, with an ease that came from years of practice.

They set off at a gentle walk down a path shaded by ancient trees.

"Loosen up, Brad. You're not auditioning for the rodeo. Enjoy the ride," said the cowboy.

She lingered behind, absorbing the moment. The sunlight danced through the leaves, casting shifting patterns on the ground. The horses' hooves kept a steady rhythm, and she found herself swaying in the saddle, in sync with Tokala's fluid movement.

They trekked for an hour through rolling hills before descending into a cool valley where a rushing creek cut through the landscape. Following the water's edge, they rounded a corner. She gasped. A tartan rug was laid out, strewn with green Stonepine logo cushions. Next to it sat an open hamper, brimming with mouth-watering food. A bottle of wine sat waiting in a silver ice bucket with two crystal glasses standing on a linen-covered tray.

"This is heaven," she said, swinging her leg over to dismount, landing elegantly on the ground.

Brad groaned as he slid off, his knees buckling and bowing. "Man, that's hard work," he said, flexing his arms out.

She put her arms around Tokala's neck. "Thank you," she whispered. The horse nuzzled her. Something within her suddenly let go and a wave of relief flooded through her.

The cowboy gathered the horses. "I gonna leave you folks, give this lot a draft of water, and head back. A jeep'll be here to pick you up in a couple hours." He tipped his hat and rode off.

They sat down, Brad reaching for the bottle. "I asked for Frog's Leap. Figured we'd skip the champagne." He poured the chilled white sauvignon blanc while she took a bite of a smoked salmon and cream cheese bagel from the hamper. Her favorite breakfast, with her favorite wine.

He handed her a glass, and raised his own. "Here's to us."

The chime of crystal on crystal rang out.

Brad rolled to one side, and putting his glass back on the tray, retrieved something from the hamper before coming up on one knee.

"What are you doing?"

"Anna Hartley, will you be my wife?"

She giggled. She hadn't seen this coming, not here, not now.

He opened out his clenched hand to reveal a small, iconic Tiffany box. Opening the lid he unveiled a ring that housed the most breathtaking diamond Anna had ever seen.

"Yes, yes, of course I will," she said.

He plucked it out and slid it onto her ring finger. Perfect fit. He kissed her. "You deserve the best."

"But," she said, "I thought we'd agreed to wait until..."

"And we have. We're through due diligence and regulatory filings. Got an email we're on track for SEC approval tomorrow. And... financing's secured way beyond IPO. Fifteen million came in this morning."

"What?" She looked from him to the brilliant jewel adorning her finger, then back to him.

"LVP are behind us one hundred percent of the way. Dwight called in yesterday to confirm the transfer was complete. I checked the account first thing. It's all there."

She threw her arms around him. Unbelievable! Scott Lyle came through in the end. "That's a miracle. Oh my God, you deserve a medal."

"We both do. It's your victory as much as mine," he said, looking out, over the top of her head to the still, deep water of the creek.

CHAPTER FORTY-EIGHT

THE 2000S

LoveLink's CEO Vikrant Chomodsky hit end call on his cell, opened his mouth and roared, thumping his fists on the new, limited edition Zeno Desk by Scolari that had arrived from Italy the week before. It had been a "gift to self" for being such a brilliant CEO.

Through the glass wall, heads popped up like meerkats from the newly installed cube farm. It was his latest strategy, inspired by a book he'd picked up at the airport, *The Kaizen Method— Enhancing Productivity through Process Calibration.* He was always chasing the next big idea, something to optimize and maximize. He'd heard the grumbles about the corporate facelift, but he'd brushed them off.

But now, right now, they were fucked. Scott Lyle had pulled all his remaining funding. The money that should have arrived first thing hadn't, and now it wasn't going to. The guy gave him some lame excuse. Bullshit. The fucker had lost faith, and no matter how much Vikrant had tried to spin the decision back around, he'd failed.

He seized his laptop, sending it spinning across the room like a frisbee. It shattered the glass wall, scattering shards and circuitry across the polished concrete floor. The barrier was gone, leaving him exposed to the growing whispers of horror from his highly paid employees.

"Get out!" he screamed at them.

Not one of them moved.

"Leave! It's fucking over!"

———

Brad used part of the LVP funds to acquire LoveLink for cents on the dollar. Vikrant exited, and the staff that remained were absorbed into the ever-growing TopMatch ranks.

With no competition within range, TopMatch sailed through IPO in record time, becoming an overnight sensation and darling of the Nasdaq. LVP played a low-key role, fronted by Dwight.

The after-party at the TopMatch offices was legendary. Cocktails, magnums of Moet flowed; Pearl Jam was flown in to play; the Tuileries did a pop-up restaurant.

Anna took Brad by the hand and led him through the crowd to his desk, where someone had stuck a giant golden trophy to the top of his monitor.

"I'm pregnant," she said, delivering the news she'd kept secret for the past eight weeks, not wanting to distract him from the final push to go public.

His face broke into the biggest smile. He looked down to her stomach, and then back up, taking her face in his hands. "My God, that's a better gift than any IPO," he said, kissing her. He hugged her close. "How long?"

She squeezed her eyes shut in the pure joy of at last sharing the news. "The doctor said ten weeks. It must have happened in Carmel."

CHAPTER FORTY-NINE

2019

Anna's eyelids grew leaden, and she was pulled into a deep sleep.

Her mind flickered through memories like an old slide projector, flicking from image to image of her working life, searching for the truth. There was a folder on that disk with her name on it.

Suddenly, in the darkest recesses of her brain, something shifted and came creeping out of the shadows. She could feel cold hard fingers trace down her body. A voice came whispering in her ear, "I'm going to fuck you into tomorrow."

She jolted awake, her heart drumming in her chest. That voice... It was Scott's.

The realization hit her like a meteor, crashing through the atmosphere, crushing her under its weight. She knew, with a sickening certainty, that the words, the actions, were true. And Brad must have known.

She felt violated, betrayed.

Her mind was now racing, a tangled web of questions and dread. How had Scott gotten to her? She'd refused him at the Circus Club. And why couldn't she remember before? Her research in cyberpsych had taught her about trauma, how it could be buried so deep that unearthing it required a seismic trigger.

Her skin crawled, red hives bubbling up on her arms. She ran to the shower, shedding her clothes like a second skin. Stepping into the warm spray, she let the water cascade over her. She scrubbed at her body, desperate to cleanse, erase, and eradicate the past that was clawing its way to the surface.

"There's no way in hell Brad would destroy it," she said aloud, her voice echoing in the steam-filled chamber. The words sparked a resolve that propelled her out of the shower and onto the cool marble floor. Brad had been meticulous about their home, every detail carefully curated. The marble, he'd insisted, was from a specific quarry in Northern Italy. Nothing was without purpose, without meaning.

She pulled on a pair of sweats, her wet hair dripping down her back, and stood at the base of the glass spiral staircase. This was Brad's masterpiece, his obsession. He'd spent hours researching, poring over the history of architecture, all the way back to Da Vinci's double-helix staircase in the Château de Chambord.

She'd campaigned for a single helix to simplify the design and get their home finished so they could move in, but Brad had been intractable. And when she'd highlighted that there were only three of them living in the place, along with a dog, that two flights of stairs was a waste, he'd gone off like a missile into a rage of ridiculousness. She'd put it down to the stress of creative perfection, but now she guessed it was driven by that bloody disk.

Part of her wanted to go down to the cellar and drink an entire bottle to numb the razor-sharp pain that sliced through to her soul.

"Keep it together, Anna," she whispered, switching on the

flashlight on her phone. She was underneath the first spiral, on her hands and knees at the first step, looking up through the semi-opaque bladder-molded glass, scanning for a thin black outline.

Methodic and thorough she worked her way up, until on tiptoe she was at her limit, and was forced to get out the aluminum stepladder that the cleaners used.

Nothing but glass. The glass that had supported all those years of home life. Jack had learned to crawl and walk on this staircase. The hours and hours she'd spent with him, holding his tiny body, and then just his hands as he figured out how to navigate its structure. 'One step, two steps, three steps more. And up we go to your bedroom door..."

As he'd grown older he and his friends had used it as an indoor climbing frame, a place to raceway, up and down on the two stair tracks.

She dragged the stepladder to the right side of the staircase, deciding on a top-down approach. Her neck ached from the awkward angle, but she was driven by a fierce determination. She shone her flashlight through the glass, squinting as the beam caught a dark shadow embedded deep within the tread. Leaning closer, she saw it—the unmistakable outline of a disk.

She clawed at the surface with her nails, a futile attempt that only left her fingertips throbbing. Frustrated, she traced the edge of the stair, searching for a way to pry it loose. It was as if the staircase was a giant, impenetrable nut.

On further inspection she could make out a complex web of carbon fiber strings embedded within the glass, holding the structure together like a suspended spiderweb. How in hell was she going to get it out?

CHAPTER FIFTY

For once his mom was calm. She wasn't talking, and her eyes were fixed on the road ahead in a kind of faraway trance.

Jack was relieved he'd called Scott the morning of the beach swim, and that he'd come straight over. His mom's descent into some weird madness had been freaking him out, and he hadn't dared share it with Alicia, or Caitlin, because if he did he thought someone would take his mom away to some kind of asylum. If he lost her too then his whole life was over.

Somehow he trusted Scott; he got the vibe that Scott cared for her. When he'd turned up, Jack knew he'd done the right thing.

He turned on his playlist that took them all the way to the school gates. He had one hand on the door handle, ready to offer his usual quick "Later," but something held him back.

"Hey, Mom," he said, his voice softening. "I love you."

The words snapped Anna out of her trance, pulling her back from the dark corners of her mind. She looked at her son, her heart swelling with a mix of love and pain. She leaned over and hugged him tight.

"I love you too," she whispered, and in that moment, the world outside faded away.

They were broken up by Gui leaping in from the back, nudging between them with a soft whine.

Anna watched Jack disappear in through the school gates, before pulling away from the curb. The drive there had been a battle, a constant struggle to maintain a facade of calm, while her mind churned with thoughts of the disk hidden within the staircase. She'd spent half the night trying to figure out how to extract it, but had yet to find a way.

Now, as she headed out into the winding hills, her foot pressed a little too heavily on the accelerator, she had time to think.

Back at the house, she pulled the car to a halt right outside the front door, the tires screeching on the gravel. She leapt out, Gui bounding after her, and went straight to the kitchen where she made a double cappuccino to fuel her mission.

With coffee in hand she got underway with googling and calling every structural engineer in a fifty-mile radius, but the responses were all the same: booked solid for weeks, if not months. Each polite refusal was like a door slamming shut, leaving her with a growing sense of desperation.

She ventured into the garage, now eerily empty of the old tech equipment that had once cluttered every surface. The shelves were bare save for a few screwdrivers and paintbrushes, their bristles stiff with disuse. She leaned against the empty cupboards, sipping her coffee, her eyes scanning the space, willing a solution to materialize from the emptiness. If she wanted answers, she would have to find them herself.

As she opened a side door leading onto the deck, a gust of salty wind swept in, carrying with it the distant rumble of waves crashing against the shore. Looking up, she saw a thick cloud bank building out across the horizon. A storm was on its way.

She pulled up the zip of her padded gilet and headed out, Gui on her heels, excited at the prospect of a beach walk. Instead, Anna turned down the side of the house, to the area where the air con systems and drainage pump were hidden. The gardeners had a lock-up shed there for various equipment to maintain the grounds. She twisted the numbers round on the plastic dial. Slot machine 777 was the code they'd all agreed upon. Easy to break, but theft crime wasn't a big thing in Stinson.

Inside, the air was thick with the scent of gasoline. She flicked on the light and scanned the small space for what tools were at her disposal.

The chainsaw looked like a good contender. She picked it up, along with the safety glasses. Nothing else looked of use, until her eyes fell upon a sledgehammer hiding behind a rake in the corner.

Time to get to work. She headed back to the house, watched the relevant YouTube tutorials, gave Gui a bone, and shut her out of harm's way in the kitchen.

The hallway stretched out before her, the glass staircase standing like a gleaming monolith, taunting her with its secret. She rehearsed the chainsaw moves—thumb grip, close contact, kickback prevention, balance, safety.

With the glasses secured, she yanked the rip cord on the chainsaw. The machine roared to life, its blade spinning around, ready for a bite.

She approached the staircase. The blade met the glass, skating and skidding across its diamond-hard surface. She tried different angles, her arms straining with the effort, the chainsaw bucking and kicking in her grip. Sweat beaded on her forehead, her breath coming in ragged gasps as she fought to maintain control. But the glass remained unyielding. Her arms trembled, her muscles burning with the strain. She gritted her teeth, determined to keep going, to find a chink in the glass's armor. But it was no use.

Finally, with a frustrated cry, she powered off the chainsaw and let it fall to the floor, her arms throbbing from the relentless effort. She sank to her knees, cradling her head in her hands, feeling the weight of her skull. Just weeks ago the brain inside was devoid of all the shit she knew now. That felt like light years away.

How had Brad lived with this burden all these years? The thought sent a shiver down her spine. He must have gone quietly mad, holding all those images in his memory, letting them fester and grow like a malignant tumor. And hers—her truth—was locked within the glass.

There was only one thing for it, and for this she needed the right accompaniment. She pulled her phone from her pocket.

The haunting sounds of Gabriel's synthesized shakuhachi flute played over the house music system. The brass and drums cut in and the vocals echoed through the space.

"Let's do this, Peter!" she said, getting up from where she'd been resting on the lower step.

She took hold of the sledgehammer, put it over her shoulder and hiked up the stairs, humming along to the classic song that she remembered her and Brad once singing along to on a trip up to Tahoe years before.

Positioning herself on the step, above the offending disk infested one, she adopted a feet apart anchoring stance and waited to sing along to the chorus before swinging it up and over like some chain gang pro.

The hammer came down, powered by all the pent-up rage that had been simmering inside her. The stairs shuddered under the blow. She didn't pause, didn't falter. She brought the hammer up and over again, smashing it down, and then again, and again, until the driving force of her anger hit a chord with the glass.

The step exploded into a thousand shards, cascading to the floor in a crystal shower. The force of the impact sent a shockwave through the staircase, triggering a domino effect that saw the lower stairs collapse in a symphony of destruction, until the entire single helix lay in ruins at her feet.

She dropped the hammer. Her breath was short and sharp.

The music faded away, leaving behind an eerie silence that settled over the scene like a shroud. She hadn't expected such catastrophic results, and she was the architect of this chaos.

Where the hell was the disk?

She took the remaining single helix steps down to the ground floor and searched through the wreckage. What if the disk had been crushed in the chaos?

And then she spotted it lying on its own, away from the sea of glass, over near the door to the utility room. It must have skittered across the floor like a stone skipping over water.

She carefully made her way towards it. The moment her fingers wrapped around the disk's black plastic casing, the impact of the destruction around her faded away. There was only one goal now: get to Brad's office.

She sank into his chair, tossing the glasses and gloves aside. Her hands trembled as she handled the old Zip drive, slotting the disk into place and waiting for the green light to flicker on. The drive hummed to life, its mechanical whir filling the silent room, and a file materialized on the desktop.

She frowned at the file extension. It wasn't a .jpg; it was a .mov. Unease washed over her as she double-clicked the file. The screen flickered to life, and the video began to play.

CHAPTER FIFTY-ONE

In the quiet of Brad's office, Anna watched the grainy footage unfold on the screen. Gui lay curled up at her feet, her warm body a small comfort amidst the storm of emotions. The scene was from a different era—the 2000s—but the horror of it was as vivid and raw as if it were happening right before her eyes.

An opulent bedroom filled the frame, a king-size bed taking center stage. A man entered the shot, his back to the camera, dressed in a blue shirt and chinos, a glass in his hand. He moved to the door and opened it, revealing another man in a dark suit, his face obscured by a large object slung over his shoulder.

"She's ready," the man in the suit said, walking to the bed. He leaned over, unloading his burden with a grunt.

Anna gasped as he stepped back, revealing her own unconscious form, clad in a white toweling robe bearing the Stonepine logo.

"I'll call you when I'm done," said the man in chinos, handing the other man an envelope.

They both turned towards the camera at the same time, and Anna's breath caught in her throat. She gripped the edge of the desk for support, her eyes wide with shock and horror. It was Scott and his driver, Gabino.

Gabino walked out, closing the door behind him. Scott knocked back the rest of his drink, his eyes fixed on Anna's sleeping form. He sat down on the bed next to her, tracing his fingers over her face before leaning in to kiss her lips.

Anna watched in disbelief as Scott loosened her robe, sliding it open to reveal her naked body. He ran his hands over her, his fingers exploring every inch of her skin. A wave of nausea rose within her, her stomach churning as she watched him violate her.

Scott stood up and crossed to the far wall of the bedroom, drawing back a sliding wood panel to reveal a backlit bar shelf. He selected a bottle of tequila, pouring himself a shot before turning his attention back to her. He filled her navel with the liquor, lowering his lips to suck it up, his actions deliberate and predatory.

Anna's breath came in ragged gasps as she watched Scott undress, his naked body a grotesque sight on the screen. He knelt at the foot of the bed, his hands stroking their way up her legs, spreading them open. He lapped and sucked at her, his tongue navigating her most intimate places.

After what felt like an eternity, he reached over to the nightstand, retrieving a condom. He ripped the packet open with his teeth, but then paused, tossing it aside. He repositioned himself between her legs, moving her knees up to give himself a full view of her. He rubbed the end of his dick against her, his words echoing through the room like a poisonous whisper.

"You had to say no, didn't you? Now look at you, you dirty little bitch," he said, leaning in close to her ear. "I'm gonna fuck you into tomorrow."

Anna's vision blurred, tears streaming down her cheeks as she watched the final, brutal act play out on the screen. A wave of horror washed over her, powerless to intervene in the scene that unfolded before her.

The bathrobe, the trip to Stonepine with Brad—the jigsaw pieces came flying together to form a picture so dark, her body went still, petrified; her blood, running cold in the wake.

CHAPTER FIFTY-TWO

THREE MONTHS BEFORE BRAD'S DEATH

The Palisades Tahoe junior ski team was out enjoying the fresh dump of snow that had fallen in the night. Brad stood at the bottom of the slope watching his son expertly navigate his way down the slalom.

It was the mid-season competition for the Eagle Cup. The caliber of talent that year was some of the best Palisades had ever seen. Rumor had it that an Olympic scout was out in the crowd somewhere.

Jack skied over to his friends who were gathered over the far side, a large group of them huddled in their red, white and blue team gear.

Brad sipped the ice-cold beer in his gloved hand and took a photo of the scoreboard. His son in first place. He sent it to Anna for when she landed in from New York. It'd be a nice surprise after her annual week of lectures at NYU.

The next skier wiped out on the last gate, and came spinning down the slope to land in the bowl. He watched them get up, unscathed. The joy of youth, being able to bounce back like that.

Over the top of their helmet he could make out Jack on the edge of the huddle talking to a girl whose long dark hair cascaded out from under her helmet. She had to be new, and for once Jack was taking an interest, leaning his head in close to hers. Brad smiled. Jack was growing up.

By the end of the race, he had been bumped to second place. The podium had been set up down by the cafe, so Brad seized the opportunity to get a coffee before the prize-giving. He needed the jolt before the long drive home.

The line was long, and by the time he came out, the podium was already crowded. He rushed back inside and took the stairs to the balcony. From his bird's-eye view he now had a clear view, so he pulled out his cell, and zoomed in.

How in hell? He froze, the camera still rolling, recording Jack having the silver medal put over his head by Scott Lyle. Time and space suspended in that instant. He wanted to vault over and punch the guy's lights out—forever.

He watched, powerless, as Scott leaned in close. They were talking. Jack was grinning, nodding his head.

Brad opened his mouth, ready to act upon the moment he'd spent his life dreading. But nothing. He was powerless.

They were on the way back home, navigating through a fresh snowstorm. Brad was gripping the steering wheel so hard he felt he was going to snap it in two.

All he could do was listen to Jack talking about the race, the prize giving, and Scott fucking Lyle. But there was nothing he could do about it.

Thank God Jack had fallen asleep two hours in. In the remaining journey time Brad's internal rage boiled over. He pulled over on the side of the road, got out, closed the door and let his simmering rage dissolve into the night.

By the time he was home, he'd managed to find the

headspace to form a plan that had him reaching for his laptop, even though it was past midnight.

Six weeks later, he launched a malware attack, striking at the heart of LVP, freezing a deal flow that sent Scott into a tailspin of pure vitriol.

CHAPTER FIFTY-THREE

2019

Caitlin rushed over the moment she'd hung up, her mind still reeling from the horrifying video Anna had described.

Now she sat watching Anna's hands shake, the ice cubes rattling in the triple-shot of whiskey she'd prescribed to calm her friend down. Outside in the hallway, she could hear Jose and his crew brushing up the broken glass and carting it away to their truck, which had been reversed up to the front door.

Anna's call had terrified her, but then a few excerpts she'd shown her from the video had pushed that fear beyond, into her soul.

How Scott Lyle could have been so depraved defied her beliefs. And how could Brad have helped it happen, engineering Anna's delivery for Scott to rape her? It was good Brad was dead, otherwise she'd kill him herself.

And then there was the timing. Was Jack really Brad's, or was he Scott's son?

"What the hell am I going to do, Cait? What if Jack and Alicia have..." The words were replaced by a gut-wrenching sob.

For once Caitlin was silent, her heart aching for her friend.

"My entire life has become some sick and twisted lie," said

Anna, her voice barely above a whisper. She wrung her hands, her fingers stretching and kneading the skin and bones.

Caitlin reached out, placing her hand gently on Anna's. "Look at me," she said, waiting for her friend to raise her eyes. She needed to be the rock that Anna could lean on, the steady hand that would guide her through this storm.

"I get that's how you feel right now. But you cannot think like that. However it came about, you have an amazing, wonderful son who is the center of your world. We're going to get through this together."

Anna took a deep breath, her shoulders rising and falling with the effort. "Brad betrayed my trust. Served me up on some platter to get TopMatch to IPO. I'd refused to do that, but not him. Oh no. He sold me to the most abhorrent, fucked-up VC in the Valley."

Caitlin listened, her stomach churning with revulsion.

"He drugged me, had me trafficked, so Scott could rape me," she continued, voice rising with each word. Her hand was now a fist. She punched her chest, as if she was trying to physically expel the pain and rage consuming her.

"Then I'm delivered back to wake up in a hotel room with my husband-to-be, who had the audacity to give me a ring he'd sold both our souls for!" She leapt to her feet, her eyes wild with a mix of fury and despair.

Caitlin watched horrified as Anna clawed at her ten-carat engagement ring and her diamond encrusted wedding band, wrenching them off, hurling them at the fireplace with a force that sent them clattering against the stone.

"But then, as if violating me wasn't enough, I find out I'm pregnant. Jesus." The last word was whimpered on a heart wrenching sob. "I mean, Cait, I can't even stomach the thought of..." Anna tailed off, her voice breaking. She was now rubbing at her temples. "I feel like I'm going insane."

Caitlin took a deep breath. "The first step is to find out the truth. We get a DNA test done."

"But Jack and Alicia? We have to stop it before it goes too far!"

Caitlin shook her head. "Not yet, not until we know for sure. I know someone who can get that answer quick." She was already pulling up the name on her phone. "Hey, Samir. I need a favor..."

While she talked, she watched Anna get up and walk towards the window. Her reflection in the rain-streaked glass revealed such a hollowed-out version of her friend that Caitlin went from deeply worried about her to a code-red angst that Anna might never, ever recover from all this. The vibrant beauty and energy was being crushed out of her by this wrecking-ball revelation.

Anna's eyes were hollow and haunted, rimmed with red. Dark circles underscored the exhaustion. Her complexion was waxen, leaving her ghostly against the stormy sky.

"COO at DNAMatch is going to fast-track the test. We can trust him, he's discreet. Courier's already on their way," Caitlin said, finally hanging up. She went over to the window and put an arm around Anna's shoulders. "We need their toothbrushes."

She guided her into the hallway. Jose and his crew had left. All remnants had been cleared up, leaving the remaining staircase looking like some fairground helter-skelter ride.

Their first stop was Jack's bathroom. Caitlin quickly whipped the head off his electric toothbrush, her movements swift and efficient. "Forgot a Ziplock. I'll be right back," she said, leaving Anna alone.

While Caitlin was opening drawers in the kitchen looking for a Ziplock bag, Anna picked up a towel off the floor. It was still damp from Jack's shower. She started to fold it, but stopped, bringing it up to her nose. She closed her eyes and inhaled. Jack. Her son.

Her mind flashed from the horrifying video of Scott thrusting into her inert body, to the hospital when Jack was born. A snapshot of Brad holding him close, saying no matter what, he'd always be there for him. *Lies.*

She finished folding the towel, placing it on the heated rail, and made her way along the landing to the master suite.

She stood before the cabinet above Brad's marble sink, her fingers touching the mirror. As it sprung open, she realized she hadn't looked in it since he'd gone. The array of men's grooming products sat neatly lined up on the glass shelves—serums, sunblocks in all SPFs, hair wax, a half empty bottle of "Oud Wood". Fresh razors and dental equipment were laid out on the bottom.

She started with the tubes, unscrewing the tops and squirting their contents out, into the sink. Her movements became more forceful and deliberate, each action fueled by a burning need to purge the memories and betrayal. She turned on the tap and watched the creamy mass slither and slip down the plughole, a symbolic cleansing of Brad's presence.

"Do not touch that toothbrush!" said Caitlin, running in, reaching across her, and grabbing Brad's Reinast Titanium toothbrush.

She dropped it into a fresh Ziplock bag with a decisive snap.

Anna's phone pinged. She reached into her back pocket, her hand shaking as she pulled it out. The home screen photo of Jack in ski gear, grinning into the camera at the top of Palisades under a clear blue sky was obscured by a new message from Scott Lyle:

Meet me at the Sausalito helipad after drop-off tomorrow. I've got to talk with you.

Her hands shook uncontrollably. She hit reply and typed rapidly.

You fucking despicable

Caitlin snatched the phone from her. "Anna, stop! This is not the time. We need to think."

"I've done all the thinking I need. Give it to me."

She tried to grab the phone, but Caitlin hid it behind her back. "No. Not right now."

"Give it back," Anna repeated, her hand outstretched, the anger flooding her veins.

Caitlin took a deep breath. Anna could see the struggle in her friend's eyes as she weighed her options. Anna knew she had to act quickly. She lunged for the phone. Caitlin tried to dodge, but she got a grip of one end. The two of them grappled for control of the device.

In the struggle, the phone slipped from Caitlin's grasp and flew across the room, hitting the marble floor with a sharp crack.

CHAPTER FIFTY-FOUR

THE MORNING OF BRAD'S DEATH

Brad watched the black stream of espresso flow into the cup, the rich aroma filling the air. It was pre-dawn, his favorite time of day, when the world was still quiet and the possibilities seemed endless.

He glanced back at his laptop, which was open on the marble kitchen worktop. The second malware attack he'd launched into the heart of LVP had hit its target, corrupting the latest slew of deal flow data. He could just imagine the chaos it was causing, the scrambling and panic as they tried to recover what was lost. He took a sip of the hot espresso, its bitter taste refreshing his senses, invigorating him for the day ahead.

He thought of Scott Lyle, probably already awake and pacing his office, his phone buzzing with urgent calls about the attack. Brad savored the image of Scott's face contorted with rage, the realization that his carefully constructed empire was under threat.

Good, Brad thought. *Let him feel what it's like to be punched in the gut, to have everything you've worked for under threat.*

Gui whined from where she sat by the back door, eager for her early morning run. Brad downed the rest of his coffee, closed his laptop, and zipped up his wetsuit. "Let's go, Gui," he said, reaching down and stroking her head.

He opened the door, Gui shot out first, her tail wagging with excitement. He followed, taking his surfboard from the locker on the deck. The fog had already rolled in, the dawn light breaking through in soft, watery beams. They followed the path out onto the cold sand, the muffled sound of waves crashing onto the shore guiding their way.

To get his blood flowing, Brad jogged up the beach, his feet finding purchase on the damp sand at the water's edge. It was his morning ritual to warm up before he headed into the ocean. Gui was somewhere ahead, no doubt on the hunt for seagulls to send squawking into the air.

With every step, he felt a growing lightness within him. He was taking action at last, striking back at the man who had wronged him. The sense of purpose filled him with a newfound energy, a drive that pushed him forward to be faster, better.

Suddenly, a figure emerged from the fog, a tall male stature coming right for him. Before he could react, the man grabbed him by the arm and made a blow to the back of his head, sending him sprawling onto the sand. Everything went black.

Gabino reached into his pocket, pulling out a syringe. With methodical movements, he pushed the needle into Brad's thigh, releasing the drug into his system. Once the syringe barrel was empty he dragged Brad's inert body onto the surfboard and launched it into the water, pushing it out into the oncoming waves.

He timed the distance by counting in his head, ensuring he was far enough out before leaving the surfboard with Brad onboard. As he turned to wade back to shore, he passed the dog whining incessantly at Brad's unmoving form.

Gabino reached the shore, his breath coming in ragged gasps as he emerged from the water. He glanced back at the churning water. With a final, satisfied nod, he checked his wetsuit pocket for the extra vials of ketamine, and disappeared into the fog.

CHAPTER FIFTY-FIVE

2019

Scott returned home to Carohill after a long day of negotiations with a new AI company that had sprung up out of Austin. Texas wasn't his favorite place to go, and the young crew had riled him by trying to play hardball. Normally he'd enjoy the cat and mouse game, but he hadn't heard back from Anna. He craved the connection. Utah had sealed his fate. He'd divorce Kristy and possess the woman who plagued his mind.

He found Alicia up in her room, busy doing her homework. "Hey, Dad. Mom's out at some fundraiser. She said to tell you she'll be back late."

"It would appear she's busier than me these days."

"How's Jack?" he said.

"Okay I guess. His mom picked him up from school. Apparently said she was really upset."

"Upset about what?"

She shrugged. "He said she'd been crying. She wouldn't take off her sunglasses."

He pulled out his phone. "I'll check in with her. Make sure everything's okay."

"Be hard to. Jack already tried calling her when she was late to pick him up. She'd smashed her phone."

Half an hour later Scott turned the wheel of his Range Rover into the Jones' Stinson driveway. He lowered the window and hit the gate intercom.

Thirty seconds passed.

He gripped the steering wheel in irritation.

Another minute.

He reached out to the control panel trying to find a way to cut the call and redial, when the gates to the swung silently open. The call cut automatically and he drove in. Jack appeared at the front door.

"Jack," he said, climbing out. "Thought there was no one home."

"Sorry, I was in a game. Had my headphones on. Mom's lying down."

"She okay?"

Jack shrugged. "I don't know anymore."

They walked inside.

"What happened here?" said Scott, seeing the staircase.

"Some kind of construction fault. Mom was in the kitchen and heard this massive crash. Good job no one was on it when it went."

"Sure is. The other part safe?"

Jack shrugged. "Guess so. She's pretty upset about it, though."

"I can imagine. She wasn't answering her phone earlier."

"It got smashed."

"This explains it."

"No it doesn't," came a voice from upstairs.

They both looked up to see Anna at the top of the steps. She looked like anything but someone who had been resting. Her eyes bored into Scott's. She held his gaze as she walked down the stairs.

"You go up and carry on with your game, Jack," she said, as she reached the bottom.

He nodded and smiled at them both and disappeared back up to his room.

Anna led Scott into Brad's study, the heavy wooden door clicking shut behind them.

Scott took a step towards her, but Anna swiftly moved behind Brad's desk, putting a barrier between them. "Take a seat," she said, her voice steady. She gestured to the leather chair opposite the desk. "I want to show you something."

He raised an eyebrow, a smirk playing at the corners of his mouth. "That staircase must have really shaken you up."

"Not as much as this," she replied, her tone hardening. She turned the monitor towards him and hit play. The video was already midway through, frozen at the moment where Scott had his fingers in her mouth, his body driving deep into hers.

Scott stiffened, his smirk vanishing. "That's clearly fake."

She leaned across the desk, her eyes blazing with anger. "How dare you even try that. I found this buried in that fucking staircase out there. You did this to me." She stabbed at the monitor with her finger. "And I wasn't the only one, was I? I know about all three of you and your sickening game. How could you?"

She reached over and slapped him hard across the face, the sound echoing through the study.

"Anna," he said, his voice a low growl.

"All those emails between 'The Three Musketeers'. You're a bunch of sick, twisted rapists, drugging and raping women for sport, in every company you invested in." She slammed her hand down on the keyboard, freeze-framing the video. "Why?"

Scott paused, his eyes narrowing as he considered his response. "The others because they were part of the deal. But you, because I wanted you. I wanted you then, Anna, and I want you now."

"You drugged and raped me," she said, her voice trembling with a mix of anger and disbelief.

"Your husband drugged you," he countered, his grip on the armrests of the chair tightening.

"You made him do it," she shot back, her voice rising.

"I made him a fair offer and he took it."

She reached out to slap him again, but he grabbed her by the wrist, his grip like a vice.

"Let go of me!" she said, struggling to pull free.

His eyes locked onto hers. "You're not going anywhere, Anna. Not until we've settled this."

CHAPTER FIFTY-SIX

Kristy walked over to the fridge and got out the rest of the bottle of Dom Perignon that they'd opened earlier. She savored Kobe's midnight blue silk shirt against her bare skin. Gossamer thin and cool, unlike the vintage wool Dior suit she'd arrived in earlier, which was a mainstay in her official charity patronage wardrobe.

She found the box of chocolates she'd brought with her and padded back to the bedroom in a state of post-coital bliss.

Kobe had his laptop open, frowning at the screen. "Says here that Elsander invested fifty-two million in a failed fintech play last year. How in hell did he come up with that kind of money?"

She topped up their glasses. "Elsander and his wife spend their winters in Dubai. They've got a place there on the water. His wife gets all her work done away from society's prying eye, while he brokers and fronts Middle Eastern deals."

She sat down next to him. "Cheers."

He looked up and smiled, clinking the Baccarat flute against hers. This woman knew everything about everyone in SF society. Together, they'd elevated ByteBeat beyond just the Brad Jones exposé column.

"Close your eyes," she said. "And open your mouth."

He did as he was told. A second later a cube of chocolate landed on his tongue. He bit down. The hit of basil and lime was intense. "Shit that's good," he said.

"It's the fusion. I have them flown in from Rome."

"You have to be kidding."

"I know what I like."

Her phone buzzed. She ignored it. But it went again and then again. She leaned over Kobe to where it lay on the rug. As she picked it up she felt his cool fingers creeping up her inner thigh. And with it another wave of desire.

"Shit," she said, reading the screen.

Message from Alicia:

> Mom, Jack called. Dad's at their house. CALL ME NOW!

Kristy leapt off the bed, hitting the call button.

"Mom, it's bad. Jack said they're locked in the cellar. You've got to do something." Alicia's voice was frantic, bordering on hysterical.

"Alicia, calm down. I'll call Dad and call you back."

She could hear her daughter crying. What the fuck had Scott gone and done?

Kristy hung up, dialed Scott. It went straight to voicemail. She hung up. Typed a message telling him to call her now. She hit send.

"What's going on?" said Kobe, now out of bed and passing her clothes.

"Get dressed."

If Kobe thought his finances were on an uptick he realized he hadn't even got beyond the starting line as he climbed into the helicopter on the roof of the Tidal Building, just four blocks from his apartment. The pilot took straight off, sweeping them up over the Bay to Stinson.

He was sat in the back with Kristy who was juggling repeat calls into Scott's phone and Anna's, both of which were going unanswered. He'd gone from being on the outside to playing a part in the story of the Joneses, and now the Lyles.

But something told him it might have been better to stay ringside.

CHAPTER FIFTY-SEVEN

Kristy and Kobe walked in through the open front door. They followed the clanging of metal against metal, which took them along the hallway, past a sculptural half-formed staircase, and into a paneled study where a monitor lay smashed on the floor. Over in one corner a panel stood open to a spiral staircase that led down to where they found Jack trying to smash open a door with a shovel. Gui was at his feet barking incessantly.

"They're in there. Scott won't let Mom go!" he said, slamming the flat of the shovel against the door again.

"Jack, stop," said Kristy.

"Mom says he raped her," he said, shaking.

Kobe reached out and took the shovel.

Kristy rapped loudly on the metal door. "Scott!"

Silence on the other side.

"Scott. Open the door."

Anna let out a muffled scream.

Kristy nodded at Kobe. He raised the shovel, bringing it down hard on the handle, but it pinged off.

"Wait," Kristy said, turning to Jack. "That doorstop up in the office."

Jack sprinted up the spiral stairs two at a time.

Seconds later he returned with the lion-shaped, antique iron doorstop that had guarded his dad's office entrance.

Another scream came from behind the locked door.

Kobe grabbed the doorstop out of Jack's hands. With a swift, powerful motion, he brought it crashing down onto the door handle. The metal groaned and bent under the force, but the lock held. He struck again, and again, each blow echoing through the hallway like a gunshot.

Finally, with a sharp crack, the lock gave way.

The journalist lowered his shoulder and drove it hard against the weakened door. It gave way with a screech of protesting metal, and he burst into a large, brick-lined cellar stocked with bottles of wine.

Jack shoved past him. "Mom, mom!" He lunged forward, shoving Scott hard. The older man was caught off guard and stumbled back, loosening his grip on Anna.

Kristy swept in, her gaze locked onto Scott, her eyes blazing with fury. "What have you done?" she demanded, leaning in close to his face.

Scott Lyle straightened, his expression darkening. "I'm reframing the past so that Anna understands," he said.

"Your husband raped me," Anna spat, her voice trembling with rage.

Kristy glared at Scott. "Is that true?"

"No," Scott replied, his voice sharp and dismissive.

"He had me drugged and then raped me," said Anna. She stood there, breathing heavily, her eyes never leaving Scott's face.

"As I said before, your pathetic husband was the one who drugged you," said Scott. "Brad and I made a deal. I gave the investment needed to take TopMatch public, in exchange for which I spent a pleasant evening with Anna."

"You mean you raped me while I was unconscious," Anna hissed, her voice laced with venom.

"The result of which we were debating when you decided to break in," said Scott. "Anna believes Jack is my son."

Kristy's hand flew to her throat, as if the words had lodged there, asphyxiating her.

"Mom?" Jack turned to his mother, his eyes wide with horror.

A heavy silence descended, broken only by Gui's soft whines. Kristy took a step towards Scott, her eyes locked onto his.

"Did you really think I didn't know about your twisted three musketeers game? I was there in Tahoe... The three of you were out on the terrace, laughing about your conquests. I left you there to carry on enjoying yourselves because of what we'd built. I didn't want to see any of that diminished. But Anna? You had to have her, didn't you? And now this, Scott? Our fucking daughter involved! What have you done?"

She raked her nails down his cheek, leaving angry red welts. Her husband pushed her away, she stumbled back. He spoke, his voice cold and detached. "You damn well know that Alicia is not my daughter."

"That's ridiculous," said Kristy.

"You slept with a fucking golf pro and got pregnant. Do you really think I wouldn't have a DNA test done as soon as she was born?" Scott retorted, his eyes narrowing.

"You drove me away," said Kristy, bitterness dripping from every syllable.

"I gave you everything you ever wanted."

"I wanted a loyal husband."

Anna stepped forward. "You will never get away with this, Scott."

Scott's eyes flashed with hostility. "You have no idea what I've already gotten away with."

———

Kobe stepped out of the cellar, out of the unravelling scene that had the hairs on the back of his neck standing on end. He pulled out his cell phone, hands shaking, and punched in the numbers for the cops.

"Give me your phone." Scott was right behind him.

Kobe ignored the order and made a run for it, his feet pounding up the steps and into the study. Scott followed hot on his heels, but Kobe didn't look back. He sped out of the room, increasing his pace through the hallway and out onto the drive. Damn. The front gates had automatically closed, sealing him in. The fog had rolled in, thick and disorienting, wrapping everything in a ghostly white pall.

He looked frantically about him, spotting a narrow path to the right. His heart pounded in his chest, his breath coming in ragged gasps as he pushed himself harder and faster.

His feet hit sand, the soft grains shifting beneath him, slowing his pace. He had to find a way to get up to the road. But the rolling white mist had wrapped him in a directionless swirl, obscuring his path, confusing his senses.

The sand was getting deeper and softer, sucking at his feet with each step. He heard the roar of the ocean, the sound growing louder. His feet started to splash in water, the cold shock of it sending a jolt through his body.

Seconds later, his legs were whipped away beneath him as Scott tackled him to the shallows. He heard the splash of his phone falling into the oncoming surf, the sound of his lifeline disappearing into the churning water.

"Get off me!" he shouted, as Scott leapt on him again, pinning him down.

The ice-cold water ran in and over him as a wave came sweeping in, the force of it stealing his breath and filling his mouth with salt. The years were stripped away and panic set in, a primal fear that gripped him like a vice. He writhed and lashed out, his limbs flailing as he fought to free himself. But Scott held firm, his grip unyielding, his weight pressing down on Kobe like a stone.

The water retreated, leaving Kobe gasping and sputtering, his body shaking. He looked up into Scott's face, seeing the cold calculation in his eyes.

"Listen to me, you blood-sucking leech. You did not see or hear anything that just happened. No calls to the cops, no press, stories or insinuations. In return, I will arrange a one-time payment of ten million dollars. If you ever break your silence I will have you silenced."

The next wave came rushing in, this time over Kobe's face. The salt stung his eyes, invaded his nose, his mouth. The sand beneath him shifted, pulled away by the retreating water. That could only mean one thing, and he could hear its roar. With a monumental effort, he arched his back, then let go, crunching his stomach muscles together, curling forward to jettison Scott's bulk off him. Scott toppled into the surf, but grabbed onto the journalist's leg, pulling him with him.

The wave took them under. The cold was intense, the dark water terrifying. Kobe emerged from the surface, gasping for air. He had to get to shore. The wave was dragging them out. He paddled, his arms flailing through the water.

A hand gripped onto his arm and pulled him down below the surface, holding him there. He punched out, releasing himself, and pushed up to catch his breath.

"A man who can't swim. That makes this so much simpler," said Scott, now face to face with him.

Kobe was flailing in the water desperate to stay afloat. Suddenly, a figure emerged from the water behind Scott. It was Anna, her eyes blazing with fury.

She screamed, lunging at Scott. She grabbed him by the shoulders, her nails digging into his flesh. Scott, caught off guard, lost his grip on Kobe and turned to face Anna.

"You think you can just get rid of people who get in your way?" Anna spat, her voice trembling with rage. "You had Brad killed, didn't you?"

Scott's eyes lit up with hostility. "Gabino took care of him. A lethal shot of ketamine, and he drowned out in the surf. Just like you're going to."

Anna flew at him, her fists flying. Scott grabbed her wrists, trying to restrain her, but she fought back with a ferocity born of pain and betrayal. They struggled in the water, their bodies thrashing against the ocean.

Suddenly, a massive wave came crashing down on them, dragging them both under. The force of the water was overwhelming, pulling them deeper into the dark, churning sea. Anna kicked and clawed her way to the surface, her lungs burning for air. Just as her consciousness began to slip and fade into the dark expanse below, she felt a tug on her shirt. Teeth latched onto the fabric, pulling her upwards.

She broke through the water, gasping and coughing, her eyes stinging from the saltwater. Gui was there, paddling frantically beside her.

She scanned quickly around them for any sign of Scott. But he was nowhere to be seen. She turned towards the shore and with a final surge of strength, she started to swim, her strokes steady and determined with Gui alongside. The waves pushed and pulled at her limp body, but she persisted.

As they neared the shallows, Anna felt sand beneath her feet. She stumbled forward, her body shaking with cold and exhaustion. Finally they were on shore. She collapsed onto the sand with Gui.

"Thank you," she said, hugging the Labrador close.

"Mom, are you okay?" Jack fell to his knees next to them.

She saw her own terror mirrored in his eyes. Over his shoulder she glimpsed Kristy tending to Kobe.

"Where's Scott?"

CHAPTER FIFTY-EIGHT

Kobe hit "publish" on his final piece for *Code Life* magazine. He stood up from his desk, stretching his stiff muscles, and stepped across to the window. The sun was setting behind the Golden Gate Bridge, its rays casting a golden glow over the city.

"The Dark Legacy of Scott Lyle," the words were now flying through the ether, landing on people's desktop, laptop and phone screens across the globe. It was a story that had taken a toll on him, both emotionally and physically, but it had made his career.

As he looked out at the gunmetal gray waters of the Bay, he couldn't help but think of Anna, of the strength and resilience she had shown in the face of unimaginable trauma. All those years married to a man who'd bargained with the devil. And then discovering that the devil was your son's father. Her strength was undeniable.

Beyond them, the countless victims who were coming forward.

And then there was Kristy, left to mop up the fallout of the eroded Lyle dynasty.

All that and more. He'd take some time out now, head out of

town for a few months to write the book, adding to the narrative as the story continued to unfold. The publishing deal would make him richer than he'd ever imagined.

He filled a crystal tumbler with ice, poured over the single malt whiskey he'd bought for the occasion, and raised a glass to the golden sky. *The Dark Legacy of Scott Lyle.* The title of his article stared back at him, a testament to the power of truth and the unyielding pursuit of justice. And as he typed, he knew that he was not just writing a story, but a call to action, a reminder that even in the darkest of times, there was still hope, still a chance for redemption and healing. And he was determined to be a part of that, no matter what it took.

"The Dark Legacy of Scott Lyle"
By Kobe Otieno

Following the grim discovery of Scott Lyle's body in the tumultuous waters of the Pacific Ocean, a sordid underbelly of his life has been laid bare, revealing a web of depravity and deceit that has shocked the world.

Magnus Lindberg and Wing Chun have been charged for their involvement in "The Three Musketeers", a sinister group of venture capitalists that preyed on women from college dorms to corporate offices. Led by Scott Lyle, this deviant trio drugged and raped countless victims, leaving a trail of trauma and devastation in their wake. The list of victims continues to grow daily as more women come forward, their voices echoing a chorus of pain and betrayal.

Lyle's estate is now under fire, facing a class-action lawsuit brought by his numerous victims. The lawsuit seeks not only financial compensation but also a reckoning for the irreparable harm inflicted by Lyle and his accomplices.

In a shocking turn of events, Lyle's henchman, Rocco

Gabino, has admitted to aiding and abetting in the drugging, trafficking, and raping of the women who fell prey to "The Three Musketeers". Gabino's confession has sent shockwaves through the Bay Area, as he has admitted guilt in the murders of leading psychologist Titus Creed, and maverick tech entrepreneur Brad Jones.

The revelations have cast a dark shadow over Lyle's once-sterling reputation, exposing a man who hid his monstrous actions behind a veneer of impenetrable success and respectability. As the investigation continues, more details emerge, painting a chilling portrait of a man who used his power and influence to exploit and destroy the lives of those around him.

The families of the victims, along with the broader community, are calling for justice and accountability. The legal system is now tasked with the daunting responsibility of bringing closure to the many lives derailed by Scott Lyle's heinous actions.

As the sun sets on Scott Lyle's legacy, it is clear that his true nature was one of perversion and cruelty. The world watches with bated breath as the legal process unfolds, hoping that justice will prevail and that the victims of Lyle's actions will find the peace and healing they deserve.

These revelations are a stark reminder that behind the facade of wealth and success, there can lurk sinister truths.

CHAPTER FIFTY-NINE

THREE MONTHS LATER

Anna and Jack closed the door behind them one last time on their Stinson home, and climbed into the car that was ready to take them to the plane.

Neither of them looked back as it moved off up the road. The place had sold quickly, to a couple who'd made a fortune in algorithms, and wanted their kids to have a wholesome life out on the coast.

Jack took a hold of his mom's hand, where it rested on Gui's back. She looked at him and smiled.

"You okay?" he said.

She nodded.

He'd grown up almost instantaneously since the truth of his parents' past, and his conception, had come to light. Alicia and he had split. Had to happen, even though he still thought about her, a lot. He was relieved he could now have a break from therapy. It was harder work than school. It'd been the same for his mom. There was no magic wand to wave. He knew now to accept it as it was, and move forward.

Anna felt lighter as the door of the Gulfstream closed and the engines kicked into action. As they took off, she looked out of the window, watching the skyscrapers of San Francisco become smaller and smaller, disappearing into the evening sky's purple hue, as they climbed above and beyond their clutches.

The steward offered her a glass of chilled champagne. She took a sip and rested her head back against the ivory headrest.

All she cared about right now was that her family was safely on board. They were all that mattered to her, except of course Caitlin, Mark and the kids, who had promised to come and visit as soon as they were settled.

Brad and Titus had been murdered. Scott had drowned. They were all gone. Left in the wake of the jet trail. She moved her fingers one by one, counting the hours until touchdown. Eleven hours. And then Tokyo. The call had taken her by surprise. The President of the University of Tokyo inviting her to head up a new faculty in cyberpsychology. She proposed it to Jack, expecting him to say no right away. Instead he'd said, "Yes, when can we go?"

EPILOGUE
FIVE YEARS LATER

Jack strode in through the carved double doors and over to the black lacquer desk. He opened the new Hermès case his mom had bought him for the occasion, and pulled out the state-of-the-art laptop he'd had custom built. Flipping open the top, he placed it on the onyx surface, claiming his birthright.

He paced over to the glass display cases to peruse the collection of ancient samurai swords. He'd heard them spoken of, but this was his first opportunity to view them up close.

Five years ago his father had bequeathed him this in his will. For five years, Kristy and her two eldest had contested it. Five days ago, it had been settled in the high court, in his favor—Jack Jones, sole heir to Lyle Venture Partners.

The blades were sharp. He could see his reflection in the polished steel. His hair had darkened since he'd left Princeton. He favored wearing it swept back, which worked well with the new tailored suit and open-neck Italian shirt.

"You ready to get started, or do you want some time in here alone?"

He turned to find Dwight in the doorway.

"Let's get to it," he said, gesturing to the desk. He walked over, sat down in the high-backed leather chair and steepled his fingers.

"Hell. You look just like him," said Dwight, taking the seat opposite. "Sorry."

Jack shrugged. "Don't apologize. I've got used to the idea. The court case brought me on side."

Dwight's shoulders relaxed. "First off, where you're sitting now is one of the most powerful positions in the valley. LVP's high-risk plays in the AI arena have paid off. Your team has done a good job."

Jack nodded. He'd been keeping track of their activities during breaks from business and law lectures.

"But before we dive into the rest, I need to say one thing. So please hear me out." Dwight leaned in, resting his hands on the desk in an open gesture. "Despite everything Brad did to you and your mom, he was, for many years, a good father. And you're a good kid, Jack. Don't forget that when you wield the full power that comes with this ride you're about to embark upon."

Jack and his mom never spoke of his dad much anymore. The hours of therapy he'd done had excavated and disposed of any feelings, good or bad, that he had for Brad Jones.

"I appreciate your concern, Dwight. But understand, I am no longer that same kid from then, and I am not my father."

Anna stepped down from the podium to a standing ovation for her keynote speech: "Truth and Lies in the Age of AI" conference.

She headed backstage, to where Caitlin was waiting, holding her phone.

"It's out," said Caitlin, passing it to her.

At the top of her news feed was a photo of Jack on the front page of *Forbes*, seated at Scott's black lacquer desk, under the headline, "Meet Tech's New Guard."

Anna closed her eyes, waiting for the past trauma to show its face, but nothing came.

THE END

ACKNOWLEDGMENTS

Thank you for joining me on this thrilling journey. While my experience in tech has informed my perspective, this story and its characters are purely fictional.

I'm deeply grateful to my editor Clare Law for her invaluable guidance, and to Betsy Reavley and Bloodhound Books for believing in this story. Thanks to the BookSparks PR team—Crystal, Taylor, Leilani and Rylee—for their passionate promotion.

To my friends for their words of encouragement, endless coffees, and keeping me sane (well, mostly).

To my family, especially my daughter, for listening to my ramblings and helping me navigate plot twists and character arcs. A big shout-out to my husband, thank you for your unwavering support.

And to my readers, your enthusiasm keeps me writing. I hope you enjoy this adventure as much as I enjoyed creating it.

With gratitude,
Susan

ABOUT THE AUTHOR

Susan Moore is an author and screenwriter whose creative journey has been fueled by the world of technology. Her work captures the essence of what it means to be human in a complex and ever-changing world. She has over three decades of experience working in the film, tech, and media, most notably at Skywalker for Lucasfilm Ltd. She has been successfully published worldwide for the 'Nat Walker Trilogy' and 'Power Families' series, and has an MA with distinction in Creative Writing from Kingston University, London.

A NOTE FROM THE PUBLISHER

Thank you for reading this book. If you enjoyed it please do consider leaving a review on Amazon to help others find it too.

We hate typos. All of our books have been rigorously edited and proofread, but sometimes mistakes do slip through. If you have spotted a typo, please do let us know and we can get it amended within hours.

info@bloodhoundbooks.com

Made in United States
Troutdale, OR
03/07/2025

29566283R00173